PRAISE FOR
A Thousand Miles

"It's impossible not to fall for Dee and Ben while they fall for each other on the journey of a lifetime, told with heart-wrenching emotional insight, undeniable passion, and laugh-out-loud humor on every single page. *A Thousand Miles* is an instant favorite."

—Emily Wibberley and
Austin Siegemund-Broka, authors of *The Roughest Draft*

"An oh-so-sweet romantic comedy that tugs on all the right heartstrings. I adored it."

—Kate Spencer, author of *In a New York Minute*

"Morrissey's dual-POV romance is full of sarcastic banter and lovable characters, but she also explores the delicate complexity of identity, loss, and reconciliation. It's a delightful, engaging gem of a read."

—BuzzFeed

"*A Thousand Miles* is a treasure trove of heartfelt warm fuzzies."

—Romance Junkies

PRAISE FOR
Love Scenes

"An endearing and entertaining read, *Love Scenes* is the romance all lovers of Hollywood need."

—Shondaland

"Real, raw, and immensely tender, *Love Scenes* is a book about second chances: in love, in work, in family. Bridget Morrissey writes with the kind of effortless warmth and complexity that elevates characters to real people you know and love, with quirks and flaws you understand."

—Emily Henry, #1 *New York Times*
bestselling author of *People We Meet on Vacation*

That
Summer Feeling

BRIDGET MORRISSEY

BERKLEY ROMANCE

NEW YORK

BERKLEY ROMANCE
Published by Berkley
An imprint of Penguin Random House LLC
penguinrandomhouse.com

Copyright © 2023 by Bridget Morrissey
Excerpt from *A Thousand Miles* copyright © 2022 by Bridget Morrissey
Penguin Random House supports copyright. Copyright fuels creativity,
encourages diverse voices, promotes free speech, and creates a vibrant
culture. Thank you for buying an authorized edition of this book and
for complying with copyright laws by not reproducing, scanning, or
distributing any part of it in any form without permission. You are
supporting writers and allowing Penguin Random House to
continue to publish books for every reader.

BERKLEY and the BERKLEY and B colophon are registered
trademarks of Penguin Random House LLC.

Library of Congress Cataloging-in-Publication Data

Names: Morrissey, Bridget, author.
Title: That summer feeling / Bridget Morrissey.
Description: First Edition. | New York: Berkley Romance, 2023.
Identifiers: LCCN 2022052036 (print) |
LCCN 2022052037 (ebook) | ISBN 9780593549247 (trade paperback)
| ISBN 9780593549254 (ebook)
Classification: LCC PS3613.O777925 T43 2023 (print) |
LCC PS3613.O777925 (ebook) | DDC 813/.6—dc23
LC record available at https://lccn.loc.gov/2022052036
LC ebook record available at https://lccn.loc.gov/2022052037

First Edition: May 2023

Printed in the United States of America
3rd Printing

Book design by Katy Riegel

For my older sisters

That Summer Feeling

Three Years Earlier

My honeymoon started with me sprinting barefoot through the airport holding a pair of sandals and a broken bracelet that may or may not have been magical. We'd left for LAX way later than I wanted to, but I didn't mention it, because I never said anything I thought might make a moment worse. Besides, our weekend of wedding festivities had been so draining that both of us deserved every extra minute of rest we could get. My new husband, Ethan, had a gift for sleeping in late and then arriving on time. I'd watched him do it enough that I decided the talent had been extended to me through our marriage.

Traffic on the 405 was the usual nightmare. We were keeping a five-mile-an-hour pace, inching toward the promise of relaxation that awaited in Cancún. Ethan said very little. He had the kind of perpetually mellow energy that made babies stop crying when he held them. It was another trait of his I hoped to acquire through our union. I was, by all accounts, too excitable for my own good. In her maid of honor speech, my older sister

Dara described me as someone who watched a true crime documentary believing that if I rooted hard enough for the people involved, their story might not end in murder after all. Then I found myself inconsolable when the death inevitably came, crying as if I were a member of the victim's immediate family.

By the time Ethan and I got dropped off at our gate, I'd taken to making up a song to coach myself through the moment, singing *This is fine, this is great* under my breath. I was always trying to find the good in my struggles, and this was me in my full glory, humming my own tune over and over as if the repetition guaranteed a successful outcome.

In the stereotypically beachy apparel I'd insisted we wear for our flight—Ethan in a floral button-down and cargo shorts, and me in a flowing white maxi dress with gladiator sandals—we took long, purposeful strides toward security, where a snaking line awaited us. We looked like textbook newlyweds, and that meant the world to me. I wanted every person who saw us to know I'd done it. I'd picked a man to love forever.

The security line moved comically slowly. As I repeated my song to myself, catching stares from strangers in the process, I checked my phone every thirty seconds, hoping my incessant eye on the time would make it stop moving. Or better yet, our flight would be delayed.

"Garland," Ethan said as he planted a kiss on my forehead. The fresh stubble on his chin grazed my sweat-slicked skin. He hated to be barefaced, but his mother had insisted on it for the wedding, so he'd shaved off his auburn beard for the first time in years. It made him look so youthful that I gasped when I walked down the aisle. He had freckles on his jawline that I'd never seen before, and two little nicks on his chin from the razor. "We'll make it."

"Our flight leaves in fourteen minutes." I illuminated my phone screen to show him the time.

"And we will be on it," he told me.

"I hope so."

He laughed softly. "Just relax. We will."

When we finally got to take off our shoes and put our belongings into bins, panic overtook me. The moment I stepped out of the body scanner, I grabbed my stuff and started running, not even bothering to put my sandals back on my feet. Ethan kept his usual pace. To him, we may as well have been strolling the beach already.

Eventually I turned my head, trying to make sure he wasn't as far away as he felt, and I ended up crashing into someone else. A very tall someone else. I was immediately torn between apologizing for not looking where I was going or running to the gate at speeds faster than ever before reached by humankind.

I chose to attempt both at the same time. "I am *so* sorry! Incredibly sorry!" I said.

To my surprise, the stranger started running after me. "Hold on," he called out. "You dropped your . . . bracelet?"

I froze.

When Dara and I were growing up, our mom and dad fought way more than they ever got along. One late night when Dara was twelve and I was ten, whispering underneath the yells of our parents' latest argument, we promised each other that we'd never let our love lives sour like they had.

Dara always said she and I had the power to bend the

world to our will. We could make impossible things happen, if only we tried hard enough. Most of the time we were too busy distracting ourselves from the constant friction in our household to put forth the kind of effort she spoke about. That night was different somehow, in the way some nights just are. An extra crackle in the air. A brighter shine to the stars. Dara and I decided to finally put our energy toward rising above the circumstances we'd been given.

Under the watchful glow of a new moon, we made bracelets out of random things we scrounged up in our shared bedroom: garden twine, beads from other jewelry, charms, and random junk like small buttons and sequins. We called the bracelets our heart promises, imbuing them with a magic we believed we created together.

As we assembled them, we came up with the rules behind the promise—we would have better lives than the ones our parents had shown us. We would find people to love with care. We'd never become bitter and stubborn as we got older. We'd be happy in our relationships.

We knew it was the kind of wish that didn't get fulfilled right away. It was something that needed to grow with us. Dara decided we had to guard each other's bracelets until we were adults. Then, whenever one of us made our promise come true, we would get our original bracelet back, as a reminder to continue living out the wish we'd made real.

Through the years, we took the job of looking after each other's bracelets very seriously. What started as a late-night childhood whim had become a very deep representation of not only our dreams but our bond. We considered ourselves the protectors of each other's contentment. We would never let the other person settle for less than they deserved.

Dara gifted mine to me on my wedding day. She called it my something old, and she tucked it into an interior pocket she'd asked the tailor to hide in my gown. I nearly cried off my makeup when she handed it over. It always felt like she knew me better than I knew myself, and it meant everything to know she approved of my marriage to Ethan. She wasn't jealous that I was younger and I'd gotten married ahead of her. She was happy for me. She believed in the love I was making legally binding.

The next day, I tied my bracelet onto my wrist for the first time ever. It looked childlike against the formfitting white dress I'd selected for my post-wedding luncheon, especially since I'd pulled my long brown hair into a sleek bun, but I didn't care. I was proud of myself for fulfilling my heart promise. Every time I looked at my arm, I saw proof that my marriage was going to be better than my parents' had been.

The man in the airport extended his hand out to pass the bracelet back to me. He was in a highlighter-green tank that showed off his muscular physique, and he had shoulder-length blond hair pulled off his face by a pair of sunglasses resting on his head. He looked to me like he surfed. Or played beach volleyball. Something sandy.

As a rule, I did not trust blond men. No real reason other than pure skepticism. But this tall, toned stranger had chased me down to return a piece of jewelry that may as well have been made during kindergarten arts and crafts. He had to be a little decent.

"Thanks," I said to him, reaching for my bracelet.

As soon as my fingers grazed his palm, I was no longer in the bright, busy airport. Instead I sat across the table from this man. We were in a large dining hall that smelled like firewood and bread. It was nighttime, and the sconces on the wall cast a buttery glow. Crickets chirped outside the logwood walls. We were surrounded by what I took to be his family—Nordic-looking blonds with beaming smiles and sun-soaked skin. There was a woman beside me, about my age. She pressed her hand against my forearm as we all laughed so hard and deep that my stomach ached. I felt the kind of soul-deep contentment I hadn't realized I'd never experienced before. I could tell I was an important part of this man's life, and everyone around me loved us both.

Quick as a blink, I returned to the crowded airport, clutching the stranger's hand. When I pulled away, startled, the man didn't seem at all disoriented.

Did he see what I saw? Does he feel like he knows me too? What just happened?

My childhood bracelet in one hand and my shoes in the other, I took off, not bothering to linger for a goodbye with the stranger I somehow *knew*. My heart pounded as hard as my bare heels did against the airport floor.

This is just your imagination trying to psych you out, I told myself as my chest heaved from the exertion. *Heart promises aren't real. They were a childhood coping mechanism, and you are on your way to your honeymoon with the man you love.*

I made it onto our flight with a few minutes to spare. Ethan arrived right before they closed the gate. It all worked out, just like he'd said it would.

We had a lovely trip together.

Day One of Summer Camp

1

Dara and I followed a winding dirt road through the Blue Ridge Mountains in Georgia, cutting sharp corners and losing our cell phone reception in the process. A ways up, the trees parted to make room for a massive overhead sign that read **Welcome to Camp Carl Cove**. The dirt road widened until it transformed into a parking lot, where rows of cars had already begun lining up.

"Are we really doing this?" I asked, nervous.

"We're absolutely doing this," Dara confirmed, no trace of hesitation in her voice.

As kids, Dara and I had always wanted to live the camp life, where for a few weeks of each summer, you left your home behind and hid away in the woods to become someone new. There was a show about summer camp on Disney Channel that we were obsessed with, *Bug Juice*, that only fueled the fantasy. We spent night after night dreaming of that kind of escape, sleeping in log cabins and cannonballing into a cold lake, free from our everyday problems. If there was mold in the corners of those cabins, it wouldn't be our job to scrub it. If the adults there were angry at one another, we wouldn't be the ones tasked with lightening their moods or offering them advice. We would be kids in the most wholesome sense. The kind of kids you only saw on TV.

Our parents never entertained the idea of sending Dara and me away, though by the way they treated us, constantly frustrated by our mere presence, they should have been eager for a chance to be child-free for a while. We'd grown up in hot, dry Arizona, and the closest Dara and I ever got to the escape we longed for was when our oldest sister, Bess—who turned sixteen the year I was born and moved out when I was two—would come around the house and take us to a lumberjack-themed mini-golf place.

Now Dara and I were in our thirties, and we'd finally made it to a real summer camp after all. It was the exact kind of impossible-seeming thing that had come to overwhelm me, because it felt too good to be true. In my experience, if life had indeed brought me a nice thing, something bad would inevitably arrive to balance it all out. I had come to depend on living in the middle. The middle didn't crush my spirit as thoroughly as the lows did.

In the distance, a pear-shaped lake glistened in the sunlight. It was the heartbeat of the campgrounds, with dirt paths spreading out around it like veins, leading to more than a dozen idyllic wooden cabins and buildings. The scene looked serene in the way vintage oil paintings did—gentle water glistening under the watchful sun, with the soft greens and browns of the trees hugging the edges.

"It looks fake," I said. "Like an art piece that would be hanging in the living room of happily retired grandparents or something."

"I was just thinking the same thing," Dara responded. "Except I think it would belong to someone young and cool."

"You're right. This is a painting for a hot girl who lives alone in a cottage surrounded by woodland animals."

Dara nodded, pleased. "My destiny."

A wooden sign staked in front said **Hello Campers**! in a crisp white font. Tim and Tommy framed either side, waving at cars as they pulled up.

One sunny afternoon back in February—exactly a year to the day after love had failed me and I'd started crashing on a blow-up mattress at Dara's apartment in Asheville and working as a rideshare driver—twin men had crawled in through the back door of my lime-green Mazda and said hello to me in a joyous singsong tone. Then they asked in perfect synchronicity how I was doing, making all of us crack up within three seconds of knowing one another. I knew then that their story would stay with me somehow.

Never could I have guessed how much.

The twins were fraternal. They made sure to clarify that when they said their names were Tim and Tommy. According to them, nearly everyone got them mixed up. Their differences had seemed immediately obvious to me, even as I clocked them through quick glances in my rearview mirror.

Tim, the slightly taller twin, had longer features and a

more outgoing personality. Tommy, the shorter one, was more aloof. He'd laughed and beamed like Tim, but he had a reservation about him that was wholly his own. He said he'd experimented with going by Thomas for a while. Recently he'd come around to using Tommy again. They were Vietnamese, and they'd been adopted at birth by a white Christian couple they did not have a relationship with anymore. They'd grown up right outside Asheville, but they lived in New York City now. They were both gay. They'd been flying into town a few times a month for a big project.

I had learned all that within five minutes of knowing them, which made for my dream ride—willing conversationalists in my back seat, eagerly sharing their hearts with me for no real reason other than that we were in the car together and we might as well chat along the way. They were so openhearted that my cheeks ached from grinning, even though our conversation veered between intense and playful at speeds far faster than my car was driving.

"What's the big project?" I'd finally asked them.

"Oh, you know. The usual. We bought a summer camp," Tim told me, bursting into laughter as he said it.

I'd heard a lot of random things over the several months I'd spent driving strangers around town. Purchasing a summer camp ranked up there among the randomest. Right behind the woman who went to different morgues asking for dead people's teeth so she could make jewelry.

The twins were very handsome, and they'd smelled fantastic. Their elegant cologne wafted up to me as the air circulated in the car. It reminded me of the pricy candles Dara liked to burn in the living room. *Musky wealth*, I called it. They both had on fitted tees that showed their penchant for exercise, and Tommy had hung a pair of expensive sunglasses on the neckline of his. Tim wore a watch that might have been worth more than my life savings. I could only imagine what kind of money they needed to purchase an entire camp.

Now I was driving my car up to the entrance of that very summer camp, and there stood the twins, beaming the same way they had four months earlier when they'd first told me about this place.

"Garland Moore!" Tim cheered when he recognized my Mazda.

Tommy gestured for us to turn left.

Even though I'd spent more of my life with my maiden name than my married name, it surprised me to hear *Moore* again. I'd only been Garland Sanders for two years, but I'd *wanted* to be Garland Sanders for what seemed like my entire life.

The twins jogged after my car. As soon as I got out, they hugged me like I was their close friend. Honestly, I felt like I was. They'd posted so many camp and life updates on their social media, it had tricked me into believing we'd spent the last few months in close contact, when really we had only shared that one fateful car ride. They couldn't believe I'd never been to sleepaway camp before, and as I drove them, I'd playfully entertained their pleas that I come for their adults-only week. I'd written the whole thing off as the kind of exchange that floated into the wind as soon as someone vacated my back seat. But Dara hadn't. When I told her about the conversation, she thought it was a sign. She insisted we go.

"Still want to leave?" she asked me as the twins made their way to my trunk to help unload our bags.

"I never said I *wanted to leave*," I whispered. "I'm really excited, actually. I'm also just scared."

"What scares you? That you'll like the experience too much?"

"Exactly," I confirmed. "Because when it's over I'll go back to my glamorous life of being a nuisance to your existence."

"When have I ever called you a nuisance?" she asked.

I pretended to pull a notebook out of my pocket. "Let's see," I said as I shuffled through imaginary pages. "April of 2006, when I left my curling iron plugged in and almost burned down the house. December of 2011, when I tripped walking into the kitchen and ruined everyone's Christmas with my rolled ankle."

"The curling iron thing was 2005." Smirking, we gave each other a beat, appreciating our ability to remember our shared history. Then Dara added, "You are welcome at my apartment for as long as you need to live there, and you know that. I don't mind the company."

I was supposed to stay for one week. One week had turned into one year and I still hadn't left. I never wanted Dara to think I planned to intrude upon her life in a permanent way. No matter what she said, I felt like I was a bother, and I hated being a bother.

"Let's make the most of this week, okay? I don't use my PTO for just anything," she continued.

I gave her a salute and headed to the trunk. She'd asked me to do this camp with her, and she never asked me for anything. I couldn't even *begin* to pay her back for all she'd done for me. The least I could do was enjoy this week, which started with checking all my anxiety at the door.

Tommy pointed to my bumper sticker. "You're divorced?" he asked me.

"Aren't we all?" I said as I popped my trunk.

Tim leaned toward me and whispered, "We saw the sticker after you dropped us off in February. He's been dying to ask you about it."

Right before I drove my car across the country to live with Dara, I'd put on a bumper sticker that said HONK IF YOU'RE DIVORCED. It was a real crowd-pleaser on highways.

I hauled my giant suitcase over the lip of my trunk, then let it thump onto the dirt. "I am the proud product of a dysfunctional marriage who went and failed her own marriage," I told Tommy. "You know what they say. *It takes a village.*"

Tommy's eyebrows crinkled with what I could only guess was pleasant shock. "I'm divorced too."

I held up my hand for a high five. "*Failed marriage* on three?"

Tommy nodded.

"One, two, three," I counted.

"*Failed marriage!*" we yelled in unison as our palms connected.

Our siblings laughed with an edge of unease. They didn't understand, and that was for the best. Dara handled her struggles the same way she handled everything else—with steadfast competence. When her appendix burst, she had me bring her laptop to the hospital so she could log in to work remotely. It wasn't that she loved her job that much. She just didn't want anyone to know anything was wrong with her. *Ever.*

I, however, wore my struggles like Girl Scout badges. My divorce was something I found myself mentioning as often as possible, as if the more I talked about it, the less painful it would feel.

In some ways, it worked. The word no longer bottomed me out. In other ways, it was a wound I poked at too much, never letting it properly heal. Ultimately, acknowledging my divorce as often as possible took the edge off other people's opinions of it. No one could ever judge me too harshly if I judged myself harder and louder than they'd ever dare.

"Quite the rollout for you, Miss Divorcée," Dara whispered to me as Tim grabbed our suitcases and started wheeling them toward the sign-in area. She always took great note of small gestures of kindness, like when a cashier gave a sincere greeting or a stranger went out of their way to pick up a piece of trash.

"It's for the both of us," I told her.

She laughed. "Please. You're the crowd-pleaser here. I'm just the bank account."

"Hey," I said softly. "You're also the *Parent Trap* enthusiast. That's a really important piece of you."

"Soon it will be a piece of you too. When you cut my hair in our cabin in the middle of the night . . ."

It sounded like she was joking, but she was being one

hundred percent serious. Ever since we'd signed up, she'd told me she wanted to use this camp to let go of her bitterness. She had a lot of resentment about the way we'd grown up and how everyone had treated us. This was her second chance at childhood. To her, letting go apparently meant re-creating what Hallie had done for Annie in *The Parent Trap*—cutting her hair. In the movie, they did it because they were secret twins about to swap lives. Dara and I were far from twins, and we already lived together. But Dara had been watching every movie and piece of media about summer camp in preparation for this week, and she'd come up with this milestone to prove she'd gotten something transformative from this experience.

That was how people used sleepaway camp in the middle school years. They hid away for a summer and returned as someone brand-new. Since the divorce, I'd cut several inches off my hair and dyed it an even darker brown. I'd also become really committed to wearing oversized T-shirts with frayed jean shorts and combat boots that took ages to break in and still gave me blisters. I didn't smile in pictures anymore. I smoldered. If anyone from camp saw my social media, they'd think I seemed mysterious and detached. Two words no one who really knew me would ever use to describe my personality. Everything about my life felt like a placeholder: where I lived, what I wore, how I moved through the world. So much had gone wrong in my life that pressing the reset button seemed not only necessary but fun. I wanted something transformative too. Who could I become to a group of strangers who'd never met me? How different could I be?

The twins continued to shower us in special attention as we

approached the main area. We definitely drew the notice of the other campers who had already arrived. There were ten to fifteen adults already there, sitting at picnic tables near the lake, watching the owners of the camp personally escort my sister and me to the sign-in table that sat just outside a tall log building aptly labeled **MAIN HALL**.

"Michelle will get you all checked in," Tommy said. "She's actually one of your roommates! And one of our *counselors*." He did air quotes as he said it.

Tim leaned in. "You're in the best cabin."

"Welcome to the show. We're Cabin Seven," Michelle said to me in greeting. I recognized her deadpan tone along with her face. The twins had recently posted the teaser trailer for her upcoming documentary. They'd met her many years ago in an adoption support group, and she'd become one of their best friends. She was a trans woman, born in Vietnam but raised in the US as well, and she'd been on a yearslong quest to find her birth family.

She had on a teal mock-neck tank top tucked into light green cigarette pants, which somehow paired fantastically with the dark red loafers she wore on her feet. She looked light-years more put together than I imagined anyone ever would be at summer camp, and I felt myself kick into turbo mode, determined to impress her as much as she impressed me.

"Hi! I'm Garland! This is my older sister Dara. I can't wait for your documentary," I blurted out.

To me, there was no use in pretending I didn't know things about people when I did, so I went out of my way to say them up front. Michelle seemed to appreciate the honesty, because her posture relaxed and her whisper of a smile turned into a real one.

"Sorry if that's weird. You don't know me at all," I continued. "If it helps even the score, I can tell you I'm here on some sort of post-divorce quest for renewal."

Michelle's smile broadened as her eyebrows quirked. "I thought I heard someone yelling something about divorce in the parking lot."

"That was me. I yell about a lot of things."

"What else do you yell about?" she asked.

"Great question. The price of frozen pizza, for one. What's going on there?" Her growing amusement fueled me. I loved making people feel at ease. "Let's see, what else? I yell about bugs, but I also try to be kind to them in case it matters in a cosmic sense."

Michelle let out a real laugh. She had a sarcastic energy that didn't seem cynical. It felt like she was laughing *with* me, understanding that even though I was telling the truth, I was mostly trying to entertain her. She handed me the paperwork, then directed her attention to my sister. "Dara, you're next door to us, in Cabin Six."

Dara cocked her head. Her grand hair-cutting plan hinged on us sharing a cabin. "Garland and I aren't together?"

"Tim and Tommy split up all the siblings," Michelle explained. "Even themselves. Cabin Six is right next to Seven. Seven is actually the smallest place here, but it has a slightly closer path to the mess hall and a better view of the lake." She handed us our keys and a map of the grounds, then snaked her manicured finger along the trail to show us how to get there.

The path wrapped around the perimeter of the lake, as all things at camp did. The layout was so simple we didn't really need a map, but it would be a nice memento to have. Proof that all of this was real.

Dara and I walked with our gaze fixed on the sky, awed by the long, lean trees that stretched up over us. She said nothing about the cabin situation, which didn't surprise me. Dara didn't like to talk about what upset her, and I knew her well enough to know I shouldn't ask. When the path split, I went left and Dara went right, both of us nodding a goodbye as we entered our separate living quarters.

Cabin Seven had a common area with a two-seater leather couch and a small wooden table and chairs. Just beyond it were two tiny bedrooms with a bathroom squeezed between them. One room had a single bed, and the other had two twins with roughly three feet of space between them.

I'd expected to be staying in bunk beds in one large room, with community bathrooms somewhere else on the property. This was decidedly nicer. Maybe the twins had renovated the cabins to be more adult-friendly? Or maybe this was how some sleepaway camps were. I had no idea either way, but I was happy with the unexpected upgrade.

Michelle had already taken the private room, so I wheeled my luggage into the shared bedroom. Eager to get back to the camp activities, I tossed my suitcase onto a bed to claim it, did a quick refresh in the bathroom, and hurried out of my cabin.

Right before I put my key into the lock, someone yelled out, "Hold on a sec!"

A white woman was running up the path, waving at me.

She wore an olive-green sports bra with matching athletic shorts that showed her well-formed legs, and she had on a *gigantic* hiking backpack. The top crested above her head and the bottom hit below her shorts. Somehow, she moved as if it didn't even exist.

When she made it closer to me, jogging up the stairs that led to the cabin, I clocked the curly shock of blond hair beneath her National Parks ball cap. Reckless tendrils were escaping her two short braids. Right as I opened the door again, about to compliment the ease with which she'd just sprinted over, she misjudged her final step. And she fell, right into my arms.

The force of her tumble pushed both of us back. The door swung all the way open, somewhat slowing our journey to the floor. She managed to squeeze me closer and spin us around so her pillow of a backpack caught the ground instead of me.

We landed with a gentle thud, everything inside her bag absorbing our fall. My body was fully smashed atop hers, flush against her matching sports set. My hands got stuck in the space between her body and her backpack. Her own hands had such a tight grip on me in return that the pressure of it almost made me cry. It had been so long since anyone had held me in that way. It made me feel like I was fragile and worth protecting.

Before my tears could form, the woman laughed. Full and deep, looking right into my eyes, her rib cage jutting up into mine as the joy moved through her in staccato bursts.

"You must be Garland," she said.

"You must be our third roommate," I guessed. I could feel

her shoulders contract as she continued laughing. That was nothing compared to the feeling of our hearts beating in unison, two wild drums of adrenaline.

"Stevie," she said breathlessly. "I think we might be stuck here."

"I think you might be right."

"Here. Hug me closer, and we can roll to the side."

We pulled together so tightly that my nose got tucked into the crook of her neck, where I could smell sunscreen and some kind of aquatic perfume. It was a familiar but uniquely comforting combination of scents. Like being wrapped in a soft towel after a long swim.

"To the left?" I suggested.

And so we rolled, hugging as close as two people could hug, until we were sideways at the entrance of our cabin, wrapped up in each other's arms.

When we wiggled ourselves free, I offered my hand to help her up.

"My preferred hello is a full-body tackle," she said when she was fully upright. Her smile had sunlight attached to it, warm and impossibly bright, shining onto me.

I could immediately tell she was someone who did hard things with ease. She'd probably hiked the mountain to get here, and the only proof of her effort was a delicate flush to her cheeks and that monstrosity of a backpack on her back. She'd managed to fall into me and make it not at all embarrassing. If anything, it made me like her more than I'd ever liked someone who'd knocked me to the floor. Not that it had ever happened before. But if it were to happen again with someone else, I suspected Stevie would maintain her first-place position.

"An underrated greeting," I said back.

"I didn't hurt you though, right?"

"Not at all. Are you hurt?"

"Of course I am," she said matter-of-factly. "Just not in the ways you can see." She smirked until I understood she was kidding, then added, "I'm sorry for barreling into you. I think I caught a loose floorboard or something."

"You're welcome to barrel into me anytime," I told her. My stomach immediately did a little flip of embarrassment.

Stevie looked me over, then tucked her hands under the straps of her gigantic backpack. "Good to know."

To direct attention away from whatever the hell I'd just said, I gestured to our home for the next week. "Isn't this cute?"

"This is perfect."

"Did you meet Michelle? She's our other cabinmate," I said. "And our counselor too. Whatever that means."

"I did. I actually got in right after you, but I dropped my brothers off at their cabins first. I didn't want to creep you out and follow you."

"You don't seem like the type of person who could creep anyone out."

"Thank god." Her gaze caught mine again as she staged a laugh of relief. She had this faint eruption of freckles across the bridge of her nose. Freckles always fascinated me. My skin didn't do that.

"Do you want to walk together to meet everyone else?" I asked.

She stared down at her outfit, plucking the fabric and then letting it fall back into place. "Should I change? You look so good, and I'm just here in this."

"You look amazing," I told her. She'd complimented me, and one of my most consistent compulsions was that I could never hear a compliment without giving one back. Plus, I meant it. She wore athletic apparel with conviction. It looked like a carefully considered ensemble on her, not something you tossed on to exercise.

I was in my usual oversized shirt, which I'd tucked into the waistband of my ripped jean shorts. At some point I'd evolved into someone who liked to wear tees that said things on them. Not in an overly basic, "but first coffee" way but a "repurpose someone's middle school gym uniform" way. The style *was* practically my uniform at this point. Dara kept teasing me, saying that the older I got, the younger I dressed. The only deviation I'd taken for arriving at camp was swapping my Docs for hiking boots.

"Garland, I hope you're not lying to me," Stevie said as she walked into our shared bedroom. She injected so much familiarity into her use of my name that I questioned whether we *had* met before. She took off her humongous backpack and tossed it onto the other bed. "I'm putting all my faith in you."

I looked again at her sports set. It sat on her like a second skin. She wore hiking boots too—a camel color, and they hit just below her calf—and hers were more worn than mine, which wasn't hard. Until that morning, I'd never put them on. It took all of one hour for me to regret them.

"I'm not lying," I said, really meaning it. She looked fantastic.

Stevie didn't even check herself in the mirror after my confirmation. Instead she headed straight for the front door, waving me on and saying, "Enough making me feel better about myself. Let's go meet the other campers. See who we're working with out here."

When we set out on the path, Dara was already ahead of us, walking alone. It was so like her. She'd disappear from restaurants or parties for twenty or thirty minutes, then return without an explanation beyond "I wanted some air." It was a good thing I had someone to walk with, or I might have been offended by how she'd gone on without me.

"That's my sister." I pointed to Dara up ahead. "She's left me to fend for myself."

"Just wait until you meet my brothers," Stevie said. "All three of them are here. One time they forgot me on the top of a mountain." When I gasped, she added, "I'm not even kidding."

"Are you the youngest?" I asked.

"Obviously. You?"

"Obviously," I confirmed, smiling. "But it's just Dara and me here. Our oldest sister, Bess, has three kids. She wasn't into the idea of finally getting to go on a vacation without them, and it's her living in the wilderness for a week."

Stevie laughed. "Bess will never know what she's missing. This place is magical. So long as you put on enough bug spray."

"Have you been here before?"

Stevie ran a hand across a tree as we passed it. "*Many* times. Every summer from ages eight to eighteen. As soon as I heard the twins were opening this up to adults, I practically crashed the website trying to sign up. It's my thirtieth-birthday gift to myself."

"When's your birthday?"

"It was at the beginning of June. But I believe in celebrating all month long."

I stopped the both of us by pressing my hand into the crook of her elbow, then bent down and picked up a rock. "I got you this," I said, giving it to her. "Happy birthday!"

"A rock? *Garland*. How did you know?"

"Please, you've been dropping hints nonstop."

"And you're the only one who's noticed them." We stood in the middle of the dirt path as a warm breeze pushed her loose curls across her face. "You know what we should do?"

Looking into her eyes, my mind went blank.

"We should form an alliance," she continued, not seeming to notice. "We know our siblings will forget about us, and who knows what kind of plans the twins have for this week. If we can't trust our family, we should trust each other."

Having never been to camp before, I didn't know if alliances happened often. Or ever. I remembered the concept from watching *Survivor* when I was younger, but I hadn't seen that show in a very long time, so my knowledge of this kind of deal was basically nonexistent. It didn't matter, though. More than anything, I appreciated the level of gravity Stevie lent the moment. It was fun to take silly things seriously. We were adults at a summer camp, after all.

"I'm in," I said in a conspiratorial whisper.

"Shake on it?" Stevie asked. She had eyes that reminded me of leaves turning in autumn. When the light caught them, there was an amber circle around the rim of her irises, a perfect complement to the yellowish green that got pulled forward by her matching workout set.

I took her hand in mine. She kept the rock there, cold in the space between our warm palms.

"It's you and me," she said. "Against everyone else."

"You and me," I echoed.

We didn't know each other. Not even a little. I knew she'd just turned thirty, but I had no idea what her job was. Where she lived. Hell, even her last name. Yet palm to palm, I felt our shared trust in my bones. A trust born of nothing but faith and circumstance.

We released our handshake and continued walking. Stray branches cracked beneath our feet, an appropriate soundtrack to the thundering boom of my heart. It had been so long since I'd made a new friend all on my own. It hadn't happened since college, and that was almost half a lifetime ago. I wanted so badly to be good at it.

"Is it normal to form alliances at camp?" I decided to ask. Now that Stevie and I were in one, I figured I could be honest with her and admit when I didn't know things.

She laughed, and the sound echoed against the cavernous trees that shaded us. It was musical and full, her laughter. She did joy like I'd already imagined she did everything else, with assuredness. "I don't think it is."

My cheeks flushed. Our interactions shot me with

adrenaline in a way that was wholly unfamiliar. I felt wild around her. Spontaneous.

My past didn't matter to her. She didn't know me as Ethan's ex-wife, or her rideshare driver, or the woman who sobbed when old people crossed the road alone, or whoever else I'd been over the course of the last thirty-two years. Her simple act of companionship reminded me I was already on my path toward reinvention.

If I wasn't ever going to love someone other than Ethan, I wanted to love *myself.* Any chance to do something new here, I had to take it. Just because I'd given up on love didn't mean I had to give up on experiencing joy.

We were approaching the main hall, where the other campers still waited around the picnic tables outside. Stevie's laughter caught the attention of most of them. A tall blond man started waving his arms at us.

"There you are," he yelled. "I was getting worried."

"I'm sure you were!" Stevie called back. "That's my brother Mason," she whispered to me. "Consider this our first alliance information session. Mason is the biggest shithead in the world."

Mason ran up to meet us. With every long stride he took in our direction, his face became a little clearer. Once he was close enough for me to make out specific features, my bones began to liquefy.

I stopped walking. Stopped breathing.

He looked *exactly* like the man from the airport—the man I'd had a premonition about when our hands connected on my heart-promise bracelet. I'd long ago convinced myself that hadn't been real. I sometimes saw that face late at night, right before I fell asleep, when my mind liked to play tricks and make me think I'd missed out on an opportunity with my soulmate or something.

It couldn't be the same guy. There was no way.

When he reached where Stevie and I stood, his broad, friendly expression morphed into something like shock. "Wait," he said to me. "I know you."

I opened my mouth to speak. No sound came out.

Instead, I fainted. Right at the feet of the man of my dreams.

2

My favorite kind of daydreaming used to be imagining all the people I could love. I did it with movie stars. Strangers on the street. Casual acquaintances. I closed my eyes, and for a brief, beautiful moment, our life together played out for me. That was how I'd moved through the world before Ethan. Then I met him the third week of my freshman year of college, and the sweet little scenarios I made up in my mind actually happened, which was how I'd decided he had to be the one.

I'd first seen him standing in another aisle of a used bookstore a good fifteen miles away from campus. For a fleeting moment, I imagined the two of us bumping into each other and falling in love, living a beautiful, uncomplicated life together where we spontaneously picnicked in the park on a random Tuesday afternoon or built a pillow fort in our living room whenever it rained. The thought was gone as fast as it came, and I kept browsing, pleased with the small dopamine hit I got from the miniature fantasy I'd created.

I'd squatted down to pet the store cat, not realizing Ethan was beside me, about to do the same thing. Our hands accidentally grazed as we both reached for the tabby. We looked at each other and laughed.

Ethan held up another copy of the book I was holding. He said, "I saw you with this, and I figured I should read it too. We can talk about it on our first date."

We quickly realized we were both students at UCLA who had happened to take a random Thursday-afternoon trip to the valley to visit a used bookstore. There was no way it was a coincidence. It was too specific and strange to be random. It had to be fate.

We got married in a small ceremony on the beach in Malibu, surrounded by loved ones. We had a beautiful honeymoon in Cancún. We bought a craftsman in Pasadena for way too much money (all Ethan's), and he let me paint the walls dark green and buy more plants than any human should ever be allowed to house indoors. It was lovely. Exactly the kind of relationship I'd always thought I should have. Aspirational. Picturesque. Safe.

Then he surprised me with a divorce over Valentine's Day dinner, and all the little head-in-the-clouds quirks about myself I once saw as wondrous now seemed like a burden.

I'd spent years wincing at the sight of surfer types. When I came across tall white men with blond hair in public, I turned in the other direction. My entire marriage to Ethan depended upon me ignoring what had happened when a stranger once brushed hands with me in the airport. What I'd experienced that day never felt like a figment of my imagination in the way my other daydream scenarios did. It felt instead like a pivotal moment of my life being revealed to me—a slip in the timeline where I glimpsed my future a little earlier than I was supposed to—and I decided that was something I could reject altogether. Not all future paths set out for me were ones I had to walk.

If anything, choosing Ethan seemed like the most romantic thing I could possibly do. I'd seen a lovely life that had nothing to do with him, and I'd turned it down in favor of the man I already knew. The steady presence I thought I could rely on. Then he told me I romanticized everything. He said I put a filter over my struggles to make them more palatable, and it prevented me from showing up to the life I had.

When I came to, sitting under the shade of a gigantic white oak tree in the middle of the mountains, it seemed possible I'd somehow escaped reality altogether and gotten trapped inside the one daydream I'd ever hid from—the man from the airport I'd seen for half a minute, several years ago.

Mason.

He stood a few feet away, gaping at me. He couldn't be real, but he was. And his sister sat directly to my right, pressing a cool compress to my forehead.

"She's awake," she said to someone I couldn't yet see. She handed me a bottle of water.

I unscrewed the lid and took a delicate sip.

Dara appeared, squatting down in front of me. "Shit, Garland. Are you okay? I've never seen you do that before in my life." She looked impressed, confused, and a little angry, which wasn't *that* far from her usual expression, but I knew the difference.

"I don't know what happened," I lied.

My airport vision was the one thing I'd never told Dara about. If I'd shared it with her, she'd have taken me too seriously. She'd have treated it like it mattered, and back then, the vision *couldn't* matter to me. It didn't match the life I'd already established for myself.

For as practical as she seemed to everyone else, Dara still believed in the magic the world could possess. Not even my divorce had gotten her down. She wasn't one of those people who evangelized *The Secret* or anything, but she did make wishes on eyelashes and coins she tossed into fountains, and she treated those wishes as law. She thought angel numbers guided her, and that randomly noticing a detail she hadn't perceived before meant she was destined to see it at that exact moment. Both of us were in our thirties, single, and living in an apartment together, and she saw it all as part of some big, beautiful cosmic plan.

I used to believe all the same things. Then Ethan served me divorce papers, and every single iota of the self-made wonder I'd dusted over my life got wiped away, revealing nothing but disenchantment. I had no interest in trying to love someone new ever again. Over and over, the only constant message the world had given was that romantic love failed me. The worst part was, I still couldn't let go of Ethan. If he were to call, I'd answer. If he wanted me to move back, I'd go. I lived my life in waiting mode, holding out for Ethan's return.

And now here I was, with the man from the airport a few feet away from me.

"I think the heat got to me or something," I made up as an excuse. It was late afternoon. A strong breeze had been blowing all day. Under the shade of thick foliage, high up in the mountains, overheating was a spectacular stretch.

"I thought maybe the sight of my brother's face scared you," Stevie joked, oblivious to how correct she was. "You wouldn't be the first."

I smiled weakly, taking another sip of water. "I feel much better now. I promise."

"The nurse still wants to see you," Stevie told me. "The twins are getting her right now. She wasn't even set up yet when you went down."

Bravely, I looked around. The other campers were watching me. Some blatantly, some in quick glances. They were a blur of unfamiliar faces, mysterious portraits of concern and fascination. The twins and an older woman, presumably the camp nurse, emerged from among them. Even though I insisted I was fine, the nurse asked me to sit in the wheelchair she'd brought.

"We'll wait to do our introductory speech until after you're back," Tommy told me.

"What a start to the week," Tim joked, patting my shoulder. "Glad you're better now. But let's be sure you're really okay."

They were being so nice that tears filled my eyes. All of this could have been very embarrassing. Everyone at camp cared for me instead of laughing at me.

Dara and Stevie came along as the nurse pushed me toward the camp infirmary.

"I've never done anything like this before," I said to Stevie. I didn't want her to regret our alliance.

"She really hasn't," Dara confirmed. "Although when we were little, I made her think there was a ghost living behind our shower curtain. Then I hid in there to scare her, and she screamed so much she damaged a vocal cord. She does love to do things to the extreme."

"I'm still afraid of what lurks behind shower curtains," I admitted. "I check in everyone's bathrooms."

"Now you can be afraid of Mason too," Stevie joked, once again hitting the nail on the head.

It wasn't meant to be that funny, but Dara laughed anyway. She must have appreciated that Stevie had immediately begun to look out for me, so she treated Stevie like an equal, which was an accomplishment when it came to my sister. She saw very few people as true peers.

To no surprise, I passed my checkup with flying colors. Nothing was wrong with me aside from something much deeper than a camp nurse could see while looking into my pupils with a flashlight. The nurse chalked it up to me being overstimulated, and I cosigned that heartily. If that kept everyone else satisfied, it was good enough for me.

The full reality of what was *actually* occurring had no proper diagnosis.

After my marriage died, I swore off the prospect of dating anyone new. I'd already had my big love story. I could never put myself through another. Not when I'd made everyone in my life fly to California for my wedding and they'd all watched me walk down the aisle and say supposedly eternal vows to someone who didn't actually want to stay with me forever.

It was embarrassing to have failed like that, especially because the reason behind our split never seemed to satisfy anyone I told. It wasn't infidelity. There was no big lie that had destroyed us. No abuse. It came down to something deceptively simple and painful—Ethan just didn't want to be me with anymore.

Even my parents hadn't understood how that could be. To them, there had to be some big *gotcha* that made getting a divorce the right move. Otherwise why wouldn't we just stick it out? How could I not convince Ethan to keep me around? I'd always known that to my parents, love meant suffering. It meant enduring everything, no matter how bad. Only something publicly shameful was worth splitting up over. Even then, a case could be made for "forgiveness."

I always thought that my parents' brand of love was the worst fate. Being trapped together and refusing to let the other one escape. I'd never prepared myself for the possibility of being rejected by someone I'd promised to spend my whole life with—a person I'd given so much of my time and energy toward loving as best I could. That was exactly why I wanted him back. I knew he was wrong about us. He was wrong about *me*.

So even if my soulmate happened to be here—and according to my own vision, he was—I wasn't about to do anything about it.

I was not going to be falling in love at summer camp.

3

After their rousing introductory speech, the twins took the campers on a tour around the grounds to show off all the options available to us over the course of the week. There were around fifty of us by my best guess, which impressed me. I was surprised so many other people could afford this, but I'd gotten so used to living without stability that I genuinely forgot other adults had it. They had jobs with insurance benefits and paid time off, not just financially stable older sisters who insisted on paying for them to come here.

Stevie and I stuck close together, exchanging the kind of empty but amusing small talk I hadn't experienced in years. I'd forgotten what it was like to whisper underneath someone else's speech. Most of the jobs I'd had didn't provide opportunities to tuck private conversations into the gaps of a public one. It made the afternoon so much more exciting than it would have been if it were only Dara and me.

She was once again doing her independent-woman bit, walking ahead of me. Being alone in public never seemed to bother her or make her anxious. As for me, the entire tour, I'd been scanning my fellow campers, inventorying things I could compliment them on if the opportunity presented itself.

Stevie's brothers were visible everywhere we went—three blond men who towered over everyone else. As the twins told us the history of the man-made lake the campgrounds had been built around, I leaned toward Stevie and asked, "They really do move around like you're not here, huh?"

I couldn't help but investigate a little. Learning more about Mason wasn't the same as trying to fall in love with him. I was a naturally curious person! I'd have done the same thing even if we didn't have a potential fated destiny.

"I think right now they want to stand up front so everyone can gape at them," Stevie told me.

"You don't want to be gaped at too?"

"Of course I do," she said. "But if I go by them, they'll huddle around me so I'm not visible. I have to cultivate my own gaping environment."

"Are they weird? Like, they hide you so that you can't date anyone?"

"God, no," Stevie said. "They just don't want me to steal women from them."

I let out an unexpectedly loud laugh. Another camper turned back and glared at me.

Right as I started to form an apology for being disruptive, Stevie nudged my shoulder and pointed to the trees beyond the campground, where a red bird sat on a low branch. "*Look.* A northern cardinal."

I attempted to whisper so the other camper would know I was somewhat trying to respect her desire for quiet. "How can you tell?"

"I spend a lot of time in nature."

"Are you a birder?"

Stevie swallowed back her laugh. Barely. It still bubbled out in the best way. Delightful as a melting chocolate chip oozing out of a cookie.

"*Are you a birder?*" she mimicked, painting my voice as something curious and a little shy. Nothing like any other impression of me I'd ever heard. "I'm not in the Audubon Society or anything, but I do like birds."

"I'd have brought some binoculars for you if I knew."

"I have some."

"Really?"

"You think I came up to the mountains without?" she asked. "There are yellow-billed cuckoos up here."

The glaring camper turned around again. "Can you two please be quiet? I can't hear."

There were few things I hated more than getting scolded by a stranger. Feeling like I was the one causing someone else trouble.

Stevie pressed her hand into my wrist. "Yeah, Garland, *please* be quiet." She had such a bottle-rocket way about her. Her every action was a concentrated burst of energy that made me want to marvel at her. She kept her hand on my wrist and guided us away from the other camper. "What's there to hear? It's the ropes course! You hold on to ropes as you make your way from one wobbly platform to the next. It's pretty self-explanatory."

She scanned the crowd with a highly focused intensity, searching for a new place for us to stand. We walked to the right side of the group until Stevie saw something that startled her. She jerked us left so intensely that I gasped.

"Sorry. Bad energy from that corner," she said. We kept walking, her hand still on my wrist, until we ended up on the far left side of the crowd. She tapped a new stranger on the shoulder. "Will it bother you if we talk?"

The person said no. Therefore, we continued.

The final stop on the tour was an extensive obstacle course complete with a rock climbing wall. I hated heights. When I got up too high, it made me painfully aware of how fleeting life could be. I didn't need to stand on the ceiling of the world to appreciate what it meant to be alive or anything. I could appreciate it very sufficiently from the ground.

Talking to Stevie provided a perfect distraction. We mused on the birds as we swatted away mosquitoes, chatting about nothing of substance while enjoying each other's company. It was delightfully simple to spend time with her. I didn't feel like I had to hoard conversational topics in case of emergency. We had an immediate ease that usually came with history or practice. We could have talked for hours.

No doubt we would have, if it weren't for the mess hall.

After the tour finished, we walked there together to have our first camp meal. The outside of the building was exactly as expected—a tall structure with the words **MESS HALL** painted above the entrance in the same lettering I'd seen everywhere else on the campgrounds.

Stevie tugged the door open, and we went inside.

That's when I saw the log walls. The long tables that sat dozens of people. The sconces with bulbs I knew glowed yellow, buttering the room when night fell. I knew because I'd been here before. In my mind. For a split second, years ago. This was the *exact* room where the vision I'd had at the airport had taken place. Where Mason and I had laughed together, so happy. So in love.

I didn't have it in me to faint again. If anything, my feet were firmer on the ground than they'd ever been. The weight of impossibility rooted me to the reality of the moment. It had all been real. Mason *and* this place. Despite never having seen this camp in my life, I'd rendered it exactly as it was, down to the granular details, like the smell of firewood that lingered in the space, and the way the tall ceilings created a drafty breeze.

After I ran away from Mason that day in the airport, I'd somehow managed to set myself on a winding, corkscrew path back to him. Despite my determination to stop being such a romantic about my own life, I didn't have the courage to continue ignoring this anymore.

I needed to purge it from my system. Be free of the burden of my prophecy, so that every little detail stopped unnerving me.

I had to tell my sister.

4

Inside the mess hall—*the* mess hall I'd conjured in my *mind*—Dara sat by herself at an empty table near the back left, looking at the walls with an idle curiosity. She'd chosen a perfect location for me to slide in across from her and reveal something weighty and shocking.

Stevie did not see my frantic beeline toward my sister as something she should politely ignore. Instead she followed me, matching my intensity as we walked. "What are we doing? It seems urgent."

"It is," I said.

"Very mysterious response. Do you think you could give me even the smallest hint as to why you've suddenly developed the attitude of a doctor who's been unexpectedly paged to perform a lifesaving surgery?"

Having Stevie around when I told Dara about the vision might benefit me. Stevie would be a good buffer, and I suspected she'd have my back in case things went sour. Plus, she was Mason's sister. Which meant she knew way more than I did about how possible all of this really was. Maybe he was married. Maybe he was queer. Maybe he was both?

"I don't have time to explain," I told her. "You're just going to have to enter the operating room with me. Scrub in, Doc."

She pretended to wash her hands as I threw myself onto the bench across from Dara.

"When I was on my way to my honeymoon," I started, staring Dara in the eyes, not bothering with a greeting.

Stevie reacted to the news of me being married with a small gasp.

"I'm divorced now," I said. "That's very important to know for what I'm about to say."

Stevie shook imaginary water off her hands, then sat beside me on the bench, so close our hips touched. "This is even better than I anticipated, and I anticipated a lot."

"I ran into your brother at the airport on my way to Cancún for my honeymoon," I told her. "He picked up something I'd dropped, then chased after me to give it back."

"That was surprisingly generous of him," Stevie said.

"What I dropped was a bracelet."

Dara gasped. "The heart-promise bracelet?"

I nodded, and then, as simply as possible, I explained to Stevie what the bracelet meant to Dara and me. Dara hadn't even heard the wildest part yet—the vision—and she was already shifting in her seat, excitement getting the better of her.

Stevie gamely kept up. "You think this bracelet represents finding the person you're meant to love forever?"

"Right. And I got mine back at my wedding. Then I dropped it at the airport, and your brother found it. When he handed it back to me, our hands touched. And I, uh, saw a vision of me with him. *Here.* In this exact mess hall. Down to every detail. We were surrounded by his family. Laughing. We were . . ."

"In love," Dara finished, staring at the antler chandelier overhead. "Garland, I can't believe you never told me this."

"You know I couldn't," I whispered.

"Of course you could," Dara countered, instantly insulted. "I would have handled it well."

It was true. She would have been as unfussed about it as she was about everything else. Unlike the rest of my family, Dara had never seen my divorce as some kind of failing on my part. Instead she'd taken the news of my split like a nurse jotting down information before the doctor entered the appointment room, gathering up the necessary details without opinion. It was another one of the countless kindnesses she'd given me, and all that time I'd been lying to her, leaving out a crucial piece of information.

I looked to Stevie. Up to that point she had been nothing but supportive of everything I threw her way. But her energy had changed as fast as mine had when I entered the mess hall. She folded her arms across her chest and angled herself away.

"I don't know," she said.

Her doubt crushed me more than expected. I wanted her to believe me, not just because I knew what I'd seen was real but because I didn't want her to think less of me for believing it myself.

"It sounds ridiculous," I admitted. "Maybe it means nothing. But it *did* happen."

"Don't say it means nothing," Dara warned. "You fainted at the sight of this guy. Obviously it means something. How could it not?"

Stevie put a hand on my shoulder. That pull between us once again set my pulse racing. It felt as if she could see through me, somehow. "Sorry. I do believe you." She paused for a second and tilted her head. "It does require an unusually high amount of faith from me up front, but I'm happy to give it. I just meant that—" She searched for the right words. "Mason can be a nightmare."

"Oh," I said softly.

"He's impulsive, for one. And not in a fun way. He gets in the worst moods. Sometimes they last for days. And he—" She paused again. "He never remembers to pick up his clothes off the floor. Or take out the trash. Doesn't matter how many times you tell him. He's been like that his entire life."

"That just sounds like a person to me," Dara snapped back.

"Thanks for telling me," I said to Stevie, forcing way too much brightness into my tone. Dara never accepted critique well, even when it didn't directly affect her, which meant I fell all over myself trying to smooth things over. The last thing I wanted was for Dara to create an enemy out of my ally. "That's really good to know."

Stevie directed her attention to my sister. "Look, if Mason really is somehow the man of Garland's dreams, I want her to know all of that."

Dara was well aware of exactly how intimidating she could

be, and Stevie had done the impossible in response—she'd held her ground.

Stevie looked at me and added, "He's just not the type of person I'd imagine for someone like you, that's all."

I had to cackle at how true that was. "Believe me. I never imagined myself with a guy like him either. I don't actually trust blond men."

Dara snickered. "That's exactly the type of weird shit she always says," she told Stevie.

"Sorry, just categorically, something is amiss there," I added, feeding on the amusement.

Everyone was smiling now, even Stevie.

"The opposites-attract love story of a lifetime," Dara said. "Except you're not opposites, you just have an irrational bias toward people you think are too good-looking."

"I fear beauty and power," I said. "I really do."

Dara made eye contact with Stevie. "She can't watch the Olympics. Too many talented, good-looking people in the same room."

"I mean, when I look at you, I have to squint," I admitted to Stevie. "It's like staring into the sun."

Stevie smacked her hands on the wooden table. The loud thwack echoed in my ears, dulling my embarrassment over what I'd just said. "Hold on. Now *I'm* too talented, good-looking, and blond? I thought this only had to do with *men*."

"It does," I said, lost in my own harebrained logic. "Don't worry. I still trust you."

"Good. Because I'm about to offer to help you date my brother, and that's not something I'd do for anyone." There was a hasty urgency to her pitch that seemed out of character. Her breathing was a little too shallow. Her speech a touch rushed. "No one here knows him better than I do. And if he's really the one you're meant to be with, I can keep him honest too."

It was hardly a minute ago that she'd been listing all of Mason's worst qualities.

"Besides, we have an alliance, don't we?" she asked in a softer tone.

I should've told her I didn't want to do this. My heart had been made up the day Ethan left me. If it wasn't going to be him, it wasn't going to be anyone. But I'd promised myself to take risks at camp, and this couldn't have been riskier.

Plus, how many people did I know as a kid who'd gone away to summer camp, then come back at the start of the school year having gotten wrapped up in a brief romantic tryst that was gone as fast as it came? What if that were me? What if it didn't have to be some big, epic thing?

Now that I'd been married and divorced and was single again, I certainly wasn't looking to put another ring on my finger. Maybe Mason could just be a summer fling. Adults could do that. A lot of adults did it all the time, in fact. That had never been me, but this was supposed to be my chance to transform myself.

I could be casual here. I could have a summer fling.

"Deal," I said, shaking Stevie's hand yet again.

5

When the sky went dark, we gathered in the event hall for the first nightly mixer. The vaulted ceiling was crisscrossed with wood beams. There was a lofted upstairs area that overlooked the ground floor. Light from wall fixtures added far too much dimension to the faces of the taxidermied deer and moose proudly displayed throughout. The whole place was huge, clearly built for crowds, with a draftiness to it that felt nostalgic somehow. Through the years, countless summer romances had bloomed and withered in this very hall. And mine was about to start. My casual, easy, low-stakes summer fling with a blond man. Not a single string attached!

Tables were scattered along the edges of the ground floor, centered around a dance floor. A large stage had been built in front of it, with a bar lining the back right, tucked under the lofted area.

Stevie scanned the crowd with the same focus she'd had

earlier on our campgrounds tour. Then she headed for the bar. "A vodka cranberry with lime," she said to the bartender. She looked back at me. "What do you want?"

"Whatever you're having."

Stevie smiled. "Make it two." She pulled a five-dollar bill from her bra and handed it over to the bartender for a tip.

She'd changed into a black cotton midi dress that hugged every inch of her with the kind of generosity that made artists want to draw, and she'd taken her hair out of the braids to let her curls flow freely. She wore very little makeup. Just a swipe of blush across her cheeks and three strokes of mascara on each eye. I knew because I'd counted, watching her as we'd gotten ready, transfixed by her ability to just *do* things. Hastily apply cream blush with her fingers and put a tiny dot on her lower lip and make it look breezily perfect, then swiftly run a mascara wand over her eyes while telling me a story about how she'd burned her thigh with a flat iron in high school and promised never to use one on her hair ever again.

"You look amazing," I said to her. "Really amazing."

Nerves made me repeat myself. We were a group of adults gathered together for what felt like a school dance, holding the same anxieties we'd had as kids but either better or worse at managing them. All day we'd been together in various places around camp, too skittish to really connect yet, waiting for the cloak of night to better disguise our nerves.

"Tell me that one more time and I might start believing you," Stevie said to me.

We'd pregamed outside the building with shots of tequila Stevie had packed in her bag and some limes she'd grabbed from the mess hall. The citrus sweetness on her breath suited her just as well as her clothing did.

"You look amazing." This time I whispered it, trying for playful.

The bartender handed over our cocktails. Stevie appraised me as she took a quick sip of her drink. "Would you believe me if I told you how amazing you look too?"

I'd put on a dark green top and black cropped jeans, then pulled my hair into a bun atop my head to keep it out of the way. It was a fine outfit. More than I'd do on a usual day. Not as youthful as my preferred looks, but Dara's comments had been echoing in my head as I'd packed for the trip, so I'd thrown in as many of my "adult"-looking clothes as I could find.

"No," I said.

She brushed a stray hair off my neck. "Well, you should." She looked into my eyes for so long I forgot what we were doing.

Then her golden god of a brother strolled into the event hall, letting out a loud whoop of excitement designed to catch the attention of everyone in his general vicinity. He'd put on *his* version of dress wear, which was a gray suit jacket over a plain white tee, tucked into board shorts. He also had on flip-flops. I wondered if the lesson he was meant to teach me was laughter. He looked ridiculous, in a somewhat endearing way.

"Am I supposed to go hang with him?" I asked Stevie.

"Absolutely not," she answered quickly. "You have to get to know me first."

"Liking somebody's family *is* important."

"Exactly. You get it."

"My ex was an only child. I only had his mom to contend with," I said.

"How'd that go?"

"She tolerated me in the most bare-bones way someone could put up with another person without ever actually speaking poorly of them."

"The good news is, *our* mom loves everyone," Stevie told me. "Even when she shouldn't. I'm ninety-nine percent sure she sent a birthday card to my ex."

Staying quiet allowed me to skip the canned laughter I normally would have offered that comment. I'd sent Ethan's mother birthday flowers back in March, and I planned to do it every year for as long as she was alive. If ever the impossible should happen and I got Ethan back, no one would ever be able to say I'd behaved inappropriately while we were apart.

"Oh god." Stevie's eyes bored into mine. "You do that, don't you?"

"How do you know that?"

"Because of the face you made when I said it."

"I made a face? I didn't mean to. I just—I want his mom to like me," I admitted. "I hate that she's probably telling people I'm the one who didn't do enough in the marriage. I'm trying to prove her wrong, I guess. Or have her regret the joy she must've felt when he told her he left me."

Never in my life had I laid out the truth that plainly. It felt exhilarating, in a "riding your bike downhill but not being sure the brakes are going to work at the end of the decline" kind of way. I actually had to wiggle my toes to remind myself I was on flat land.

"No amount of kindness you pay those types of people will ever change their minds," Stevie said.

"I'll still try," I told her. "Just in case."

"You and my mom can end up in a lifelong battle, then."

"Wait until she sees what I can do with a Fourth of July fruit basket," I joked. "Arbor Day tree-planting kits? Your mother doesn't stand a chance against me."

Stevie pressed her hand over her heart. "*Finally.* Someone who can knock that nice lady down a few pegs."

Mason approached us, snapping his fingers as he walked up. "Our fainter!" he said to me. "You good?"

The heat of the embarrassment that crawled up to my cheeks could've cooked an egg. "Oh yeah! All good! Better than ever."

Mason nodded. "We do know each other, right?"

"You gave me my jewelry back in the airport once." It felt odd to leave out the details now that Stevie knew them too, but the prospect of explaining to Mason that we might be destined to be together seemed like something that should come after we'd learned the color of each other's eyes, at least. Anything more than what we had.

He scratched his head. "Nice! Well, it's good to see you again."

If he'd had the same vision as me, he was much better at making it seem insignificant. All the same, there was kind of an exquisite simplicity to his friendliness. It seemed earnest and unpolished.

"You too," I said to him.

I prided myself on being able to hold a conversation with

anyone. Finding the briefest thread of connection with a complete stranger was something I enjoyed being good at. It was not often, if ever, that I lost my ability to think. Standing there with Mason—nursing a vodka cranberry after having had a shot of tequila, already knowing I was making mistakes with my alcohol intake and, more broadly, with my life—any idea of what we should talk about completely left me. The task of getting to know someone from the ground up was daunting under normal circumstances. But the extra layer? The unexplainable vision and our potentially intertwined fates made me overthink everything. I didn't know how to downplay it enough to make sure he knew I didn't want anything serious, because what could sound more serious than telling a perfect stranger you'd seen your future with them?

"You know, Garland has her own coffee maker here," Stevie offered up to fill the silence. "I think it's the same as that one you asked for last Christmas."

Mason's eyes—it was too dark to really be sure, but they seemed to be green, if they were anything like Stevie's—lit up. "No way! A Ratio Eight pour over? No one in my family would get it for me."

"It was almost six hundred dollars, dude. Get it for yourself," Stevie said. "Or . . . maybe you can borrow Garland's?"

Stevie had so generously attempted to open the door to a connection between Mason and me, but she'd picked the one topic that led us further away from territory I knew.

"It's actually my sister's," I explained. "She couldn't fit it in her bag, so I had to pack it in mine. She was really concerned that the coffee up here wouldn't be any good." I pointed to

Dara, who was being her typical self, standing in a back corner watching everyone else. When I waved at her, she returned the favor by throwing up the middle finger. *Come over here*, I mouthed, to which she replied *no* and kept on standing alone.

"Do *you* like coffee?" Mason asked me.

All I could think to say back was "Absolutely. It's so good. Coffee rocks."

Stevie choked on her drink. Vodka cranberry shot out through her nostrils in shocked laughter.

Mason—sweet, oblivious Mason—looked around for some kind of clue as to what was so funny. When he couldn't find it, he said, "I'm gonna get a drink, I'll be back in one sec." Then he did the very slick thing I'd always admired in confident men—he patted my shoulder and squeezed it before walking off.

"Coffee *rocks*," Stevie teased once Mason was out of earshot. She could do a great impression of me. It made me feel understood in a different way than I'd ever felt before. Most people picked up on my optimism. Stevie captured my vulnerability. The worries I hid behind the hope I projected.

"Why did I say that?" I asked, laughing with her. "I'm a mess. I haven't had to flirt in years. It makes me want to die inside."

Stevie tapped her pointer finger against her tooth, then rested the same finger against her nose. Whatever she was thinking about, she was thinking it very intensely, until finally she offered, a little cryptically, "Mason's not a complicated guy."

She switched to staring at her brother. She was very good

at looking at people. She had no qualms about where she focused her attention. It was forward, like her. Honest.

"He likes you," she continued. "I can tell because he's doing his cool-guy thing. Like the shoulder grab."

"The shoulder grab," I echoed, feeling the burn of where his hand had touched my skin. It embarrassed me that she'd noticed. That they had a sibling shorthand she could pick up on that told her how he felt.

"Plus, I may or may not have told him to pay closer attention to you," she admitted.

It was my turn to choke on my drink. "You did *what*?"

"Don't worry, I didn't tell him about your vision. He wouldn't know what to do with that kind of information anyway. Mason's not really down with the universe sending us signs or anything like that. In fact, most of the time he can't see what's right in front of his face. So I did a little pointing on your behalf. That's all."

It made me feel like a baby fawn, stumbling through the world. Somehow Stevie, a stranger by all metrics, kept anticipating the paths I was going to take and clearing away any debris that might make me fall on my face. I didn't know how to feel like I'd earned that when all I'd done in return was talk to her.

"Just be yourself with him. That'll be more than enough," she said.

"You've really got a lot of faith in me. Even after 'coffee rocks'?"

She found my eyes again—just once, fleetingly—before

looking down at her drink. "Having faith in you is a part of our pact, isn't it?"

"Do you know what's funny? I don't even know your last name." We'd already spent most of the day together, except for whatever moment she'd stolen away to tell her brother to notice me, and we hadn't even thought to cover the basics.

"Magnusson," she answered. "Anything else you need to know?"

"Everything," I said honestly. "But I'll settle for the quick hits first."

Stevie grinned. "Okay, let's see. Our dad was born in Sweden, but he moved to the States when he was a teen. Our mom's from Rhode Island. We were all born in Vancouver. Then we moved to Connecticut when I was three. Then Idaho. Then New Mexico. Then Florida."

"Wow."

"Before you even ask, we got out of Canada too early for the whole niceness thing to really settle in. Only our oldest brother, Andrew, absorbed the Canadian spirit. The rest of us are, as my dad sometimes says, 'aggressively American.'"

"Where do you live now?"

"It's a long story, but I kind of live nowhere." She paused, then added, "Mason's still in Florida."

She was good at incorporating her brother into our conversations, but I wanted to know more about *her*. What did it mean to live nowhere? Mason, the Florida resident himself, returned with a beer and a mission, and I lost my opportunity to ask.

"We need to play beer pong," he told me. "You and me against Stevie and our brother Andrew."

Before I could protest, which was what I always did when it came to anything that required competition, Mason guided me toward the staircase that led to the lofted section of the hall. He kept his hand on my back in that same confident way he'd squeezed my shoulder, and I hated how it reminded me of Ethan.

It occurred to me then—at the base of the stairs in the middle of the event hall—that it was because this was the first real trip I'd ever taken without him. We didn't go on vacations in my childhood. Only in college, when I'd cobbled together enough money through a part-time job and a healthy dose of financial ignorance, did I ever take trips for fun. Because that was something Ethan did.

"Oh, you're out for blood," Mason said to me. He thought I was pausing to mentally prepare to annihilate everyone at beer pong, not having a full-scale internal crisis over my capacity to love again after having my heart broken.

"Something like that." I downed the last swig of my drink and headed up the stairs.

The loft had a beer pong table, a single chair, and a huge painting of the lake that looked to be straight from the 1970s. Exactly the kind of gentle, dreamy landscape work I'd imagined someone would do of this place.

Andrew, the oldest Magnusson brother, grabbed Mason by the shoulder and roughed up his hair, then kissed him on the cheek like he hadn't seen him in weeks.

"This is Garland," Mason told him afterward.

Andrew offered me a gigantic bear hug, which I took readily. "I've seen you. You're Stevie's friend."

I smiled. I liked being known as Stevie's friend.

"She's *my* friend too," Mason corrected, which made me laugh, because we'd said all of ten words to each other.

Andrew let me go. "She's *my* friend too," he said in good-hearted mockery. A family trait, it seemed. He had the same build as Mason, but a more weathered face. He looked like he lived his life out on a boat. I could picture him with a flowing blue shirt, half-unbuttoned, navigating a steering wheel with one hand and holding a cigar in the other.

"Right?" he asked me. "We're friends, aren't we?"

"Of course," I said. "The best of friends."

Andrew high-fived me, then pointed to the other Magnus-son brother, who sat sideways in the leather chair, sulking. "Best friend, that lunk over there is Frank."

Frank offered up a sad wave.

"He hates to come in last," Andrew explained. "He lost the first game, and we had to ban him from playing any more for the night. He's not in the best of moods right now."

"Welcome to life with my brothers! You'd never know all of us were adults, would you?" Stevie had come up the stairs, and she stood a few paces behind me with a smirk on her face, taking in the scene before her. "I told you, Andrew's the nicest one. Right?"

"Not you?" I asked.

Frank readjusted his position in his pouting corner, moving closer to sitting upright. "Stevie's only nice if you earn it."

"I don't believe that," I challenged. "She was nice to me right away."

It didn't seem possible, and the light was a little too low to really tell, but Stevie seemed to blush. "Please. I clotheslined you at the front door."

"That's not normal?"

She grinned at me. "I only do that for the best of people."

Mason cleared his throat. "Let's get going. Me and Gar against Stevie and Andrew."

Gar was hands down the worst nickname anyone had ever tried to give me, but I swallowed back the urge to say anything about it. Beer pong reminded me of college, which reminded me of Ethan yet again, and I was doing my level best to stop myself from seeming too moody. I could be Gar, if Gar kept the mood light.

Ethan was beginning to turn into a representation of ideas instead of the man he was. Ethan was longing. He was knowledge in a crowd. He was the first eyes I found when something silly happened. No amount of alcohol could chase off the surfacing pains of what I'd lost. He'd have told everyone I don't like beer. He'd have made sure to excuse me from the competition.

As much as I missed that, I didn't want to be someone who needed another person to do work for them anymore. And it wasn't that I didn't like beer so much as I didn't want to drink it in a random frat house with strangers. I'd never bothered to explain that to Ethan in the first place. I just let him do what he thought was right, because that was easier than trying to get him to understand a nuance that only made sense to me.

"Good luck," Stevie whispered before she met Andrew on the other side of the table. "We've had tequila, vodka, and now we're about to have beer. We better be on our best behavior."

We weren't on the same team, but she was still on my side. "No need to waste your luck on me. I am very bad at beer pong."

She laughed as she walked away. I took my spot beside Mason.

"Please tell me you're good at this," he said to me.

The truth was, I could have been good if I really cared. I just hated the way people rested all their hopes and dreams on something so deeply trivial, like a game of beer pong in the loft of a campground event hall.

"*Mm.*" It was a noise, not a confirmation or denial.

Mason accepted it as an answer all the same, which was good. I didn't want to ruin any of this precious newness between us by spoiling his hopes. This would be a great test of our ability to be teammates. Maybe he didn't have to be the guy who protected me by stopping me from playing. Maybe he'd be the one who made competing worth it.

When we started the game, I threw the little ball so far past the table that Andrew had to go running to save it from falling onto the main floor.

"Sorry!" I told Mason, who could not hide his wince.

As the game went on and it became clear I was not going to get any better, panic set in. Mason was being friendly about his disappointment, but it couldn't be long before that disappointment turned into outright resentment. I felt so terrible about it that the beer didn't even taste bad going down. When we lost, I chugged the last cup gladly. At least it would eventually quiet my ability to process my own panic.

"Nice game," Andrew said with unearned kindness. "Should we play another?"

Stevie started nodding her head. Then she looked across the table at me, and a tiny mountain range of concern sprouted between her brows. "Actually, I wanna dance," she said.

Andrew seemed as surprised to hear this as I was. "Are you sure? There are a lot of *people* down there."

People was usually a word meant to indicate a group. The way Andrew said it made it clear that there was one *specific* person downstairs the Magnussons did not want to see. I couldn't imagine a world where anyone disliked any of them. Especially not Stevie. She reminded me of the sun, not just because of her bright hair and beaming smile, but the way she pulled you into her orbit.

"I'm sure," Stevie told him. "C'mon. Let's go dance."

6

By midnight, the lights overhead had changed to a pulsing purple and blue. The breeze that pushed into the hall from the open doors, keeping the air from getting too stale, developed a real bite to it. Cold enough for a coat, if you didn't have your heart rate up as high as I did out on the dance floor. The band had been playing what I took to calling hee-haw music, only because it made me yell out "Hee-haw!" every time they kicked off a new song. We as a society do not yell the words *hee-haw* enough, and once I discovered how much joy came from doing so, I became an unstoppable hee-hawing force of nature.

Mason could not dance. Not in the technical sense. He was all limbs and commitment. Several drinks deep, we started making up our own choreography together. It reminded me of being at a friend's house and coming up with a performance to convince our parents to let us have a sleepover. Every so often, someone we didn't know would join us, until we had a large group of campers united in our brand of chaos.

It was the most fun I'd had in solidly a decade. Maybe longer. Even Dara joined in with the dancing. Her fearlessness knew no bounds in this way. She'd gone the whole night without talking to anyone, yet she slapped her hand on her shoe alongside us, grapevining across the floor.

The only person missing from the magic was Stevie. Almost as soon as we'd gone down the stairs, she'd disappeared. Every time I tried to step away to find her, Mason pulled me into another dance, or Dara brought me a new drink, and it distracted me from uncovering where Stevie had gone. I felt her absence like hunger, a dull ache in my belly that grew with time, until the drinks made my head swim so much I couldn't remember what to do about the feeling besides agonize over it.

The lead singer of the band asked for the lights to be dimmed. "It's time to slow things down here so everybody can get a good night's rest before tomorrow," he said.

I booed. *Loudly.*

The lead singer laughed, recognizing that my taunting was in good fun. "Don't worry, Garland, we're here every night. There will be plenty more good times where this came from. We need to make it to tomorrow to get there, though."

I didn't remember giving him my name, but I couldn't really remember a single thing at that moment other than that I missed Stevie, and I loved to dance, and if given the chance, I was going to yell "Hee-haw!" again.

"Campers," the lead singer continued, inciting a big laugh from me. It would never stop being funny that I was a *camper.*

"We want you to look around and find someone in this crowd to share a special dance with. Doesn't matter if you know them well or not. It's probably better if you don't. But we're gonna close this out with one last song, and all we ask is that you treat this like what it is—a summer-camp slow dance."

They started playing a country cover of "Hero" by Enrique Iglesias, the very song I had slow danced to with Lyle Holter in seventh grade. He'd sweat so much his hands had left imprints on my silky T.J. Maxx dress, and we took a disposable camera picture together that didn't get developed properly. All you could see were our awkward torsos, leaving generous space for the Holy Spirit between us.

Mason put a hand on my shoulder again and squeezed. "Wanna dance this one with me?"

"Sure," I said.

His arms around my waist were much more confident than the seventh-grade take on this, but I felt just as nervous. Maybe even more so. Even though I was drunker than the day was long, I could still feel the uncertainty of my footwork and hand placement. I never understood why as kids we didn't pull each other close enough to avoid making eye contact. At least Mason gave me that courtesy. I rested my head against his sweaty torso, combing the crowd for Stevie one last time. I'd started doubting my memory of her face. I needed to look at her longer so I could never lose track of her again.

When the song finished, it became clear that Mason had been holding me up more than dancing with me. All the liquor in my system had turned me liquid myself. I was maybe ten minutes away from passing out or vomiting. I could see only the outlines of things. My thoughts. My hands. The world itself.

"Night night," I said to Mason, patting him on the head and wandering off, finding myself in front of a wall instead of the very large open door. "Whoops."

After a few course corrections, someone had a hand on my biceps.

"It was the cocktail Dara got you after beer pong. That's what did you in."

The voice was Stevie's. That effortless, low confidence. She spoke like she never questioned her own words. Like she always knew exactly what she wanted to say and how she wanted to say it.

"I missed you so much," I said, poking her freckled nose. "Where'd you go?"

Her hand moved from my biceps to the entirety of my back. "You really are drunk, aren't you?"

I kept poking her freckles as she led us toward our cabin. "No."

"Did you have a good time with Mason? I saw you two slow dancing."

"He's so tall," I told her.

"Yes, he's very tall."

"How come you didn't dance with anybody?"

"How do you know I didn't?"

"Because I was looking for you," I slurred. "Obviously."

"Obviously," she repeated.

We were outside now, trudging along the dirt paths we'd walked all day, following lamplit markers to Cabin Seven.

"You didn't answer," I noted.

"I was drinking water," she said, guiding me up the stairs. "Something I suggest you do too."

"You were drinking water for *hours*? That's a lie!" I had a well-documented boldness to me when I was drunk. I said things without consideration for whether the other person would be offended by the level of truth I was communicating.

Stevie did not respond.

The light inside our cabin glowed bright against the darkness. When we stumbled through the door together, we found our roommate, Michelle, sitting in the common area eating a bowl of cereal. She had on a matching pajama set and fuzzy slippers.

"You two closed it down," she said.

"I wish you were there!" I told her, suddenly swept up in sincere regret. I wanted to know her better, and I'd lost a whole day's worth of opportunity to do that. "We missed you so much!"

"Oh, I was there," she informed me. "I saw you leading your dance class. But I couldn't get through your army of fans to talk to you."

"We needed you," I assured her, even though I had no idea if she liked to dance. In that moment, I really believed myself. "I was telling everyone, 'We need Michelle!'"

Stevie looked past me. "She's very drunk."

"And you're not?" Michelle asked her.

"Not so much."

Stevie's hair was so pretty. So curly. Soft ringlets. Just lovely.

"Can I braid your hair?" I asked her.

"Maybe in a bit. Let's get you changed first."

"Okay." I wandered off into what I thought was our room, only to discover I was in the hall closet. "Whoops!"

Stevie got behind me again. Her hands were so warm, they heated me from the inside out. She had them on my waist, pulling me toward our room. "This way."

I flopped face-first onto my bed, unable to resist the temptation. Distantly, I could understand I wasn't behaving properly, but I couldn't hold on to the thought long enough to change my actions. Only between bursts of sleeping did I realize Stevie was gingerly slipping off my shoes.

"We need to brush your teeth and get you in pajamas," she insisted.

"No!" I yelled, then laughed. "I'm gonna sleep now."

She tried again, this time nudging my shoulder. Instead of responding, I pulled her on top of me like a blanket. "C'mon. Sleep with me."

She pried herself away. "I'm going to get you a glass of water. Okay?"

"No! Come to bed!" I pulled her back down. It felt so nice to have her lie on top of me. Why would she want to get up? Where could be better than here?

She still smelled like a cherished memory. Like I'd known her all my life, but somehow I'd forgotten her until today. The sunscreen mixed with the watery scent on her skin reminded me of even more safe things. Lying on my back on a pool float. Making a wish on a dandelion puff under the high-noon heat of a long summer day.

If she got up again, I didn't feel it.

The last thing I remembered was the comfort of her body atop mine.

Day Two of Summer Camp

7

The next morning greeted me with a splitting headache and an alarm that went off with the sunrise. Light sliced in through the slatted blinds, insulting me with the promise of a new day. On the nightstand between my bed and Stevie's, a tall glass of water awaited me, along with some medicine and a croissant. There was a little note that read *You'll need this when you wake up. See you out there, ally.*

It took a lot of effort to get myself upright, but I drank the water readily and took the medicine with my croissant. Stevie and Michelle were already gone. Morning people, it seemed. Something I could genuinely never be, though my recurring alarm still kept the faith. The best part of my job as a rideshare driver was setting my own hours. I preferred to start my day around noon and be done with work by five.

By the time I'd showered and dressed myself, I felt slightly less like a hollowed-out husk of a human, not that it was any accomplishment. Last night's drinks came up my throat in five-minute intervals. Little reminders of the decisions I'd made, though I couldn't really remember any of them.

What had I said? What had I *done*?

I emerged from my cabin in big sunglasses and an oversized hoodie, hoping to make it to the mess hall without incident. Somehow, campers still recognized me.

"Garland! So much fun last night!" one of them yelled out. "Hee-haw!"

"Hee-haw!" Another person echoed.

I had no idea who they were. Or what *hee-haw* meant. Hand over my heart, if I got asked to explain the origins of that phrase or be thrown into a lightless cave for the next hundred years, I'd have kissed my life goodbye and moved into the darkness.

"If it isn't Garland Moore," Tommy said when I made my somewhat dramatic entrance into the mess hall. It wasn't the theatrical sunglasses and gigantic hoodie that made my arrival notable. Campers were letting out genuine whoops of appreciation at the sight of me.

Tim patted the spot beside him. "Hee-haw!"

I groaned. "Why does everyone keep saying that?"

The question elicited *raucous* laughter from the twins.

"You don't remember?" Tommy asked. "You turned it into your own personal catchphrase last night. Everyone's been calling the mixer hee-haw night."

They smelled fantastic, as usual. Unfortunately, musky wealth wasn't the best solution for a hangover. I bit back the urge to taste even more of the previous night's drinks.

"I have very little memory of that," I told them honestly. "Why didn't I say 'yeehaw' instead?"

Tommy laughed again. "No one knows. That's the magic of it." He was wearing a Camp Carl Cove shirt that looked vintage. It had a gigantic cross on it.

Tim had on a newer version of the same shirt, and the cross had been replaced with a picture of a tree. I knew instantly that I needed one of my own. It felt like exactly the kind of niche thing I'd grown to love wearing. I pictured myself climbing inside the picture, living in the shirt portrait, free from the hee-hawing reality I'd built for myself without conscious effort.

"What's with the cross on the shirt?" I asked Tommy.

He looked down at it. "This place was originally a Christian camp. They're the ones who built the campgrounds and dug their own lake and all that. When new owners bought this place, they kept the original name, so our parents didn't realize it wasn't a God thing anymore. We sure weren't going to be the ones to tell them. This is the original camp shirt design. I got it my first year coming here."

"I really love it," I told him. I wanted to say more, but my headache made me pinch the space between my eyebrows instead.

"Enough about shirts. Please go get something to eat," Tim said to me. "You look like you're going to faint again."

I scurried off toward the food line, where breakfast was served buffet-style. Eggs, hash browns, pancakes, and all kinds of meat. The scent of bacon reminded me of Saturday mornings in the kitchen when my dad was in a good enough mood to make everybody food. Hash browns were mornings in Dara's apartment, when I'd decided to impress her with some home cooking. The smell of breakfast food always reminded me of hope. It was almost enough to make me feel better.

Waiting in line, I passed out countless friendly hellos to strangers who seemed to love me. I pretended to know them for fear of insulting anyone else with my lack of memory. When I got back to my seat, the twins ran me through the previous night's events until I developed a coloring book outline's worth of memories from the evening. Too many types of alcohol. Mason and me having a certified blast. Hee-haw. Falling asleep with a blanket on me. Perfectly warm.

Tommy pulled my sunglasses down to the tip of my nose to get a good look at the exhaustion I'd attempted to cover up. "You must be feeling it all today," he said.

"You really were the life of the party," Tim assured me again. "I knew you'd be the right kind of person to invite to camp."

My cheeks flushed. I hated not being able to control every aspect of my behavior. Worse, I hated how successful I'd been at making friends I didn't remember.

"And don't you just love Stevie?" Tim continued. "You two rooming together with Michelle might make for my favorite cabin. Just saying."

"Did Stevie tell you she used to go to this camp with us when we were kids?" Tommy asked.

"She mentioned coming here, but I didn't realize that meant you all knew one another then," I said. "I guess I should have."

Tim grinned. "She recruited more people to come this week than anyone else. We love her to pieces."

Even though I'd only met her yesterday, it fit with the Stevie I'd come to know. Generous and supportive without anything expected in return. She'd been helping me since the moment I arrived, and I still hadn't done anything to return it. What if she thought I didn't value her? That I wasn't showing up?

"Do you know where she is?" I asked.

"Probably on a morning hike."

That made sense too. I knew she loved birds. She had weathered hiking boots. She wore a National Parks ball cap. She was an outdoor kind of woman. Every piece of information slotted into place, not so much a Stevie puzzle piece finding its home but instead a Stevie painting I could see from a distance, and I was continuously stepping closer, making sense of all the details.

"She used to love this spot by the south edge of the lake, farthest from the buildings," Tommy said. "If you follow the curve, there's a small part of the water that gets wedged between the trees. It's a little hideout. I bet she's there."

I finished breakfast as fast as I could, then headed to the spot the twins had described. As predicted, Stevie sat by the water with her knees up to her chin, using a pair of binoculars to gaze into the trees. She wore another matching athletic set, this time a plum color, with an oversized white flannel over it.

Her two small braids framed her face, tucked underneath a ball cap again.

There was a calmness to this part of the campgrounds that didn't feel possible to explain. Pictures couldn't grab the energy here. Even the sun seemed to understand, because the rays of light sliced through the gaps in the greenery with gentle reverence.

"Look at you," I said to announce myself. "Present in nature. Not a phone in sight."

Stevie set her binoculars down to pull her phone from the pocket of her shorts. "I was on this five seconds ago. You happened to walk up at the right time. Not that I get any reception here. But I was trying."

"Don't spoil the moment."

"You're right. Sorry. I was here communing with the wind, free from the prison of technology. Just me and the birds."

"Find any yellow-billed cuckoos, like you hoped?" I asked.

"Only some Acadian flycatchers."

"I thought I heard Acadian flycatchers this morning."

She grinned at me, and my heart suddenly ached. Like an actual, tangible hurt that made me press my hand against my chest in surprise.

"You okay?" she asked.

"Oh." I looked down at my hand on my shirt as if noticing the gesture myself. "Yeah. Still feeling the weight of last night's decisions. Mind if I sit?"

"You're always welcome wherever I am."

My heart ached harder. As if little construction workers lived in there and they'd started building something new without a permit. "I wanted to thank you for everything you did yesterday," I said as I settled beside her. "And for the food and medicine this morning."

"Please. I'm the one who should be thanking you. You got my brother to line dance."

"Is that what you'd call what we were doing? I don't remember it super well, but I think I'd call it 'middle schoolers who've had too many Pixy Stix deciding they know how to jig.'" As we laughed, I picked up her binoculars and looked at the trees. "There it is. Just like I thought. The Acadian flycatcher."

"Did you enjoy your slow dance with him?" Stevie asked.

I was glad to have my attention on the trees, where in truth I saw nothing but blurred greenery. The details of my slow dance with Mason were about as racy as the seventh-grade swaying I'd done with Lyle Holter. Probably even less, since I'd touched three different naked bodies since then and therefore a fully clothed drunken twirl around the room was the equivalent of a handshake at my ripe age. But it still embarrassed me to talk about it with her. I didn't know what to say other than "I think it was nice."

Nice was easy. Nice was casual.

"Good," Stevie said.

Nice and good. The best of friends.

"Totally," I said. "By the way, do you think birds are real?"

Stevie fell apart, laughing so hard she genuinely startled some wildlife. We heard the frantic, scattering rustle in the forest beyond the edge of the campgrounds. "That's a conspiracy theory some random guy started to mock other conspiracy theories," she said.

"Oh, I know. But what if it's so completely off base it circles back around to being right?" I pretended to adjust the focus of the binoculars. It only made the scenery even more blurred. "Fucking CIA drones," I muttered. "Or FBI. One of those guys."

"Watching our every movement."

"Tracking our thoughts."

"Memorizing our behaviors."

"See?" I said. "You get it."

Stevie didn't laugh so much as let out a long hiss of breath, the kind that stretched out into a contented sigh. "You're doing the color games, right?"

When Dara signed us up for the camp, there was a choice to opt in to the competitive element of the week: the color games. Four teams—Red, Yellow, Green, and Blue—would compete daily in various morning contests, earning points depending on where they placed. The winning color team at the end of camp would walk away with a trophy and half off camp tuition for the following year.

Dara immediately wanted to do it, not allowing me a moment to protest. I'd put it out of my mind, hoping it would be at best something she forgot about or at worst something I didn't have to invest in very seriously. Now Stevie—intense, committed, fullhearted Stevie—was asking me if I planned to participate.

"I am," I said, leaving it up to her to interpret my tone as she pleased.

"Thank god." She opted for relief. The worst of the interpretations.

"I'm not sure you'll be thanking Him at the end of the week."

Stevie scooted until she was sitting behind me in a straddle. "You know, you'd probably see a lot more if you turned the binoculars around." Her legs framed either side of my body, and her arms hovered just above mine, wrapped around me like an open bear hug. Then she secured her hands atop my own and flipped the binoculars around.

At once, the world opened up. Every leaf came into focus, their spindly veins holding droplets of dew that were suddenly so plump I could nearly taste the water on my tongue. My heart's construction crew hammered away with reckless abandon as I found a small brown bird resting on a branch.

"Wow," I gasped. "I think I see a yellow-billed cuckoo."

"Stop it. No, you don't," Stevie said.

I leaned forward—not very far, not breaking our touch—but enough to be playful. "Oh yeah. The . . . plume gives it away. That rich green? I'd know it anywhere."

"Why would a *yellow*-billed cuckoo be *green*?"

"That's the thing. This one is."

"Incredible," she said. "The second I get reception, I'm calling the Audubon Society and letting them know."

"Thank you." I continued inspecting the very ordinary-looking brown bird. "Never seen anything like this in my thirty-two years of life. Maybe they can call this the Magnusson-Moore cuckoo. I'm willing to share credit for the discovery. Only because you lent me the binoculars."

"That means a lot to me, seeing as I'm the one who fostered this new passion you have for birds."

"I will always credit the passion you foster in me," I said.

Stevie scooted back until she was no longer touching me.

This was not the first time I'd managed to say something inappropriate, but I sincerely hoped it would be the last. It wasn't in my nature to make suggestive jokes, so the urge I had to do it around Stevie mystified me. If I'd offended her, she didn't give me time to apologize. She just pulled her phone from her shorts pocket and said, "Shit. We need to get to the main hall for the team announcements."

"I think we have some time. The twins were still eating breakfast when I left to find you."

"So? We need good seats. We have to see everyone's faces when they call out what teams people are on. You can tell by someone's face whether or not they're gonna take the competition seriously."

I hoped she could not see in my face exactly how little I wanted to participate in this. She clearly did not see my abysmal beer pong effort as the looming bad omen she should have. Talk about a missed sign.

Our steps fell into a matching rhythm as we emerged from our hidden alcove and set ourselves back on the regular paths. The synchronized walking made me think of a processional.

Maybe if I changed my mind and I *did* end up marrying her brother, my wedding would be nontraditional. As most second weddings were. Perhaps Stevie could walk me down the aisle? She was the key to all of it. It would make sense.

I shook my head, stopping myself. It was another one of my classic daydream scenarios. Mason and I had drunkenly swayed to Enrique Iglesias, and not at all passionately at that, and I was already imagining my alternative second wedding with him despite not wanting to get married ever again or expecting anything serious to happen with Mason.

There was no way to know my future if I never stayed in the present. So I took to looking at the trees again. Breathing in and out.

Appreciating that I was alive and I was here, and that was the best I could do.

8

When Stevie and I made it to the main hall, all three of her brothers arrived right behind us, breaking into a sprint to grab seats. Running was completely unnecessary. The other campers were filing in one or two at a time with no sense of urgency, and every single one of them opted to leave the first two rows vacant.

"Hee-haw!" Mason called out as he sailed past me. He fell into his seat, and his brothers swiftly followed suit until all three of them had crash-landed in the front row, nearly knocking over the remaining chairs.

Stevie and I took spots beside them. Immediately, all four of the Magnusson siblings started speculating about who would be on what team. They engaged in truly nauseating levels of competitive banter, shit talking one another, making bets on who would win and who would come in last.

Frank the poor sport received most of the antagonization.

They loved to remind him of what a sourpuss he could be, and it was the exact kind of ribbing I wasn't built for. It made me feel so bad for Frank, and also grateful to my own sister. She could be competitive too, but she knew me well enough to know I couldn't handle being dragged through the mud for my faults.

Mason encouraged most of the insulting, I noticed. That would be a fight we'd have later on. We'd have to discuss how he needed to be more supportive. He'd probably tell me I didn't care enough to try and win. I saw it all unfolding, and I had to stop myself again.

Stay in the present, Garland. Stay here.

In the very last row, I spotted Dara sitting with legs crossed, chatting with two people I recognized from yesterday as her cabinmates. Thanks to the name and pronoun tags Tim and Tommy had everyone wear, I'd learned their names were Aja and DJ. Aja was a beautiful Black woman with an infectious, beaming smile, and DJ was a white nonbinary person who wore a button-down with cats on it. They had a disposable camera on a lanyard around their neck. Dara looked at ease with them. I never understood how she made friends so quickly, because it seemed to me like she didn't put in much effort, and effort was practically my middle name.

Tim and Tommy arrived, starting with a speech about how excited they were to be able to do this. They'd had the entire competitive element of the camp planned without their input so that they could participate too. They'd been so thorough with every facet of this experience, it really did feel like a completely different world from the one all of us knew outside

camp. No one was bound to their jobs or their personal con-
nections here in the mountains. Instead we were defined by
our cabin numbers and, soon, our color teams. Our names
were going to be picked out of a hat to ensure the teams were
randomized.

"About eighty percent of our campers signed up to participate in the color games, so we're lucky enough to have eight
members on each color team!" Tim said excitedly.

The Camp Carl Cove alumni among us clapped. I didn't
actually know if they were all alumni, but I figured they had
to be, because who else would get that excited over learning
how many people were going to be on a team?

"Eight's a good number," Stevie whispered, confirming my
theory.

"Fantastic," I said. "Easy to say. Fun to write."

She gave me her bottle-rocket laugh, her joy charging
straight for the ceiling. Tim and Tommy both paused to look
at her, then pressed on as if the interruption didn't surprise
them much.

"We're going to start with Blue Team." Tommy waved his
fingers over the bowl of names. "The first member is . . . Garland Moore!"

The Magnussons absolutely *lost* it, hooting and hollering
like I'd been drafted onto the nation's leading sports team,
even though no one knew what I was capable of, including—
but not limited to—me. I had *no* idea what I was going to do
with these little competitions. I'd told myself to take risks at
camp, and becoming someone who cared about winning was
not exactly in my definition of risky.

Having been anointed the first person picked, I found it sort of implied that I stand up and wave. Draft pick number one, accepting my honor. The other campers hee-hawed at the sight of me. It got so rowdy that Tim and Tommy had to tell everyone to quiet down so they could continue.

"You're already a camp legend!" Mason said when the cheers died off.

"Am I?"

He gave me a hilariously stern grimace. I was obviously the world's most clueless adult for not realizing the incredible impact I'd had on Camp Carl Cove's social ecosystem.

"I'm honored to have made an impression," I corrected.

The twins continued picking names for Blue Team. Four people got called after me, and I hadn't yet met a single one of them. I was going to have to compete, and I didn't even have a *friend* to make it worthwhile? At least not a friend I remembered. Dara's roommate Aja had been put on my team, and I was at least eighty percent sure I'd never actually spoken to her, but the drunken hee-haw night complicated my memory.

The seventh name they selected for Blue Team ended up being Tommy, who drew a crowd reaction even bigger than the one I'd received. He handled the moment with poise, bowing and waving everyone off in his understated and elegant Tommy way.

His presence on my team should have been a gift, because he *was* my friend, but the cheers reminded me that this was his camp. He'd orchestrated all of this. And he'd done it with so much care. I couldn't slack off with him around.

There was one slot left on Blue Team, and I wished hard on

every shooting star that might be passing over every unseen galaxy that it would be Stevie. She was the only one I wanted by my side, even though she cared way more about this than I did.

"And the final member of Blue Team is—" Tim started.

"Stevie!" Tommy finished, grinning as wide as I'd ever seen him grin as he read her name off a slip of paper.

My relief could have fueled power plants. Revived extinct animals. I had probably had happier occurrences in my life, but at that exact moment, I couldn't recall when. "If it isn't lucky number eight herself," I said to Stevie.

"Easy to say and fun to write. Exactly what my teachers used to tell my parents at school conferences." She put her hand atop my forearm. Something cold and smooth pressed into my skin.

"What's that?" I asked.

"My birthday gift from you. Now the honorary mascot of *our* team." She picked up her hand and showed me the rock tucked into her palm. "Our alliance is preserved."

"Cabin Seven Blue Team, home of Garland, Stevie, and Rock 'The Rock' Johnson," I said.

"Toss us anywhere and we'll land with a bang."

Two people who worked for the camp found the Blue Team members in the audience and handed us shirts. They were a bright cobalt, and they had CAMP CARL COVE written across the front in the same font as the entrance sign, with BLUE TEAM in bold letters below.

I held mine up to my chest. "Cabin Seven Blue Team until the end of time."

"Or the end of the week," Stevie said.

"It's turning into one and the same for me."

When Stevie smiled at me, it was with the melancholic knowing of someone who'd been through this process before. "Camp always ends," she said.

This was my chance to give her the advice I'd been giving myself all morning. "C'mon. Let's not think about the ending before we've even begun."

The twins continued picking the names of other teams out of a hat. Dara got put on Red Team with Mason. The two of them would appreciate their shared desire never to do less than their best. My cabinmate Michelle was on Green Team with both of Stevie's other brothers and Tim. I knew no one on Yellow Team. No one yet, at least.

When all the names had been called and everyone had put their color shirts on over their other clothing, I looked around at the sea of red, yellow, green, and blue. Stevie was right. Camp would end. And I wanted to savor each moment before it did. Even though all of this was completely silly to me, it still warmed my heart to see everyone participate. Some of the team members were way older than me. Into their fifties or sixties, by my best visual guess. And they still wore their color shirts.

"Scouting the competition?" Stevie asked.

"You know me," I said. "Always looking for ways to win."

"I don't care about winning," she told me. "We just have to beat Mason. That's all."

It took only three seconds of looking at Mason to know he was good at most physical things. And all of twenty-four hours with him to know he loved to be the victor. "I'm pretty sure beating Mason would require winning."

Stevie smirked. "*Exactly*."

"Then let's win," I said, fighting off the urge to run into the forest until the campgrounds disappeared.

Stevie was my ally.

For her, I would try.

9

The woman who'd shushed Stevie and me yesterday was on our team, because why wouldn't she be? Why wouldn't this competition I didn't really want to participate in have yet another challenging element to it?

Her name was Julianne. She was married to a man on Yellow Team, and they had matching Mickey and Minnie Mouse tattoos on their calves. For reasons unknown to me, she wore three different water bottles on a tool-belt-style fanny pack. I didn't recognize her at first on account of the fact that my head still hurt a bit, and it was embarrassing to look at the faces of all these people who knew me as the life of the party when I couldn't come up with their names without glancing at their name tags. But as soon as our teams gathered by color outside the main hall and I heard her quick, disappointed hello, I knew exactly who she was. All week we'd be wearing the same color—temporarily bonding us against our will.

"I'm sorry about yesterday," Stevie told her as we stood around in an awkward semicircle with our new teammates. "No hard feelings?"

"Yeah," Julianne said in a clipped tone. Then she walked off to talk to her husband over by Yellow Team.

Stevie shrugged. "Well, I tried."

If I were her, and someone I didn't know quasi-rejected my apology like that, I'd probably start digging until I created that lightless hee-haw cave for me to live inside.

We'd been asked to pick a captain, and luckily we had an enthusiastic candidate in Aja, Dara's cabinmate. She was the exact kind of outspoken extrovert who went out of her way to introduce herself as an extrovert. Her hand shot into the air as soon as the prospect of choosing captains was announced. She ran uncontested, because she had an infectious energy we collectively knew could not be topped when it came to choosing a leader. Her excitement even tricked me into believing I liked this. If not the actual competition, then the community that came from being a part of a team.

"I can do this," I said aloud, riding the temporary high of my joy.

The two camp employees who'd passed out our shirts turned out to be the color-game referees. They instructed us to follow them to the site of our first competition.

Stevie put her hand on my head as we walked. "Of course you can. Julianne might kick your ass if you don't."

When Stevie and I laughed, Julianne whipped her head around and glared. There was no way she'd heard us, but it was like instinctively, she knew.

Tommy caught up to us and said, "I hope you two are being nice."

It mortified me that anyone would think I was anything but, even if it was a joke. "I am!" I said, clearly too emphatically, because Tommy laughed in a *That's our Garland, always worrying* way that made me feel very exposed.

"That's just how Julianne is," he said. "At least, I think. I don't actually know her, but from what I've seen so far, I don't think it's personal."

"Oh, no. It's personal," Stevie told him. "I was being an asshole and talking over you guys yesterday when you were taking us around the campgrounds, and she got mad at me for it."

Her admitting such a thing to Tommy's face made me consider how I could order flowers for him and have them delivered to camp, just so he knew we didn't mean to offend him.

He shook his head and said affectionately, "You really have not changed."

"Yes I have," Stevie told Tommy. "I'm *much* gayer now."

"Please," Tommy snapped back. "Don't forget that picture of us when we were like twelve, and you're in the overalls, backward cap, and cowboy boots. It's in the gay rights museum now."

She laughed heartily at that one. "Right beside the image of you as the yellow Power Ranger from costume night."

"Trini was a formative part of every Asian's life back then. Especially a gay Vietnamese one's. May she rest in peace."

They bantered with an ease I longed to experience for myself. It made me want to have memories to contribute one day.

Stories we could revisit over next year's campfire. History between us that we'd be able to laugh about in the future.

All my joy and hope washed away when I saw the first challenge. We'd visited the ropes course on yesterday's tour, and I'd immediately dismissed it. I knew I'd never voluntarily do it, not remembering that my participation in the color games *was* voluntary.

Mason, who'd been voted captain of Red Team, craned his neck over the crowd to find Stevie. "Do you see what I see?" he yelled.

"Oh god," she muttered to me. "If he wins this one, he will never shut up about it."

"Why?" I managed to ask through the panic that was rising like high tide inside me.

"Because we used to do this course every summer. Like four times a day. I'm not even joking. Mason and I raced each other so many times, the counselors told us our competitiveness was making the ropes less inspiring for our other campers, and they banned us from going on it anymore."

"What team?" Captain Aja yelled to us.

"BLUE TEAM!" the rest responded, innately understanding the call-and-response nature of her question.

I only mouthed along. The actual sound got lost in the taste of resurfacing bile in my throat.

My eyes were on Dara, who'd already put her attention on me, reading my mind in the way only she could. She knew that this wasn't something I wanted to do, but she couldn't help me here. She wasn't on my team.

If I hadn't gotten so close to Stevie, I'd forfeit right away.

Despite how she said it, I knew she cared about winning, not just beating Mason. Winning required my participation.

The referees explained the rules. We'd go through the course one team at a time. The team with the fastest time would win. Only six members per team needed to complete the course, meaning we could have two members per team sit out.

A gift! A sign! A reward from the universe! I wouldn't have to conquer my fear of heights after all!

The oldest member of our team, a white woman named Marge in her early sixties with hair dyed the color of a glass of merlot and eyebrows tattooed on in thick unbroken lines, yelled out, "Welp! One of them is just gonna have to be me!" and sat down exactly where she stood. "My knees don't work for shit. Sorry, Blue! If we do puzzles tomorrow, I'm your gal."

The referees explained to us that they had factored in the possibility of each team not having certain competitors participate due to various accessibility issues, so the challenges were balanced between physical and mental, to hopefully cater to different strengths and sensibilities.

Every challenge was worth forty points for the winner, thirty for second place, twenty for third place, and ten for fourth. The team who'd earned the most cumulative points by the end of the last challenge would be the overall winner, getting that grand prize of half off tuition.

Just as I cleared my throat to announce myself as the second person from Blue Team who would sit out, Julianne nominated herself.

"I'm afraid of heights," she told us, sitting beside Marge.

No, I'm *afraid of heights*, I thought but did not say.

My opportunity window had closed as quickly as it had opened up.

I was trapped.

The six remaining team members looked at one another, silently agreeing that we could all make it through this first course. It was that exact kind of overly serious intensity I hated most about competing against other adults. It wasn't silly, or fun, or any of the things I thought it should have been. Aja pulled us into a team huddle, and everyone began strategizing like this was a battle of honor, of dignity, of life and death. It was a ropes course at an adult sleepaway camp!

I was smart enough to know that no one wanted that perspective check, so I listened and nodded, doing my best to draw very little attention to my growing panic. Maybe if I pretended it didn't exist, it would go away. That had never worked before, but all of us were capable of change!

The referees picked our competition order from a hat. Blue Team got pulled first, because again, of course we did. Why wouldn't we be?

"This is gonna be so fun," Stevie said to me, vibrating with excitement. It was an actual thing I could see on her—a soft drum of anticipation that made her hands shake.

We reached the base of a wide ladder, where the referees instructed us to put on helmets.

"I need water," I announced. I had a matter of minutes, if not seconds, before I fell apart. I started shoving into people, pushing against the sea of blue shirts.

Stevie caught me quickly and pulled me over to a spot

beside Red Team. My sister shot me a familiar glare. *Are you going to be okay?*

Stevie turned me until we were face-to-face. "What's going on?"

I wanted to tell her everything was fine, but the truth fell out of my mouth first, surprising us both. "I'm afraid of heights too."

Stevie looked from me, to the course, to me again.

"Oh," she said. "Shit."

The ropes were easily thirty feet up. Maybe more. I wasn't good at estimating that stuff. Worse, they were designed to feel unstable. There was no way it was actually safe. If my vision weren't starting to go black around the edges, I could better assess the hundreds of ways I'd surely die up there.

"I could help," Stevie said. "I could hold your hand."

"Maybe if I close my eyes, I won't even notice that I'm holding on to wobbling ropes as I leap from tiny log to tiny log like Tarzan."

"Exactly."

I looked at her palm, soft and sure. If I disappointed her now, this early into our alliance, it would resurface later.

When Ethan served me papers, he referenced a moment that had happened before we even got married. We'd been in the grocery store together when a man started screaming at an employee. Ethan had decided to interject.

Ethan was a calm person by nature, but the adrenaline rush of his split-second decision gave him way too much nervous energy. He went in jittery and intense and a little uncertain of himself, and the angry man picked up on it immediately.

The man left the employee alone and started screaming at Ethan instead.

I thought for sure Ethan would stay composed. He was *always* composed. But for reasons I'd never understood, Ethan started screaming back. Next thing I knew, the man and Ethan were yelling at each other, almost fist-fighting, and neither of them even knew why.

I had to walk away. I was embarrassed the whole thing was happening at all. Ethan so rarely got angry at anything, I thought that moment was *not* the time to suddenly test out the limits of his emotional landscape. The whole incident ended with Ethan and the man both getting escorted out of the store.

Ethan and I had driven home in silence, neither of us daring to mention what had just occurred. The incident didn't come up again until that fateful Valentine's dinner, well over four years after the fact. Ethan brought it up to explain to me how I'd never really been his teammate. I didn't jump in to support him that day in the grocery store, which to him meant I never accounted for him in the way he accounted for me.

Nothing could have hurt me worse. It haunted me to know I could let someone down and not realize it. I tried to be so vigilant, never letting a moment pass by without playing it back and making sure I was the optimal version of myself—friendly and giving and considerate. I let small things slide in the name of keeping the peace. How could I have helped that day? What could I have possibly contributed to that altercation? Why did Ethan hold on to it for years and years without ever bringing it up?

If I didn't go across the ropes with Stevie, would it change the fabric of our relationship in some small but significant way?

"Let's go," I said to her, lacing my fingers through hers and walking us back to the ladder.

"All good?" Captain Aja asked when we returned.

"All good!" I assured her, injecting cheer into my voice.

I would show up this time. I would be the person everyone needed.

Stevie couldn't hold my hand as we climbed up the ladder, so I stared at her shoes instead, thinking of all the times she'd been here before. It comforted me to imagine young Stevie, scrappy and determined, chasing her big brother up this very ladder. Wanting so badly to beat him. To be seen as a contender.

The distraction worked until we got to the top and I saw the distance between me and the ground. I saw my sister and Mason as red blobs. I saw the end of my life. Worse, it wasn't the highlight reel playing for me. It was all my failures. The moments I hadn't shown up.

I saw Ethan, dressed in an ill-fitting suit, meeting me at the courthouse to file our divorce papers. I'd die without proving to him that he didn't have to walk away from me. I could be a teammate. I *was* a teammate.

Stevie put her arms around me, hugging me from the back. The front of her helmet pressed into the side of mine as she said, "Listen. All you have to do is hold my hand."

"We're gonna lose if you do that," I told her. "You have to

grab the ropes to stay stable. If you hold me, you won't have a good enough grip to move quickly."

"You underestimate how good I am at multitasking."

We got strapped into harnesses. But harnesses broke all the time, didn't they? How many times did harnesses get used before they gave out? Were these ones brand-new?

When the whistle blew for us to begin, Stevie pulled me forward.

My feet did not move.

"Come on, Garland," she said, the barest hint of annoyance in her tone. "Trust me."

It wasn't that I didn't trust her. I did. More than made sense for how long we'd known each other. The problem was me. It always was. I didn't trust that I could stay out of my own head long enough to finish the course.

My body knew best. And my body said no.

"I'm so sorry," I told her as tears filled my eyes. Our teammates had started to look back. They were yelling our names. Screaming for us to get started. "I can't do this."

"Fuck," Stevie whispered. A single syllable, harboring a world of disappointment.

She let go of my hand and took off after our teammates. She caught up to them easily, then passed them, maneuvering smoothly beyond where they struggled along the course, until she was the first to reach the other side.

It didn't matter, because I never moved.

Our team had lost before we'd even begun.

10

As we sat on the bleachers watching the other teams complete their turns, Stevie projected an impenetrable force field of disappointment. I wouldn't have been surprised if it could be seen from the farthest rungs of our universe. Black holes might have closed up out of fear.

Every time a competitor managed to make it to the other side, I apologized. One person on Green Team fell into the netting and I apologized for them falling. With each apology, Stevie said some variation of "It's okay," then continued to behave as if it were not okay in the slightest.

Red Team competed last. Mason moved across the ropes exactly as I expected he would, like they'd built the course just for him and he was excited to demonstrate for the rest of us mere mortals how easily he could complete this. He got to the other side well before the rest of his team.

Dara finished next, and the two of them high-fived each other, then screamed and cheered for everyone else.

We didn't know the official times yet. It seemed from my mental calculations that Red Team had easily beaten everyone else. I wondered how we would have placed if I'd done my part. It was terrible that we'd never know. Because I hadn't moved.

"I'm really sorry," I said for what may have been the *Guinness World Records* holder for number of times a person could apologize for the same thing.

This time Stevie waited, saying nothing for so long I almost apologized again. Then she squared herself toward me, putting her hands on my shoulders.

"Listen," she said with a surprisingly gentle touch. "*Please* stop apologizing to me. You were genuinely scared. That's not something I could ever be mad at you for. I just have a hard time losing. It's completely my problem. Nothing to do with you. I'd be like this even if we'd gone across. Probably even if we won."

"But *I'm* the reason we lost," I reminded her.

"Garland, I promise you, there is not a single person here who does not know that. The ghosts of past campers have already issued the announcement in their local ghost paper. *Garland Moore loses ropes course for Blue Team.* They will use this news to haunt the future children who attend this camp. By mortals and dead alike, you will be feared." She looked right at me. Down into the core of me, where I was hurting the worst, feeling all the deepest kinds of disappointment. "My reaction has nothing to do with you and everything to do with me. I need you to believe me."

It scared me, even though I did think she was telling me the truth. She was just handling the loss with little grace, and I wished she would care less, if only so she wouldn't be so hurt by the result. Then again, I wished *I* would care less about most things, and that only ever seemed to make me care more.

After Red Team climbed down the ladder, they strolled proudly to the bleachers to sit with the rest of us. Their collective energy was that of champions. Shoulders pulled back. Chins held high. They knew what they'd accomplished. The referees came over to read the results, not that anyone needed to hear them to know.

Red Team took first place, earning forty points.

Blue came in dead last, grabbing only ten.

Another apology surfaced on my tongue. This time for my entire team. I stood up in the middle of our cobalt blob on the bleachers and put both my hands atop my heart. "I'm so sorry, everyone," I said, tears spilling out of my eyes. "I won't let that happen again."

"You were scared," Aja said. "Now we know. Next time just tell us beforehand so we can figure it out."

"I will," I promised.

The referees dismissed us, and all the teams started shuffling off in various directions, ready to spend the rest of their day however they pleased.

"Couldn't make it happen, huh?" Frank yelled down from the top of the bleachers. He had his hands on his hips and his Green Team shirt wrapped around the back of his neck like a towel. His team had come in third, but he didn't want to be the target, so he'd decided to start the Stevie antagonization.

"It's only the first competition, fuckhead," Stevie yelled back, twice as loudly and with three times the confidence. I took a step up the bleachers, thinking she wanted us to go and talk to him, but she pressed her hand against my arm, holding me back.

"Yeah, and you're in last!" Frank reminded her.

"That's a familiar place for you! Have any tips for me?" she asked.

Suddenly, a set of strong arms wrapped around the back of me and tilted me off the ground until my feet faced the sky. My legs flailed for purchase. I was a captured cockroach, desperate to be set free.

"What happened up there?" Mason asked me, his breath hot in my ear.

"I don't know," I said.

He placed me down, then put a hand on Stevie's head. "Sorry about last place. That sucks." When he looked at me, he smiled with utmost sincerity. "This is why Stevie could never beat me. She's too soft. I would have carried you on my back across the ropes."

Stevie's hands clenched into fists.

Something otherworldly possessed me. A courage I'd never felt before straightened my spine. "Absolutely not," I said.

Mason's cheeks got as red as his team shirt, and his eyes lit up. "You don't think I could?"

"I'm sure you could. But I wouldn't have let you," I told him. "It wasn't Stevie's fault I didn't do the course. It was no one's fault but mine."

Mason looked at his sister. "I don't know. I think I could've convinced you to make it happen."

The casual dismissal of her made my blood boil. "If anyone in the world was going to get me across that course, it would've been Stevie. So if this is a competition between you two, she wins. Every time."

He put on his poutiest puppy-dog eyes. "I don't win? Not even once?"

The vision I'd had of the two of us laughing in the mess hall seemed miles, if not oceans, away from where we were. He may have been attractive to someone else, but *I* wasn't attracted to him. I wondered how I ever would be. If the difference this time was that the attraction was meant to sneak up on me. Become something that just existed, not something I could see by imagining little vignettes of our life together.

"Not even once," I told him.

I wasn't going to lie to him about my allegiance to Stevie. If I'd done anything with Ethan, it was lie. I kept quiet when I was nervous. I didn't say what bothered me. That day in the grocery store, I hadn't wanted him to interject. At least not in the way he had. He'd gone about it all wrong, and I'd never said anything about it.

This would be how I'd practice getting better. Saying the tough things out loud. For Mason, or Ethan.

No.

For *myself.*

Mason took my comment as a challenge, which was a common thread among the Magnusson family. "We'll see about that," he told me.

Andrew appeared. "C'mon. We're booked for the Jet Skis

on the lake in fifteen minutes." He called up to Frank, who still stood at the top of the bleachers. "Let's go!"

The three of them headed toward the water.

"You really are perfect for Mason," Stevie told me once they were out of earshot. The rest of the competitors around us had already left, leaving us completely alone. "I've never seen anyone stand up to him like that before."

"I did it for you," I told her.

She paused for a long while, staring at the ground. Then she started nodding to herself. "Yeah. This will be very good for him."

"What?"

She gave me that look again. The spotlight-onto-my-soul look. "Dating you."

"Oh."

Every discussion of Mason turned my thoughts into a desert. Any concept of what I should say shriveled up. It was so much easier to talk to Stevie about literally anything else. The quality of the soil under our feet would have interested me more. Ethan worked at the landscaping company his family owned, and from the secondhand knowledge I'd picked up, I thought the dirt seemed to be well hydrated.

"This isn't an apology," I said as a precursor. "But you need to know it all the same. I promise that tomorrow, whatever the challenge is, I'm gonna make sure our team wins. I know I let you down at the ropes course, but I plan to show up for you as much as I can everywhere else."

Stevie didn't seem to hear me, despite looking right at my mouth. "He doesn't have enough people to give him perspective."

We were the only two people talking, and we were having two different conversations. To test it, I asked, "Does he think birds are real?"

She didn't even smile. Her focus on me had become something that went beyond words, so I gave up trying to use them. I became hyperaware of my feet on the well-hydrated soil. The sounds of the maybe-real birds up in the trees. She would know their names. What it was they sang to us in that moment. Fast, trilling melodies I'd never paid attention to before, matching the chaotic beat of my heart.

"Garland," she finally whispered. "I have to tell you something."

My whole body leaned forward. Pulled toward her. I felt disoriented, almost like I did when I was up too high. It wasn't fear so much as hatred. I *hated* feeling out of control, and there I was, stone-cold sober with the lingering hangover to prove it, and I may as well have been walking a tightrope between mountains while downing shots of tequila. I didn't know what was going on, and I hated how much it terrified me. Worse, I didn't understand why the terror seemed to excite me.

"I don't think it's a good idea for us to spend this much time together anymore," she continued. "I think that I—"

"Stevie?" a woman called out.

Stevie's head whipped around so fast, she actually hurt herself, grabbing her neck to nurse the sudden strain. When she saw the woman who'd called to her, she stumbled back, looking as disoriented as I'd felt only moments before.

"Allison," she said. "What do you want?"

11

Short of becoming a bird myself, I did everything in my power to get away from Stevie and Allison as fast as possible. I needed more air than the sky could give me, and more space than the earth could offer.

Dara happened to be at the picnic tables near the lake, coloring a picture.

"Arts and crafts time?" I said to her as I walked up. The shake in my voice caught my own attention.

"Can't get anything past you." She was shading in a black-and-white version of the same Camp Carl Cove picture that had been on Tim's shirt. "The official thing is happening in the main hall. But people were like, color matching their crayons with textures in the room. I knew if I invested that much effort in the contest, it would get ugly. So I came outside."

"Making lots of new friends," I said.

She set down her yellow colored pencil to look at me.

"Actually, I am. Most of them wanted to go on the Jet Skis, and you know that's not my journey in life."

"Aren't we supposed to be making the most of camp?"

"Says the one of us who refused to do the ropes course."

I nodded. "Harsh but true. Congrats on first place, by the way."

She tugged proudly on her red shirt. "Thank you. Where's your friend?"

I didn't want to say that Stevie was talking to someone she clearly knew. Maybe it was because Stevie had just gotten done saying she didn't think we should spend any more time together, and it embarrassed me that I'd had a friend for all of twenty-four hours and she was already backing out of the relationship. Dara was the only person in my life who'd never really abandoned me.

"Her name is Stevie, and you know that," I said to her, cleverly avoiding the real question. "Don't forget, she's Mason's sister."

I wanted to be sure Dara understood that I was getting closer to Stevie as a way to know Mason better. When drunk, Mason and I were apparently the resident dance hall maniacs, cutting rugs for the community at large. But under the harsh judgment of day, with nothing but nature to soften the blows of truth, getting to know Mason proved to be a difficult task. I needed Stevie as my buffer.

I hadn't dated anyone since Ethan, and I'd never dated anyone *casually*, whatever the hell that meant. I didn't know how to get around showing Mason all my flaws while learning his at the same time. Having Stevie around made all of that seem less daunting.

Quite honestly, I didn't want to learn any more of Mason's bad traits. I'd have to find it in me to be more assertive and tell him to stop when I thought he was crossing a line. Or maybe it wasn't up to me to ask him to change. That might have been the problem last time. I thought in my head that Ethan should be different, and I never said it. Maybe I was wrong for even thinking it. Maybe I needed to change the way I reacted. None of us was perfect, and I had to stop expecting that from a partner.

My head hurt. And not in the hangover way. *This* was exactly why I didn't need to fall in love again. I'd done it once, and once really was enough for me.

"Mason's cool," Dara said simply. "He's a good fit for you."

"Everyone seems to think that," I replied, annoyed at the repeated insistence on my compatibility with him. Even my own heart-promise bracelet supported it.

What exactly made us great? The idea that our story sounded sweet when told aloud? I'd done that already. I'd met my husband in a bookstore petting the same cat, and here I was in the mountains—single and confused—watching my sister fill in a coloring-book page. Clearly that hadn't worked for me. Nothing worked for me.

My face must've shown my conflicting feelings, because Dara said, "You and Mason are like the king and queen of this camp right now. Everyone on Red Team freaked out when I told them you're my sister. They thought you threw the ropes course so Mason could win."

No one had ever cared that Dara and I were associated with each other. She ran in completely different crowds from me in school, and neither of us helped or hurt each other's reputations. The only place it came up was in the classroom, when a teacher would find out she was my older sister and they'd expect me to be as quietly diligent as she was. Instead I was excitable, impatient, forgetful. Crying when my assignments weren't in my bag. Raising my hand to answer questions I didn't know, just so that they didn't have to suffer up front without a volunteering student.

"Ew," I said. "I'd never do that."

"Obviously I know that." Dara rolled her eyes. "But the story is cute."

"That's all it is. A story."

She looked over at the water. "Then go Jet Ski with him! Turn the story into reality! Aren't we supposed to be making the most of camp?"

I rolled my eyes the same way she had. The difference being I was already standing up. Far be it from me to turn down a suggestion from my sister.

"When are we cutting your hair?" I asked her before walking away.

"It's not time yet," she said.

"My only request is that you don't wake me up in the middle of the night for it."

"Who do you think I am? I'm not trying to scar you for life. I don't want to have you sleep with the lights on for the next two years again." She used a second brown to shade in the tree she was coloring, adding dimension to her already very impressive coloring sheet. "I'm just not ready yet. But I will be. Soon. And you'll be the first to know."

It occurred to me then that I'd never seen Dara with different hair. It was always nearly waist length and her natural shade of brown. I was the one who had a hair change for every season. As soon as Ethan had divorced me, I'd chopped mine off myself, cutting it to just below my chin and embracing the jagged hairline I'd concocted. Cutting Dara's hair was a pretty big deal, and she'd undersold it so much, I hadn't fully comprehended the gravity.

"I didn't bring hair-cutting scissors," I told her.

She looked up as she said, "I did. Obviously."

"Obviously," I echoed.

She shooed me off. "Go Jet Ski! You're distracting me from my *process*."

Along the edge of the lake, Mason and his brothers slapped each other with towels. Such golden boys in all senses, free with themselves and their bodies. I forgot people could be like that as adults. They could be playful and harmlessly aggressive with one another. Roughhouse for the thrill of it.

Mason had just put Frank into a headlock when he saw me. "Garland! Put on a suit and take a ride with me!"

If I went on the Jet Skis, I could ask Mason about who Allison was and why everything suddenly became very intense and awkward as soon as Stevie saw her. Just to get the context, of course. I was naturally curious! I ran to my cabin, threw on my green one-piece, then headed out to the lake.

"Where's Stevie? This is the first time I've seen you without her," Mason noticed, setting the stage for my inquiries with such a flawless ease, I had to pause for a second to marvel at it.

"She's with Allison?" I painted it as a question, watching the Magnusson boys' faces very carefully as I did so.

Frank staggered back like he'd not only seen one of those camp ghosts Stevie joked about earlier, but he'd been personally gut punched by said ghost. "Are you kidding?"

"She showed up over by the bleachers," I continued, fascinated by their reactions. Allison meant something to them, that much was clear.

Mason gazed out at the water. "What the hell?"

I hoped with every fiber of my being that they would give me the gossip. They were being so strange and dramatic, I needed to know everything they knew about Allison and then some. No detail was too small or specific. I wasn't sure if that much outward eagerness would serve me, so I opted for concerned interest. "She seemed really intense," I guessed. I'd seen maybe six seconds of their interaction, but it did have a fervent burning weirdness to it that had practically set my feet on fire.

"She's the worst," Andrew said, his first contribution to the Allison conversation. His brief but brutal assessment unleashed a tirade from the other brothers. It was like unlocking a new level of Magnusson insider knowledge.

"A fucking nightmare," Frank added.

Mason shook his head. "She cheated on Stevie. The whole time they were together."

Aha. There it was.

Allison was Stevie's ex. The one her mom sent cards to, I bet.

Stevie's ex was *here*. And she'd made the kind of mistake that other people saw as worthy of breaking up over. It was true. It did make my blood run cold, thinking of Stevie being hurt in that way. She didn't deserve that.

All this new information swam through my head, pushing against a back current of everything I thought I knew. I remembered all the times Stevie had scanned the crowd as if looking for someone. What Andrew had said to her in the loft after beer pong. How Stevie had all but vanished when we'd gone back downstairs. It was all because of Allison, who had *very* cool bangs. I mentally removed my reminder to compliment her on them. I had exactly zero kindness to offer that woman.

"Why is she here?" I asked Mason.

"Because she signed up to come to camp with us." There was a low hiss to Mason's voice that I'd never once heard. A seriousness he didn't have even when he was hassling Stevie about losing. This was his bottomed-out truth. Angry and almost feral. "They broke up about four times over the course of us registering. The last time was in April, and Allison swore she wasn't coming. Then we got here, and there she was. I told her she better leave Stevie alone. So far she has. Until right now."

"I think she came to camp because she realized her deposit wasn't refundable," Andrew offered. "It *was* a lot of money."

"No. She wanted to come ruin Stevie's life even more," Frank corrected.

It was easy to imagine them here as kids. Frank was definitely the crier, getting worked up by anything and everything. Andrew was the one who took it upon himself to be the helper. Mason, with his casual charm and effortless strength, was the star.

And then there was Stevie.

Stevie was the Swiss Army knife of this family. Clearly there was no role she couldn't take. No part she couldn't play. She'd told me yesterday that her brothers had once forgotten her on a mountain. I'd assumed then that they were negligent or they didn't really care about her. That didn't seem true in the slightest. If anything, they'd probably lost track of her on account of the fact that she had a way of being whatever she needed to be, and they'd assumed she'd find them when necessary.

"Maybe I should have stayed with Stevie," I said to them. I regretted how I'd fled, but I'd gotten so flustered. She'd just finished saying she didn't want to spend so much time with me, which made no sense. Both of us clearly enjoyed each other's company.

"There's no point in trying to get between Stevie and Allison," Mason told me. "They're gonna do what they're gonna do."

As much as I didn't like it, it seemed my time being Stevie's ally really was over. It sucked, but the signs were there, and I'd told myself to follow them. I was supposed to take every opportunity. Unless it involved heights. Then I could take an opportunity to set a boundary for myself. The opportunity to redefine an opportunity!

"So we can't help?" I confirmed for posterity's sake. Stevie would find a way to help me. She'd try, at least. Then she'd know when it was time to let go. Like when she took off across the ropes course. She knew when to surrender. A skill just as important as knowing when to push.

"Unless you wanna run in circles, no, we can't help," Mason told me. "But we can ride the Jet Skis?"

That simplicity of his logic charmed me. To his credit, I'd never tried to forget anything by getting on a fast water vehicle and whizzing around. There might have been merit to the solution.

"Well, then," I said. "Hee-haw!"

Mason pumped his fist. "Hee-haw! Let's go!"

We walked to the edge of the dock, where a Jet Ski was tethered to the side. Mason climbed on first. I stepped on behind him, wrapping my arms around his torso as I settled into my seat. He was so fit, it was like holding on to a slab of rock. Actually, I'd recently held a rock and it was smoother than Mason. He was so rigid and taut, rough in his strength, that I felt burdened by the effort he'd put into his body. Not ashamed of my softness but overwhelmed by the contrast. Even if we were to have a casual fling, I worried I'd be stressed the whole time.

"We're going fast," he told me.

"Famous last wor—"

He pressed the gas with such ferocity that my cheeks got sucked back into my ears, swallowing the end of my prophetic sentence. I'd never tasted so much of my own spit in my life. It was impossible to focus on anything but the immediate situation. The mist of water drenching my face and the feel of the wind at high speeds. The smell of the air. My lungs breathing in and out. As we soared across the lake, my worries and disappointments could not catch me at the speeds we were traveling.

Mason was right.

Jet Skis *could* fix things.

He did figure eights in the lake with impressive ease. The edge he cut splashed so much water in my face that it reminded me of standing in front of a running hose as a kid. A simple kind of bliss.

By the time we pulled back in to the dock, I could've napped for hours. Or completed a triathlon. Either option made perfect sense to me. The ground suddenly felt so still and steady I couldn't believe we moved ourselves across it, because we'd been flying through the water so easily that walking seemed comically slow by contrast. My first few steps on land, I stumbled.

"That was fun," I told Mason, disbelieving.

Scary things could be fun. I'd forgotten. Maybe I'd never known at all. I'd been too afraid to find out. Funny how that worked.

All the worries and disappointments I'd shed on the water were eager to meet me again once I got my bearings on land. How long had Stevie dated Allison? When did she find out about the cheating? What kind of relationship did they have? Did the family like Allison before the breakup? Where *was* Stevie?

As if beckoned by my incessant thoughts of her, Stevie—no Allison in sight—found us by the water. She took in the scene before her—me and Mason toweling off, with Andrew and Frank sitting at a picnic table arm-wrestling each other. All four of us stopped what we were doing to stare at her in silent awe.

"Let's eat," she said.

The brothers and I shot up in near-perfect unison. I almost laughed at our eagerness. We were all *dying* to know what had happened with Stevie and Allison.

12

So much for getting the scoop. Throughout our meal, Stevie had an almost supernatural calm about her. Nothing like the extroverted go-getter I'd come to know. That woman had been replaced with someone so neutral she could have startled a Buckingham guard with her commitment to not budging.

I followed her brothers' cues regarding Allison. None of them asked about her, so I didn't either. In fact, I didn't say much of anything at all. It was a skill I'd never mastered, sitting with a group of people and contributing nothing but my presence. I understood why Dara did it. By saying nothing, I could see everything.

I kept thinking of the story of Stevie's brothers forgetting her atop the mountain. I'd expected to meet three airheads who didn't think about anyone other than themselves. Especially when we'd watched them on the campgrounds tour and they'd stood at the front of the group, towering over everyone, demanding notice.

Now that I knew them a little better, what I found instead were three guys who really loved their sister but did not know how to handle her pain. They were so worried about her, it seemed to immobilize them. Frank could hardly eat, he spent so much of our meal biting his tongue and sighing. Andrew put his hand on Stevie's back more than once, double pats of support that seemed to be all he could muster. And Mason kept guard. Every time a camper came through the mess hall doors, he made a point to turn his whole body toward them and watch, as if they might morph into Allison at any point.

It was a sweet revelation. I liked seeing how loved Stevie was.

Throughout our meal, I learned that the Magnussons spent most Christmases together in Vermont. I learned that Frank became a firefighter because he wanted to rescue cats from trees. Andrew had never eaten pork before. Stevie collected feathers. Mason hated the sound of paper crinkling. Our conversation had a calculated randomness to it, everyone offering up interesting factoids and details about themselves to keep the mood light, avoiding the subject of Allison at all costs.

Stevie and I walked back to our cabin and discussed how much we enjoyed the breeze that settled over the campgrounds when dusk turned to dark. Allison lingered at the corner of every topic of conversation. So did what Stevie had said to me right before Allison showed up. She'd asked for distance between us. I didn't agree with that request, so I wasn't going to be the one to bring it up again. Judging by how closely she stuck to me, strolling campgrounds paths with our shoulders sometimes touching, she didn't agree either.

By the time we'd showered and started getting ready for the nightly mixer, Stevie had *almost* defrosted back to her normal self. She rummaged through her luggage for an outfit in a way that involved our whole cabin, shouting for Michelle to come into our room and help out.

"What did you two do after the ropes course?" Michelle asked Stevie and me, standing in our doorframe. She was genuinely oblivious to the whole ex-girlfriend element, so she engaged without any extra layer of caution.

I looked right at Stevie, who shifted gears back to Buckingham guard neutral with impressive ease. "Garland went on the Jet Skis with my brother."

I was fine with her ignoring the Allison thing in front of her siblings, because I understood better than anyone that sometimes it was hard to talk about relationship issues in front of the people who'd likely had a front-row view to the reasons those problems existed. But I was supposed to be her ally. We had to talk about Allison at some point, and Michelle was a better conversation participant than most. She was a documentarian, after all. Her whole career revolved around getting to the heart of things.

"That is indeed what I did," I said to Michelle. "I guess Stevie didn't exist in the hours between the end of the competition and the time she met her brothers and me for dinner."

"I was attending to some personal matters," Stevie said.

I cocked my head. *"Mm."*

Up to that point, Michelle wore a *Mona Lisa* smirk at all

times, the kind of buried expression you could spend a lifetime trying to decode. A perfect complement to her declara-
tive fashion sense. But her brows shot up and her eyes widened
with full-bloom curiosity as Stevie and I spoke. She cranked
her head back and forth between us like she was tracking a
tennis match and Stevie and I were smacking the shit out of
the ball.

It might have helped that Stevie and I were also elbow-
deep in our respective luggage, tossing out clothes with reckless abandon. I'd packed entirely too many adult outfits, all
thanks to Dara's comment. As a result, I'd brought only two
of my vintage graphic tees, and I'd already worn one of them
yesterday. Nothing I'd brought with me spoke to the energy I
wanted to convey at the mixer. It had been such a strange day,
living up to the impression I'd made the night before. I enjoyed being liked, but I wanted a more accurate version of
me to be seen, and I wasn't the person I'd packed into this
luggage.

"What did *you* do?" I asked Michelle.

"I'm on a tight deadline with the documentary, so I wanted
to get some work done on it, but the twins wouldn't allow it,"
she said. "They forced me to color with them."

Stevie laughed as she threw a shirt over her head, clearly as
frustrated with her clothing as I was with mine. I wondered
what she wanted to see in her bag that she couldn't find. She
always looked right to me.

"That sounds like Tim and Tommy," she said to Michelle.
"Even when we were kids, they'd ask all of us to pretend like
our real life didn't exist here."

Michelle gave a sad little laugh. "Probably because their real life wasn't very easy."

When I'd first met the twins, they'd told me about their history with a practiced breeziness, hitting all the life milestones without diving very deep into how they'd been affected by them. I thought of Tommy and me high-fiving over our respective divorces. I knew I did that as a coping mechanism. Being loud about my divorce made the quiet, consuming sadness of it harder for people to reach. They couldn't coax it out over all my yelling and car horn honking. Tommy would understand that better than anyone. What it felt like to carry that kind of public failure with you everywhere you went. How you constantly had to decide who you were in relation to it.

"I guess adults don't really revive a summer camp unless they're looking to heal something," I said.

I knew Dara had come to this camp to let go of her bitterness, and I'd come here for reinvention. I hadn't considered that everyone here was probably doing something similar. A quiet understanding permeated the room. All of us had come for different reasons, but the heart of them was the same— summer camp was a place for us to heal.

"I shouldn't say they forced me to color, because I do like to do that," Michelle said, hinting at earlier regret. "It was a hell of a strong suggestion, though." She went into her room and returned with a very impressive version of the same coloring sheet Dara had been shading in by the lake. "Lucky for me, I won best picture. I even won a prize." There was her deadpan demeanor again. The expert flat tone, matched with a perfectly placid expression. "It's a T-shirt I will never wear."

"A Camp Carl Cove shirt? Like the ones Tim and Tommy have?" I asked.

"How did you know?" Michelle got the shirt from her room to make sure I knew what she meant. It was a white ringer tee with green trim and green font, and the strange little picture screen-printed onto the front.

"I just—I love the shirt so much," I admitted. "It was a guess."

Michelle turned the tee toward her, staring at it with her *Mona Lisa* best, looking for whatever it was I saw in it. "Do you really love it? It's yours if you want it. I could never pull this off."

"I'd love to have it. Thank you," I said. It flattered me that Michelle didn't believe she could wear my kind of look. She could quite obviously make anything look cool.

This was the kind of everyday magic that awed me even more than the "heart-promise vision, see my future" type of mystique. Michelle had received something I desperately wished for, and she had no desire to keep it. It was a small thing, not so much coincidence as a pure stroke of luck, but the surge of joy in my chest that came from the stars aligning in my favor reminded me of what a gift it was to feel connected to the wonder of life, even if the wonder was a Camp Carl Cove T-shirt. But if I put on that shirt, I'd feel like exactly the person I wanted to be, and that was a gift I'd thought I'd never receive.

Michelle tossed it over. I ran to the bathroom to throw it on and examine myself in the mirror. If I squinted a lot, I almost looked thirteen. I didn't *ever* want to be that actual age again because it had been absolute hell. I was perfectly thrilled to be thirty-two. But I wanted to do right by thirteen-year-old Garland. To pay tribute to her. Give her the confidence she so desperately needed. Show her that life might have been hard then, but one day she'd grow up and the past would be just that, something that was behind her. Something she had to keep walking away from in order to grow. And in the silly little camp shirt, I could do that for her. For me.

"See?" Michelle said when I came back into the room. "You look better than I ever could."

Stevie stole a single glance over her shoulder. She said nothing, and still I felt it again. The heart hammer. More like a jolt. Something deep inside me attempting to leap out and be seen.

"Ugh. I'm just gonna wear this." She grabbed something from the very bottom of her bag and disappeared into the bathroom with it.

"As your counselor, I don't think I'm supposed to suggest this, but do you want to drink?" Michelle asked me while we waited for Stevie. There was an innocent, conspiratorial energy to her request that created sudden and powerful community between us.

"This is a perfect time for me to ask what the hell it means to be our counselor," I said.

"I have to make sure you're accounted for every night. That's the main job. But I also have to watch that you're not doing drugs or committing crimes."

I threw up my hands. "There goes my night."

Stevie came out of the bathroom in a baby-blue mini

sundress and cowboy boots. She'd taken her curls out of the braids again and let them loose in a cascade of golden ringlets. She had an aura around her that glowed. "Be honest, do I look ridiculous?"

I took the opportunity to scan her again, as if I hadn't already gotten a thorough look the first time.

"I know," she said. "This is too honky-tonk. I don't know what I was thinking."

"No," I said, too urgently. "It's perfect. You look perfect."

Stevie stopped. "See?" she said to Michelle. "This is what Garland does. She makes me believe untrue things."

"You do look honky-tonk," Michelle deadpanned. "But who says that's bad? We're literally in Georgia."

She started humming a song the band had played the night before. "Chattahoochee" by Alan Jackson. The tune lit up a corner of my memory. I remembered myself the night prior, boot-scooting across the dance floor with Mason as the band performed it. Now Michelle was the vocalist, and Stevie took to making up a line dance in our room as Michelle turned her humming into full-blown singing. When she reached a stopping point, Stevie did one last knee kick before taking her well-earned bow.

"Honky-tonk suits you," Michelle told her afterward. "I say go for the dress."

When Stevie looked my way, my whole body flushed. "My opinion hasn't changed," I told her. "You look perfect. Just like I said."

She didn't roll her eyes or throw up her hands. Instead she gave me a nod, almost shy, and headed for the door.

"Last call for someone to drink with me before we go," Michelle said.

Stevie said "Hell yeah" and made a U-turn to get her tequila.

"Just one shot," I said. "But that's it for me today. Truly." I still planned to have as much fun as the night before, without forgetting a single moment of it.

The three of us huddled in the living room with the alcohol in the exact way I suspected we would have if we were teens and the illicit item were a gross bottle of rum stolen from one of our parents' home collections. Not that I really knew for sure. There was so much I felt like I'd missed in life. I had so few opportunities to test those kinds of boundaries as a kid because I was trying to survive instead. To not get in the way of anything. I felt the burn of that loss in me. All that I'd never gotten to be when I was younger.

I couldn't go back. But I could continue to honor that younger version of myself going forward.

"To Cabin Seven," Michelle offered as our cheer.

"To Cabin Seven!" Stevie and I responded.

We took our shots, turned off the music, and danced our way out of our cabin together.

13

A band of musicians framed the entrance of the event hall. Five people in a varying array of flannel and denim, ages thirty to seventy-five by my best guess, were each holding their individual instruments and staring at me. Mean mugging, to be more exact.

"You guys look ready to be photographed for an album cover," I said, hoping to cut the tension. Surely I was projecting and they weren't actually angry with me. "If we tossed a couch out front, you could be Crosby, Stills, and Nash. Plus some extras. Bonus-edition band members!"

A white guy in his early sixties turned up the volume on his vengeful glare, smoldering with displeasure. Beads of perspiration broke through on my face. I always started sweating on my nose first, and I could feel the cold pinpricks of nerves sprouting up above my nostrils.

The man and I stared at each other—me panicked, him

furious—until suddenly, *triumphantly*, his anger collapsed, and a megawatt grin filled the vacancy. "We're messing with you," he said in a manner that suggested he believed I knew very well he was kidding.

I did not know he was kidding. Not until he pulled me in for a hug best described as *Wow, I can't believe I just saw my best friend driving down the same street as me! We've both pulled over to greet each other because we have to celebrate this beautiful coincidence to the fullest.* I had a disco glitter flashback of me talking to this guy several times the night prior. Screaming requests in his face. Booing at him?

"Don't you worry," he said as he held me. A sweet Georgia lilt coated his words, flowing out from beneath his impressive handlebar mustache. "We went and learned your song for you."

Another band member, a Black man with graying locs and the kind of rich bass voice that vibrated into my toes, stepped forward holding a guitar. "We spent all day working on it. It sure is a fun one."

I could not bear the thought of breaking it to these musicians that I had no idea what I'd requested. So with the utmost sincerity, I said, "I'm so excited! I can't wait to hear it!" because that much was true. It would be very exciting to know what song I'd forced this poor group into spending their day learning.

The youngest member of the band, a genderqueer thirtysomething with a buzzed head and dozens of pins on their denim vest, stepped forward. "We waited out here to tell you. I was pretty excited to get to use this thing on it!"

They held up a fiddle.

I did not think I knew any fiddle songs. None were coming to mind, at least.

"We are definitely going to go on a journey together!" I told them.

With that, the band made room for Stevie, Michelle, and me to enter the hall. I couldn't help but look around for Allison. If Stevie was the sun, that woman was like the moon. Jet-black hair. Jet-black clothes. Frustratingly cool bangs I reminded myself I could not respect.

Allison made me question why I wanted to wear T-shirts with phrases on them. I'd never even heard her say a single word other than Stevie's name, and I'd already started making a little mental tally of things I did that didn't seem like something she would do. She had the confidence to attend an entire week of camp in hopes of getting Stevie back. I knew I'd *never* do something like that. I'd begged Ethan to take me back exactly once. Sobbing and shaking on our kitchen floor, pleading with him to reconsider. He didn't even move. Not to hold me. Not to help me. He said "This is for the best" and left me lying there.

I fled Los Angeles as soon as we filed our papers at the courthouse. Even seeing him by accident would have been too much of an indignity. If he wasn't remembering me splayed out on the kitchen floor begging for him to take me back, *I* sure would have been.

Then again, Ethan showing up at this camp was everything I'd ever dreamed of happening. Perhaps that's what Stevie felt, deep in her heart. Maybe she couldn't speak about it because she didn't yet trust it. That Allison was really here with good intentions.

I always believed in redemption, even when I probably shouldn't. Allison had cheated, and it infuriated *me*, but I wasn't Stevie. I knew what it was to have other people think they had the correct opinion of your love life. Only Stevie could decide how grievous that mistake had been. If she didn't think it was that bad, then that was her decision to make.

It didn't mean *I* had to be nice to Allison, though.

I found her at the bar, sitting on one of the stools in front of the counter. Stevie clocked her at the same time as me, and she did not head for drinks like she had the night before. Instead she went toward a random table along the other side of the hall and plopped down, forcing herself to appear unaffected. I could still tell she was rattled. It was in everything she did not say. All the places she would not go. It was her version of yelling over the quiet parts.

This was why her brothers had a hard time navigating her pain. She worked very hard to disguise her feelings. Much like the force field she'd projected after we'd lost the ropes course, I *felt* her reaction all the same. She could try to hide, but I could see the truth.

Allison was not the moon, I decided. That was too much of a compliment. She was a storm cloud, blocking Stevie's sun. Our allyship had not been compromised by Allison's presence. If anything, she'd strengthened it. I would do whatever it took to protect Stevie. To make sure her week continued to be good.

"Do you want me to get you a drink?" I asked, gesturing to the bar with the very visible Allison sitting with a foot looped through her stool, scanning the crowd.

"No, no," Stevie said quickly. "I'm good. I don't want one."

I tried on my best impersonation of her, intensifying my gaze until it cut through her, moving the storm clouds until I saw the brightness of her smile. Joy pushed against the corners of her mouth, fighting to prevent itself from being revealed.

"Steven Magnusson, you want a drink," I said.

She burst into the full, bright laugh I'd already come to depend on. "My name is Stephanie. And I don't want anything," she said, not even bothering to make it sound like it was true.

"Don't you lie to me, Steven Magnusson. You are the master of mixing liquors and wearing matching sports sets. You want a vodka cranberry with lime. I know you do. Don't forget, I have *visions*."

"And you're having one of me?"

I closed my eyes and pretended to conjure up a prophecy. "Yes." I nodded as if seeing it all come together. "You are having your drink, but you are also . . ." I smiled. "Wow. Steven. You're dancing. With *me*. We're having a great time. Not at all worried about anyone else here." I opened my eyes and found Stevie looking at me. No longer smiling.

"Then I guess I need a drink," she said in her low, serious way.

Borrowing a move straight from Mason's handbook, I squeezed her shoulder before heading to the bar, faking the confidence I needed to walk right past Allison and act like I didn't care that she was there.

"Are you Stevie's friend?" she asked as soon as I approached. She was forthright in a way I hadn't anticipated. I was determined to stop it from scaring me off.

"*Something like that*," I told her, leaving it up to her interpretation. More than anything, I wanted this storm cloud of a woman to regret her decision to attend camp.

Allison leaned in, dropping her voice to a staged whisper. "Is she avoiding me?"

Stevie herself had told me nothing about Allison, so I was well within my rights to pretend I had no idea who she was. "She didn't say anything. Do you guys know each other or something?"

Allison had to laugh. When my face didn't break as she expected, she went quiet. She couldn't read me, which made me feel wild with power. I'd never tried to be anything but nice to a complete stranger before. This wasn't me being mean either. I didn't know what I was being, but it worked all the same, unsettling her in the exact way I hoped it would.

"We lived together for a year," she eventually told me, speaking in a totally different register of her voice. "I saw you with her all of yesterday. She wouldn't even look at me." She'd taken to scanning me top to bottom, appraising my every inch, deciding if I was someone worthy of knowing Stevie.

God help me, in the Camp Carl Cove T-shirt and Docs, I wanted to be.

"Oh," I said, as if remembering. "Her roommate!" Now I was using my brightness to its full effect, employing my Garland-the-friendly-stranger tone in a way I never had before.

"Her girlfriend," Allison corrected.

I colored my reaction not with shock but a sort of pity. "Hm. She definitely didn't say anything about *that* to me."

Maybe I *was* being mean. I didn't like knowing this woman had hurt Stevie. Embarrassed her in front of her friends and family. Cheated on her. She wasn't worth birthday cards. Why had Stevie's mother done that?

Why did *I* do that for people who didn't deserve it?

I leaned over the counter and ordered a single vodka cranberry with a squeeze of lime in the same way that Stevie had the night before.

Allison had run out of words to say. Or she figured they'd be wasted on me, because I'd shown that I wasn't going to give her a single ounce of power in the situation. I waited for the drink in silence, confident that Stevie was watching every single moment of this interaction.

When I came back with her drink, Stevie asked zero questions about what Allison had said. She was prideful, that much I knew, but the levels she'd go to for her pride continued to surprise me. She had to want to know what Allison and I had talked about. Instead she said, "I believe we have a vision to fulfill," and grabbed my hand to lead us to the dance floor.

When the band saw my feet hit the parquet, the lead singer stopped singing to tell me, "We're playing your song next!"

"Can't wait to hear it!" I called out. Then I turned to Stevie and whispered, "Literally. Because I have no idea what they're going to play."

She smiled at me. I hoped Allison could see. She hadn't taken Stevie's light. No matter how much she'd tried to, Stevie was still Stevie.

We danced together through the end of the current song, a heart-thumping folksy tune that made me remember exactly why I'd started yelling *hee-haw* the night before. The music *required* it.

Stevie moved similarly to her brother in that she did not care about embarrassing herself. But she had way more rhythm than him, and a much better sense of what style of movement the music required. She danced with the exact same conviction as she did all other things in life, and her commitment demanded a match from me. I didn't need alcohol to do this with her like I had with Mason.

I wouldn't like that, I realized. Drinking would dull my ability to feel her energy. To remember each moment in its completion. By the last chorus, we jumped up and down, singing lyrics to each other's faces. It was so easy to rise to her level and stay there, lost in the beat.

After the applause died down, the lead singer set up the next song. "Last night, one of our campers had a big ask of us. And she asked it so much we had to go home and figure out what it was she kept shouting at us to play. So we spent all afternoon on this. We even printed off the lyrics just to be sure we don't mess this one up. Garland, this one is for you. Hee-haw!"

At that, the band started playing "Hoedown Throwdown" from *Hannah Montana: The Movie*.

"*This* is what you requested over and over?" Stevie asked me. She was genuinely on the verge of falling to the floor in amusement.

"Oh my god. I guess so," I told her. "I saw the movie in theaters when it came out. I was in college. I didn't realize it made this much of an impression."

"Stop it," Stevie said. Not in a dramatic way. In a serious one. She was laughing so hard she'd started using me to hold herself upright. "I can't take this."

The lead singer sang out the commands of the song.

"I'm so sorry, Steven, but I'm going to have to do a choreographed dance now," I said. "I owe this not just to the band but to the me of last night who insisted this get played."

I headed to the spot in front of the stage and began dancing the hoedown throwdown in proper, hitting moves I'd learned long ago, stored in some long-neglected part of my brain that harbored all kinds of random silly things I thought I'd never again do. Lucky for me, there were two other campers who also knew the dance. They joined my movements. Soon, other people got behind us to follow along and learn it. By the second chorus, we'd built a little army of Hannah Montana dancers. Including Stevie.

The cowboy boots and sundress she'd put on for the night's event couldn't have looked better for the moment we were having. We danced side by side, beaming under the disco lights, having too much fun to worry about anyone else in the room. There was only her and me. The whole moment was so joyful I felt wild with it.

No matter how old I got, I could always find new ways to be young again.

14

My feet went numb from stomping the ground. Beads of sweat dropped from my hairline onto the floor. At some point, Mason tried to join Stevie and me, but we'd become so exclusionary he eventually left, dancing somewhere else.

I didn't look.

Allison watched the whole thing from the sidelines. Whenever I felt like I didn't have enough energy to keep going, the heat of her stare fueled me. She hated every moment of this, and she deserved to hate it, because she'd hurt Stevie.

At my most tired, when even Allison's ire wasn't enough to keep me going, I watched the way the light caught Stevie. Disco-ball prisms sparkled like jewels against her glistening skin. She made me afraid to blink, because to miss even a single second was to miss something revelatory. I would dance with her until the music stopped. Even then, if she wanted to keep going, I'd create music for us.

When the band played a slow song—the first of the night—
she made a move to leave the floor. I pressed my hand on her
shoulder to stop her, then turned my palm over in offering.

"May I?" I asked.

Her smile faded faster than I expected. "Not Mason?"

Even his name sounded wrong in that moment. Insulting,
almost. "No. You and me."

Her puzzled expression did not budge. No breakthrough of
understanding, and certainly not one of interest.

In a rush to explain myself, I added, "We need to make
Allison jealous. I kind of made it seem like you and I had
something going on when I talked to her earlier. This will help
sell it."

At that, Stevie backed up and turned on her heel. Her pace
increased with every step until she was practically running,
rushing out the barn doors and into the night. Her cowboy
boots stomped so hard that dirt clouds puffed up around her
every step.

"Stevie, wait," I called out, chasing after her.

When we were far enough away from the event hall that
the thrum of the live music sounded more like a memory than
reality, and the air nipped at our skin, making both of us
shiver, Stevie stopped moving.

"I'm sorry. I never should have said that," I told her. I was
desperate for her to turn around and look at me. "She was just
making you doubt yourself, and that really pissed me off. I
wanted her to feel bad for trying to ruin your trip. Now I see
that I look like an asshole, inserting myself into your love life.
That was really inappropriate of me."

Stevie finally turned around. She stared at me in that way only she could. Open-mouthed. Unflinching. Fighting against the chill that had her teeth chattering.

"Do you want me to go tell her I was lying?" I asked, trying to find a way to fix the mess I'd made. "That would make me want to die, but I'd do it for you."

"No," she said. "You don't have to be a distraction prop in my love life. Thank you, though."

That wasn't what I felt like I was. Until Stevie stormed off, I'd felt with complete certainty that I was doing the right thing. In reality, I'd not only made the wrong choice, I'd cheapened myself to Stevie in the process.

"I just wanted to help you as much as you've helped me," I told her, fighting back tears. She'd probably think I was crying to weaponize my emotions against her. That's how Ethan felt. Like I cried to make him feel worse, when in reality, my tear ducts operated separately from the rest of me. They just turned on, faulty faucets in my eyeballs incapable of being repaired.

"I'm pretty positive slow dancing with you won't help me one bit," she said. Her honesty had no malice to it. The truth stung anyway.

"I also just wanted to," I admitted. "Dance with you." The words sparked against the dark, charging the space between us.

Stevie sighed. "This is why I told you it wasn't a good idea for us to spend this much time together."

Allison had a real flair for timing. I had to give her that. She came outside at that exact moment and said, "What's going on?"

A perfect question, really. As perfect as her bangs.

"Nothing," Stevie told her, clipped. She was caught in what I guessed would be her worst nightmare, because I'd upset her, but so had Allison, for much longer and in far worse ways, and she couldn't appear completely fine to either of us, because we both knew too much.

Allison, sensing the vulnerability, walked up to Stevie and put a hand on her neck, forcing an intimacy between them that made me roll my eyes. "Please just listen to me," she whispered.

I wanted to evaporate. Turn to dust.

That was exactly what Allison hoped I'd feel, I realized, watching her behave as if I weren't right there in my Camp Carl Cove T-shirt, tears rimming my eyes, clearly an active part of this moment. I'd run away from them last time. I needed to stay put this round. I couldn't abandon Stevie, even though we'd just been fighting.

No, not fighting. We'd been doing *something*. I owed it to both of us to stick around and find out what that something was.

"Stop it," Stevie said to Allison, the barest hint of hurt cutting through the blunt force of her request. She looked at me then—a quick glance where her eyes went saucer wide and her lips folded together—before returning to her usual gravity-holding expression.

I held my hand out to Stevie, taking a page from Allison's handbook and ignoring Allison's entire existence in the process. "Let's go inside," I said. "Dance with me."

Stevie and I were on the ropes course again. Except this time it was me who could provide a safe path to the other side.

She stared at the shake in my fingers. I couldn't say if it was the cold or nerves that made me tremble. Maybe both.

I told myself it would be okay if she rejected my offer. After all, I hadn't actually gone across the ropes with her. She had every right to ignore my request to whisk her back to the very place she'd stormed away from barely two minutes ago *because* of me.

But Stevie, brave Stevie, grabbed on to me, tucking her palm into mine.

"Okay," she said, so soft it nearly broke me.

Stepping past Allison without granting her a single moment of acknowledgment, I led Stevie back to our spot on the dance floor. The slow song hadn't yet ended, though I swore we'd lived an entire lifetime outside just then. Sparkles from the disco ball moved in a lazy circle around us, swirling with the easy beat of the music.

The shake in my hands stopped once I had Stevie in my arms. I thought of how she'd grabbed on to me when she tripped at our doorstep. The way she'd been so careful, so exact with me, even while stumbling. She'd found a way to cushion my fall. I needed that cushion again, because I'd never held a woman in a slow dance. Not even jokingly. At least not that I could remember. Not like *this*.

Stevie had give to her that made me warm. I liked pressing my fingers into her flesh and feeling her skin make room for me. And the smell of her only got better up close. I could learn it now, break it down from the inside out, so I could put something new along with it in my brain, forever associating it with Stevie's head on my shoulder. Her arms around the small of my back. The heave of her chest, breathing deep against my own. It would go into my catalog of best scents, beside a blown-out birthday candle or the sky after rain.

I didn't like Mason. I never had. Not for a single second.

I liked Stevie.

No.

That wasn't enough.

I had a full-on crush on her. A heart-stirring, hands-shaking, forget-how-to-breathe crush.

I didn't like her freckles because they were cute. I liked them because they were hers, and I liked every single thing about her, and in fact I'd spent two days straight thinking of only her, and oh god, I had never felt less prepared to continue existing, because the framing of my entire world had changed in a millisecond. She was so delicate, so precious and fragile, and I was the one holding her, not knowing exactly how much care I needed to take until it was too late.

The song ended, and she whispered a gentle thank-you to me. Then she walked through the open doors and out of the hall, leaving me alone in the middle of the dance floor.

I had to let her go. I'd spent the last two days following her everywhere, and if I went after her then, I didn't know what it would mean. Only that it would mean too much. Way more than I'd planned to have anything mean here.

Instead I stood with disco lights swirling against me, wondering who the hell I was anymore.

Day Three of Summer Camp

—
15
—

Stevie's bed was three feet from mine. Thirty-six inches. One long jump, really. Not that I'd spent all night fixating on the distance, tossing and turning, judging my every movement. That was not how any rational adult with a crush behaved. Adults didn't even have crushes. They had attractions. Sensations. Arousals? Something way more sophisticated than me, heartsick and overwhelmed, obsessing over the woman sleeping a baseball bat's length away from me. (At 4:41 a.m., I'd spent an embarrassingly long time forcing my phone to find Wi-Fi, holding it skyward like an offering toward the gods of reception, until I could google things that were three feet long.)

Stevie's alarm went off at six on the dot. Like the gloriously beautiful early riser she was, she obeyed it without even hitting snooze. I lay in bed with my eyes half-open, workshopping ways to be casual. What did I usually say in the mornings?

Oh. Hey. How'd you sleep?

Mm. Nice beds here, yeah?

Do you think we go somewhere real when we dream?

She left the room before I could decide, and a boulder of my anxiety walked out with her. For the first time in hours, I could breathe.

Then a heaping dose of longing moved right into the vacancy. I missed her already.

Crushes—or attractions, or sensations, or arousals, or *whatever*—did not get any easier with age. If anything, I felt even less prepared for the revelation that I liked Stevie than I would have been in seventh grade. I thought I knew everything there was to know about myself, when in reality I'd been ignoring my own truth in favor of keeping things from getting too complicated. Now it had all come crashing down on me, and I was thirty-two years old and I had a crush on a woman at summer camp, and it seemed like the most intense thing to ever happen in my entire life.

If I really thought about it—and I had all night, every agonizing hour in my twin-sized bed that was all of one golf club away from Stevie—when I imagined hands on me, they were a woman's. When I saw myself struggling and I pictured the shoulder I would most want to cry on, it was a woman's. When I asked myself who I liked to travel with, or who took the best pictures of me, or who made experiences the most fun, it was a woman. I'd tricked myself into thinking that meant friendship, because sometimes it did. But I'd spent my whole life muting the part of myself that wanted more from women. Now that part of me was screaming, a speaker turned up so high the sound almost hurt—wild and sharp and very, very loud.

Eventually the sun hit my face in the same way it had the morning before. The blinds had those gaps in them that seemed to align with my irises. This time, the sun reminded me of Stevie, and Stevie was beautiful, and I'd never been so desperate for a confidant to talk me down, because at this rate I was going to pretend to sleep until the day ended, if only because thinking of Stevie caused me physical distress.

I couldn't tell Dara I was betraying the vision. She'd been so hurt when she found out I'd kept it from her in the first place. It would only be worse if she knew I was actively going against it now. Her pain was the last thing I needed on top of all my other sensations bearing down on me.

My options were the twins or Michelle. The twins already knew Stevie, which compromised them in this situation.

Michelle it was.

She sat on the couch in our common area with headphones and her laptop, doing work before anyone could catch her and get upset. Except me, I guessed. But she seemed to know I'd never get upset with her.

I tapped her on the shoulder. "Do you have a second?"

"Sure." She took off her headphones. There was a frame of an orphanage up on her screen.

"I'm an asshole," I said, looking at it. Michelle with her real, important job, and me moving through the world like a contestant on *The Bachelor*, ready to unload my big special feelings without a moment's notice. "It's not important. Never mind."

"Please. Stop me from spending my time on this. I need someone else to do it, because clearly I will not."

"Michelle, stop spending your time on this! I've been telling you over and over!"

She closed her laptop with a definitive smack. "Thank you. What's up?"

"How do you know when you like someone? Like, romantically?" I asked before I could second-guess how ridiculous it sounded to look another adult in the eye and inquire about one of life's most commonly experienced sensations. Especially since the first thing I'd ever told her was that I was divorced. Clearly love was not new territory for me.

Michelle did not react like it was an absurd thing to ask. Instead she leaned back to think it over, a dreamy look on her face as she combed through her own memories. "For me, it's always when I'm in a place without them," she said. "If I notice that they're gone, or I miss what they'd add to something. That's usually when I realize I'm in trouble. Even if I see someone at a party who I think is cute, and they leave before I get a chance to know them, I'm like, 'Damn.' Basically, I have to lose you to realize I want you around."

For some reason I'd hoped her words might resonate less. Instead she managed to double down on what I already knew. The second I'd met Stevie, I'd spent the rest of the time looking for ways to be around her. Hating every moment I wasn't. She snuck into my heart unannounced and staked a claim to land I didn't realize was up for grabs. I swore I'd closed myself off, and she'd found a broken gate and walked right through, not even bothering to announce herself.

"Yeah, totally," I said to Michelle, trying to keep it in.

Before Stevie, there had been an obvious set of parameters to my romantic attractions. I liked men because that was what I'd always seen as the obvious choice for me to make. I knew a lot of queer people, and the certainty with which they'd decided upon their queerness intimidated me. They spoke of knowing it since childhood, understanding they were different before they could even articulate how. I never felt like I knew anything about myself for certain.

My resistance to committing to one way of being now seemed doubly obvious in retrospect. Not all paths set out for me were ones I had to travel. That's what I'd told myself when I'd first ignored the Mason vision all those years ago at the airport. I knew I had the ability to go in any direction with it, and I chose to go toward being a nice woman who married a nice man at a reasonable age, settling down in a nice house to live a nice life. There were always other roads available. It didn't matter if I never took them. They existed. They were real.

I was real.

I liked men. And women. Anyone, really. And I hadn't let myself hold space for it, because I'd been so obsessed with ticking off boxes for the life I thought I needed to have that I didn't pay much attention to the life I *wanted* to have.

Michelle clocked my withholding right away. She moved her laptop from the tops of her thighs to a safer spot on the coffee table so she could sit up straighter. "Why? Do you like someone here?"

"I might," I said. *The understatement of the year.*

Michelle wiggled her fingers together. "Oh! Can I guess who?"

If she guessed Mason, I feared I might scream. If she guessed Stevie, I feared I might cry. Because if it was that obvious to someone else, how hadn't I seen it? Why didn't I know myself enough to know this was who I was? Who I'd always been?

"I wish you wouldn't," I told her honestly. She nodded like she understood. "Knowing myself is fucking complicated."

She laughed heartily at that. "Tell me about it."

"It's scary, taking risks."

"It doesn't really get easier either."

"Probably because the older we get, the more we realize just how much opportunity there is to fail," I said.

"But there's also so much life we miss out on when we hold ourselves back," she responded. "You can never get those moments back. The best you can do is be truer to yourself going forward."

"You're really right."

"Do you know what's true to me right now?" she asked. The moment felt really important. I wanted to say something profound. Unfortunately, nothing profound came to mind. "I'm hungry," she said, filling the gap of silence.

I had to laugh. "And here I thought we were having this soul-deep conversation!"

"Sometimes having breakfast is the deepest thing you could possibly do," she told me.

"Then we better go to breakfast."

Stevie wasn't in the mess hall. She'd likely gone to her

bird-watching corner again. I was too nervous to approach her there, and while I felt her absence, I had an opportunity to get to know some of the other campers better, and I wanted to take it. To make real friends.

Michelle and I sat with the twins. We spent our meal running through the previous day's events. What we'd enjoyed. What had been funny. It was easy conversation. Nothing too deep at first glance.

Still, I understood what Michelle had meant about breakfast. Sharing a meal with people was one of life's simplest pleasures. In the right company, breaking bread together, walking through the mundanities in our lives felt revelatory. Our simple chatter held so much space for me.

I'd always thought I needed to earn my place in order to be accepted. Turned out, existing was the only thing required in earning my authentic life. Hour by hour, with the help of friends and crushes alike, I was remembering how to do that. To really exist. Not just survive. To be myself in all my completion.

And I liked who I was becoming.

16

I didn't find Stevie until I headed toward the main hall for the color games. She waited at one of the outdoor picnic tables with the rest of our team. Seeing her in profile, chatting casually, holding her own in the world, had my stomach in knots. Every step I took felt like a new kind of courage.

"Hello!" I said to everyone. My voice had a way of fluctuating when I was nervous, reaching into the top register and shrieking out syllables. Stevie would no doubt notice, because she noticed everything about me. "Great to see all of you. Blue is looking good on us this morning!"

The rest of the team appreciated my excitement. Stevie did not so much as glance at me. She'd been talking to Tommy, who held his hair in his hands. It was exceptionally windy outside, and he fought the elements to maintain his perfect coif.

"*Tommy*," I said. "Any idea what we're doing today?"

He scowled. "Stop it. You know they haven't told me any-thing. I'm a team player, not a cheater."

He said it with a blood-oath level of sincerity, and it shocked me a little to realize I found that necessary. I'd let a shadow of doubt creep in regarding what Tim and Tommy might know about the competitions, even though their insider knowledge would be a benefit to our team instead of a setback. Somehow I was turning into one of those people who valued the integrity of the game or something.

"I'm hoping for some kind of puzzle," Julianne said quietly. It was the first time she'd ever entertained anything I brought up. Even Stevie had to gape at Julianne's acknowledgment of me.

"Are you good at them?" I asked her.

"My husband and I set the record time at the escape room in Plano," she told me with obvious pride.

"Then I'm hoping for a puzzle too."

She accepted my comment with a flat line of a grin, which was pretty damn good considering where we'd started.

Stevie stood up from the picnic table. "I'm not really feel-ing well," she announced. "I'd like to sit out today's challenge, if that's okay."

There was no reason to doubt her. She'd given everything to yesterday's competition. We all knew she cared. But she'd seemed completely fine until I approached. She'd been laugh-ing and chatting with her usual ease, surely reminiscing with Tommy about camp memories from years past.

There was no doubt in my mind that this had to do with me.

When I'd gotten back to our cabin from the mixer, she was already asleep in her bed. The last thing I wanted to do was wake her up and force her to talk to me about the conversation we'd had before our slow dance. I was too busy processing the earthshaking revelation that I was downright obsessed with her and hadn't previously realized why. Now I feared the worst. I'd pushed her away right when I figured out it was the last thing I ever wanted to do.

She *had* to be avoiding me. I stared in her direction, trying to prompt answers with my eyes. I couldn't believe I hadn't noticed my own feelings toward her before now. She sucked the air out of my lungs. She made me want to do random things like sing.

"We'll just have to win it for you, then," I told her, too loudly. I looked every other member of our team in the eye and said, "We have to. Okay?" The words sounded comical coming from me. But Stevie needed to see that I could be serious.

She continued avoiding my eye as she said "Thanks for understanding" to our team, then headed off toward the cabins.

Tommy cocked his head, as confused as I was. "Hope she's okay," he said.

"Everybody else feeling good?" Captain Aja asked. "Speak now or forever hold your peace."

The rest of us nodded.

The referees walked us over to the opposite side of the lake, farthest from all the buildings. We were in a clearing. All the trees encircled a wide-open field, where no visible sign of a challenge awaited us except one large rock in the center of the grass.

"Today's challenge is a scavenger hunt," one of the referees announced. "Each team will be given a list of tasks, and the first team to return to this spot with everything properly completed will win."

Now, *this* was a challenge I could do, uniquely catered to my habit of storing little details to cherish and remember. I jittered with excitement, and so did Julianne, who saw this as something puzzle-adjacent and declared "We'll be winning this" with a genuinely inspiring amount of confidence.

The referees handed out the lists and gave us a few minutes to strategize before we were allowed to begin. Our team of six decided to divide up into three groups of two to maximize our coverage, breaking the list down into pieces and assigning them to each pair. Tommy and Aja chose to work together, picking the most obscure list items to complete. Our leaders, doing the hard stuff. Julianne got partnered with Sky—a wiry young person with a rotating collection of unique eyeglasses and all of twenty-two years old, by my guess—who really loved bugs and therefore told us they'd be very good at "seeing what others could not," which sparked Julianne's interest enough to request their partnership. By process of elimination, I got paired with Marge, the brassy older woman who'd sat out yesterday's round due to her bad knees.

Our last teammate, Laurie, who'd kind of become synonymous with Sky because they'd been everywhere together, told us she'd be the second one to sit out because she wasn't sure she'd be helpful enough to contribute.

"Thank you for that honesty," Aja told her.

Laurie said, "That's what teammates do. We tell each other the truth."

The referees blew a whistle for us to begin. Marge pulled me by the arm, and off we went. Without cell phone reception to fact-check things, we relied on our individual knowledge to complete our tasks. Marge swore she knew how to fulfill the first item on our section of the list—*Find something native to this area*.

"I don't mess around," she told me as I boosted her up so she could reach into a tree and grab a leaf she promised was indigenous to Georgia.

"Of course not," I said.

"And I don't like when people are flighty," she added. It seemed to be a thinly veiled insult. A bold one, considering I cupped her small, fragile ankle in my hands. "You gotta show up, you know?"

Normally the last thing I'd ever want was a confrontation, and certainly not one with a teammate I barely knew. The crush situation had recalibrated my brain enough to make me newly bold. "If this is your way of telling me I messed up yesterday, I know," I said.

She plucked the leaf, then looked down at me, where I was literally *bowing to the earth* to keep her safe. "It is, yeah."

"I'm not flighty," I informed her. "I just get scared sometimes."

She grabbed hold of my shoulder to step off my palms. "The older you get, the more you realize there's a damn good reason to be afraid of just about every single thing in life. So you might as well do it all, because the fear sure doesn't care either way."

We continued on to the next item on our list—*Collect a gift from the previous owners.* All the prompts were brain challenges as much as scavenger hunt items.

"I gotta say, I don't know shit about the previous owners," Marge noted, holding her shaky finger over the words. She wore bright red nail polish that didn't have a single chip, and she smelled like cigarette smoke covered by floral perfume. "I came here back in the seventies. I don't remember them very well anymore."

"Those were the Christian camp people," I said, gazing out at the lake to think. How could we collect a gift from the previous owners? What constituted a gift? "What are things you can collect?" I asked Marge.

"Coins. Feathers. Stamps," she listed.

"Stevie collects feathers," I told Marge, who truly could not have cared less.

The water rocked itself to its own gentle lullaby as I turned the prompt over in my mind.

Then it hit me.

"I know what we can do," I said, tripping over my own words in my excited haste. "I'll be right back."

I sprinted to the mess hall. Other color team members watched me with a jealous kind of curiosity, wondering what I'd found on the list that could possibly make me move with such urgency. When I got back to Marge with my supplies, I squatted down and collected lake water in a cup. After I filled it up, I took a hair tie off my wrist and a napkin I'd grabbed from inside, and I covered the top of the water to keep it from spilling.

"Wanna tell me what the hell you're doing?" Marge asked.

"The original owners built the lake themselves!" I said. "A gift from them! That we can collect!"

Marge took the cup from my hands and held it up to examine the contents. "Hmm. Clever. Good job."

My cheeks warmed. "Thanks."

Marge and I proved to be a good team. We completed our tasks long before any other pair returned to our agreed-upon meeting spot, which gave us lots of time to chat. I learned that when Marge had come to Camp Carl Cove back in the seventies, she'd met her current husband here. They'd dated for the week, then gone their separate ways, each marrying other people. They'd found each other again later in life. Now they were grandparents, and they'd come back as an anniversary gift from their children.

"If you wanna hear me talk more about it, I was just on a big podcast," she told me.

"You were on a podcast?" I asked, sure I'd misunderstood. Marge had the kind of old-school, *I don't mess with the internet* energy that made me think she wouldn't know what a podcast was, much less be a guest on one. It had to be a word she was misusing. Maybe she'd done a school project for her grand-child and they'd said the word *podcast* and she'd run with it.

"I work part-time as a waitress in Chicago, and this couple that always comes in to see me roped me into it," she explained.

"The girl, Dee, she's got a big show where you talk about your life and your secrets and all that kind of shit. *Did I Forget to Tell You.* That's the name, if you want to look it up."

I actually knew of the podcast. It *was* a big one.

"I will," I assured Marge.

"Dee invited me to her wedding," she told me with pride. "I guess I was there when she first got back together with her fiancé. They consider me a big part of their love story or something. I don't really get it, but that's okay. I'll still go. I love an open bar. And Dee snagged a very handsome guy, lemme tell you. She got lucky. It's rare to find a man like that anymore."

"Lucky for me, I'm looking more at women these days," I blurted out, which constituted me coming out for the first time, and I'd done it to Marge, my crotchety, brass-tacks teammate with bad knees and big opinions.

"Oh. That's fine," she told me. "Love who ya love. It's sure not bothering me."

"Thanks, Marge," I said. "I will."

I decided I'd probably never do that again, and everyone else could just mind their business when it came to my identity, which made it even better. Marge had no idea she'd won the prize of being my first official ally. No wonder a random podcaster had invited her to their wedding. Marge had *presence*. And she made big deals small, in a comforting way.

Tommy and Aja sprinted to our meeting spot, shocked to find that Marge and I had beaten them there by several minutes. We all showed one another what we'd found, pleased with the creative ways we'd fulfilled the list's tasks. Sky and Julianne came in a few minutes after that. Julianne was simultaneously so blown away to be the last pair to return and so confident in her findings that she said, "No time to review everything. Let's turn it in. Trust me."

Five of us ran to the referees, with Marge behind, walking at a comfortable clip. We were the first to submit materials, and all six of us held hands as the referees reviewed the items on our list. When they got to my cup of water, I explained my reasoning, and they nodded and checked the box.

With much gravitas, one of the referees said, "Congratulations, Blue Team. You've won today's challenge."

We erupted into screams that could surely be heard across the campgrounds. Except Marge, of course, who stood and grinned, then said, "Okay. I'm gonna go see what my husband's doing. Nice work."

Red Team came in moments later. While their materials got approved, I overheard my sister and Mason arguing.

"I told you we should've broken up the tasks," Dara said.

"It's too late now," he said back.

In the end, Red Team got second place. Yellow Team came in third, with Green Team in last. When the referees read out the updated rankings, we learned that because of our win, we'd moved into second in the overall rankings. Red Team still held their overall lead, but it was close.

I felt so proud, not only of my team but of myself. We'd come up with a plan and executed it without hesitation. When I saw Stevie again, I hoped she would tell me she was proud too. Not that I needed it. I just wanted her to see that what I'd done was as much for me as it was for her.

Not only could I try new things, I could be good at them.

17

The wind picked up as the day went on, until it whipped so hard that I was swallowing my own hair. That was after I'd tied it back into a ponytail. Out of the corner of my eye, through the strands of brown that had become glued to my eye socket, I caught a glimpse of Stevie talking to Allison outside the mess hall, so I skipped the lunch I was no longer very hungry for and went to the water, where the Magnusson brothers tended to camp out.

"Gar! Let's go out in a rowboat!" Mason yelled.

Despite my lack of feelings for him—and my abundance of feelings for his sister—my vision continued to plague me. I'd spent the first two days of camp allergic to any information about him. Now that I'd removed all the romantic pressure from the situation, I found myself genuinely intrigued. How could the universe think *Mason* was the one for me?

For the second time in as many days, I found myself getting

ready to spend time on the water with him. I ran to my cabin and threw on a sweatshirt over my tee. The wind had enough chill to it that I wanted something to keep me from shivering. When I came back outside, I found Mason once again arguing with my sister. This time they were bickering over whether we should go out on the water at all.

"It's too windy," Dara said, using her *you're possibly the least intelligent person alive* voice. He had no way of knowing how rare it was for her to care about anyone enough to tell them they were making a bad decision.

"We'll be fine," Mason said to her. "Hand on my heart." He did a little bow in her direction, to which she scowled heavily. "I promise to keep your sister safe."

A scowl was a sign of affection from Dara. It meant she was watching. That she didn't agree, but she at least saw you as worthy enough to pay attention to. Mason broke out into a wide grin, somehow understanding this about my sister.

In that moment, all the stars aligned. Birds flocked into the formation of an arrow. The little ache of satisfaction started pinging in my chest, like I'd set a timer the night Dara and I had made our bracelets and finally, twenty years later, it was going off.

My heart-promise vision wasn't about Mason and me.

It was about Mason and *Dara*.

They were both ambitious, competitive, and competent. Where Mason was goofy and naive, Dara was serious and insightful. He could bring a lightness to her steps. She could give him a healthy dose of support when he needed it most. They were each other's perfect complements.

How did it take me this long to realize that I, the keeper of Dara's heart promise, had to be the one to find a way to fulfill it for her? It had been clear for a long time that she'd never do it for herself. She needed her nudge from the universe, and in this case, I was the one who carried the wisdom of the cosmos inside me.

"Dara!" I yelled, acting like I hadn't overheard her fighting with Mason. "Come on the rowboat with us! It's going to be so fun!"

It would be the perfect chance to get them to connect. I would be their orchestrator. That was what I shined at best. Lifting my sister up. Putting her best foot forward for her. Making others see the good in her when she tried so hard to keep it a secret.

"It's too windy," she told me, using the exact same tone she'd used on Mason.

"No, it's not," Mason muttered.

Dara really brought color to his personality in a way that I did not. It made so much sense. Too much sense! It sparked me forward, eager now to see this through.

"We won't know who is right about that until we get out there, now will we?" I challenged. As expected, it was the exact prompt that put us where we needed to be. Dara loved being right, which was basically the same as winning. She couldn't resist.

She headed for the supply room to get us life jackets. When she returned, she tossed one to me, and right when I pulled it over my head, she said, "Look! It's Garland's best friend. I better go get her so she can join us too."

I got lost in flotation device foam upon hearing that, scrambling like a headless zombie, waving my arms around. Who should assist me but Mason, who took the opportunity to try and make the moment meaningful. He eased the life jacket down over my head, then pulled my hair out from the back so it was no longer trapped. It would have been sweet if I weren't seeing all his decisions under a blacklight. The choices had stains on them I couldn't help noticing now that I'd uncovered the full truth about my vision.

He'd only taken a shine to me because Stevie had told him he should. She'd said he needed direction, and she'd pointed his compass the wrong way. He wasn't here with me because he wanted to be. He was here because someone he trusted had told him it was a good idea. It was up to me to point him in an even better direction. Focus his attention on my secretly sweet, privately generous, quietly hilarious older sister. His *real* soulmate.

I broke out of the moment Mason had tried his hardest to make meaningful by issuing a perfunctory "Thanks" and shifting my gaze to Stevie.

Seeing her felt like jumping in a moving elevator, a surprising gravity tug that jolted my heart. She still wore her Blue Team shirt with her usual braids under her ball cap. She hadn't gone to our cabin to sleep off her supposed illness. She'd been talking to Allison by the mess hall. I hated not knowing what any of it meant.

"We're going out in the rowboat," Dara told her. Not a request but a fact.

"It's pretty windy," Stevie noted.

Dara almost injured herself cranking her neck to glare at Mason, who said "It'll be fun" and started tugging the boat into the water.

Stevie had no reason to say no. What was she going to do? Tell my sister and her brother that she was avoiding me? She'd never be able to explain why, because she hadn't even explained it to me.

"Fine," she said.

I felt sure that if I so much as touched her, it would shock me. Not only because I had so many feelings for her, but because she *definitely* had some feelings about me. What they were, I didn't exactly know, but they made everything heady and tilting, slanting the flat ground enough to make me feel perpetually off-balance.

Mustering up as much bravery as possible, I started to ask, "Do you want me to get you a lifejack—" and she cut me off with a quick, incisive *no* that made me go very still.

"Let's go!" Mason waved us forward, blessing us with an escape from the awkwardness that had settled atop our strained interaction.

My sister took one side of the oars and Mason took the other. They were seated directly across from each other on the boat, with me behind Dara, and Stevie behind Mason.

Mason and Dara worked together in a seamless way, matching each other's pace without any discussion, gliding through the choppy water with ease. I wanted to highlight how impressive I found this, but Stevie's presence set me more and more sideways the longer we spent together. Soon enough I'd be flat on the ground, incapable of fighting the force.

My goal was to make Mason love my sister. Stevie's goal was still to make Mason love *me*. What a colossal mess I'd made.

Once we got a sufficient distance from shore, the wind made everything incredibly loud. "DARA'S VERY GOOD AT ROCK CLIMBING," I yelled to Mason, determined to accomplish what I'd set out to do.

He said, "YEAH! I'M REALLY GOOD AT ROCK CLIMBING!"

"NO! DARA!" I screamed so hard my throat felt raw. I pointed at my sister. "DARA ROCK CLIMBS!"

"OH! COOL!" Mason yelled back.

I imagined their life together. They would make their fancy pour-over coffee for each other with increasingly unique, hard-to-source beans, forever in a competition over who could brew the best cup. On Dara's grumpier days, Mason would bring her smiley face pancakes in bed. When Mason got a little too intense about something, Dara would put a hand atop his and say, "I'm here. What do you need?" They'd take thirty-mile bike rides together for fun. It would be perfect.

If only the wind would stop trying to ruin everything with its violence.

The boat rocked. I hated every single second of it, but no one else called chicken, so I pressed on with my mission. Another thing to add to my tally of risks.

I nudged my sister, who rowed valiantly, putting every ounce of muscle she had into it, scowling at the water while very likely thinking Mason was a brainless sack of muscle for proposing we do this.

"Mason loves coffee!" I told her.

She ignored me.

"He complimented that machine you made me bring."

This made her look at me, but only to glare.

"YOU AND DARA SHOULD DO THE ROCK CLIMBING WALL TOGETHER," I yelled over to Mason.

"SURE," Mason yelled.

Stevie finally took her eyes off the water and granted me the honor of her attention. She had a puzzled look on her face, which was better than nothing and hurt much less than how dismissive she'd been earlier. I could feel her analyzing me, trying to understand why I wanted Mason to hang out with Dara.

Pushing against the current, I stood up so I could switch sides with Mason. That way, he could talk to Dara without needing to scream.

"I'LL ROW," I told him. I was practically in a middle split to keep from toppling over. The boat did not just rock. It shook so violently from side to side, it was almost taking on water.

"Hey, Garland," Stevie said tentatively. "You should probably sit."

"I WANT TO ROW!" I yelled.

"Sit down!" Stevie commanded, right as she herself stood up.

With both of us upright, the swaying went from violent to terminal. Our rowboat tipped over, and all four of us got plunged into the lake.

18

The icy water shocked my system as I spun in the washing machine of the lake. There was only the sharp sting of water in my nostrils and the disorienting feeling of falling while floating. My life jacket shot me upward, and I emerged on the surface with a baptismal gasp.

Mason and Dara popped up next. The three of us bobbed for half a second, coughing up water and fighting off shock, before my stomach somersaulted on its own.

"Stevie," I whispered. She hadn't put on a life jacket.

Scrambling, shaking, my fingers fighting my every move, I unbuckled mine so I could go under to look for her.

On a normal day, the lake was relatively clear. The combination of the wind plus the rowboat had sent a current through the water, and all I could see were foggy clouds of bubbles and dirt. I'd swim to the bottom and back to find her, letting my lungs burn and my eyes turn red from willing myself to see her. I'd do whatever it took.

Reaching out as I swam down, my hands collided with the soft tumble of her body. I could feel her panic as she kicked and thrashed. I grabbed her tight, and her frantic scrambling stopped. She stilled enough for me to pull both of us up.

We emerged together, another huge, cleansing breath on both of our lips. I didn't want to let her go, not even when Mason swam over with my life jacket, giving it to us to hold. Paddling desperately toward the shoreline, I thought of nothing but land and stability and keeping Stevie safe. She shook in my arms, so much more fragile than the Stevie most people got to know.

Andrew and Frank had seen everything unfold. Andrew waded in to help us out of the water while Frank offered each of us a towel.

"Are you all right?" Andrew asked, inspecting both Stevie and me. It touched my heart that his concern was not limited to his sister alone, though I hadn't earned it, seeing as I was the reason we'd been thrown into the water in the first place.

Stevie didn't answer him. She just wrapped herself in the towel, shivering, shocked, and silent.

"I'm so sorry," I told her, only once. It had to be said. More than any other time I'd spoken it. She met my eye with the most soul-piercing flicker, then let her attention drop to the ground. I grabbed a towel and stood trembling beneath it, unable to process all that had happened.

Mason and Dara swam in after us with the rowboat, their shared competence once again highlighted by this event. I hadn't even looked back for them. As soon as I'd realized Stevie was under, I'd abandoned the boat and all sense of space and time.

My sister—with the bitter, waterlogged look of a half-drowned rat—huffed her way toward dry ground. I'd made a mess with my recklessness in the exact way she'd taught me not to do. She'd always begged me to stop trying to force good spirits onto people who didn't want them, because when we made less noise we attracted less attention and we stood a slightly better chance of our parents being in a good mood. But my urge to be different from her always reared its head. I thought if I could just show her how my way worked, she'd understand she didn't have to be so put together. Hiding our pain wasn't going to fix anything. Tap-dancing over it sure might make us feel a little better!

No matter how many times it ended in disaster, I could never seem to train myself enough to stop trying. I found myself in trouble spots I could never anticipate. Like overturning a rowboat trying to play matchmaker.

Teeth chattering, Dara completed her self-appointed tasks with her levelheaded diligence, checking off every item on the list before she handled her own comfort. Only after she'd returned the boat to the shed, confirmed that Stevie was okay, and brushed the random dirt and debris off her legs did she walk over to the stack of towels that Frank had set down on the picnic bench and put one around her shoulders.

"I'm going to go shower," she announced.

Pulled by guilt, I followed her, my soggy clothing dripping rivers behind my every step. "I didn't mean for that to happen," I told her. Adrenaline had me walking too fast and talking too loudly, but I still couldn't catch her. "I'm really sorry."

"I don't understand what you were trying to do," she said.

"I wanted you and Mason to have a chance to talk."

"Why? I'm not the one who saw a happily ever after with him."

"I don't think it was *my* happily ever after that I saw." I paused, letting that concept linger. It landed with substantial intrigue, slowing Dara's steps. "I think I saw yours."

This made her stop completely. We collided, and her towel fell from her shoulders. She scrambled to pick it up. The sandy dirt that formed the campgrounds' walking paths had already coated it with a thin layer of grime. "What are you saying?"

"I'm saying I don't think I'm the one who is meant to be with Mason. I think *you* are."

She took off again, now holding her towel over her arm. Her shoulders shook as she blazed down the path. "You can't be serious."

"I am." I forced calmness into my voice so she'd take me seriously. "I don't feel anything for him. It's because he's meant to be with you. I mean, think about it. You were the one who'd held on to my bracelet all those years. *That* was the bracelet he picked up in the airport. It had all kinds of Dara energy all over it instead of mine. You know? It makes sense."

My logic wouldn't work on many people, but it would on her.

"There's only one problem," she said. We were in the space between our cabins, lingering on the pathways.

"What?"

She jogged up the steps of Cabin Six. "I don't feel anything for Mason either."

"Maybe not yet. You have to give it time," I said. She did not dignify me with so much as a glance. "You're always so closed off to love," I continued. "Open your heart up a little! Let that tall, blond Swedish man make a home there!"

"No," she said decisively, turning toward her door.

"C'mon! How can you know if you don't at least try?"

She kept her back to me as she said, "Because I want to be alone, Garland."

"No, you don't," I told her. "You're just saying that because you're scared. You can't avoid love forever."

"I'm not avoiding love, or whatever else it is you seem to think I've been doing for the last thirty-four years of my life. Being by myself is not a flaw. It's a *feature*. So no, I'm not the one who will be falling in love with Mason. End of discussion." She opened and closed the door of her cabin, locking it before I could so much as come up with a single word in response.

She'd always been the one to tell me that true love existed. That we could find it. And now she'd told me she didn't want it, and she didn't even seem to be apologetic about it.

I'd never get to give her the heart-promise bracelet? For as seriously as we took it, she didn't want it? From now until forever, I'd be holding on to two people's unfulfilled hopes and wishes?

It didn't hurt as much as make me hollow. So much of me had been filled up with the beliefs Dara and I shared. In my darkest moments, they were the foundation pieces I clung to, reminding me of all the good that awaited me in the future. And Dara had snapped her fingers and vanished all of it in one clean break.

Defeated, I went to Stevie's hideout by the edge of the lake. I'd given three solid days to following my initial rule—trying it all, being open to risks. For all the courage I thought I was demonstrating, all I'd done was create a mess in other people's lives. It was time to close the door. There would be no reinvention here. I had to keep myself from causing any further harm.

With the blanket of trees far above my head and the gentle hushing rock of the lake beyond my feet, I lay down on the hardened dirt. I wanted to be alone. Truly alone.

I couldn't hurt anyone where no one could find me.

19

When I woke up, the trees blocked the light of the stars, enveloping me in a darkness so absolute I went hot and panicky. I couldn't even see the outline of my own body. The gentle lapping of the water was all that kept me sane. I knew the entire camp had been built around the lake, and I'd never be lost so long as I stayed near it.

Crawling on all fours, I moved toward the swooshing sound until my palms were wet. I patted all around me, feeling for the seam of the shoreline so I could follow it. *Why did I do this?* I asked myself over and over. Another case of me trying to do the right thing and making a mess. Though I was the only one paying for it right now, lost and alone and terrified in a way that drenched me to the core.

My speed could not have been much faster than a snail's. At some point, the darkness broke enough for me to see things like the shape of my own fingers, but it didn't help calm the fear. At once, a bright, piercing light shone into my eyes, rendering me immobile.

"What the hell have you been doing?"

I couldn't see the person, but I knew the voice. It was Stevie. And she was *mad*.

When I lifted myself up, her flashlight moved lower in response, no longer beaming straight into my eyeballs. It allowed me to catch a quick look at her face. She was furious. Even the hand she had wrapped around her phone seemed overly tense, squeezing tight enough that the white pads of her fingertips were visible around the edge of the light.

"I fell asleep," I told her, wiping my dirty palms against my clothing. "I was trying to find my way back to the campgrounds."

"I thought you went missing," she said. "I haven't seen you in hours."

"I wanted to be by myself. I've been making such a royal mess of things, I figured everyone needed some Garland-free time."

"You thought the appropriate solution was to come to my hideout? No one knew where you were," Stevie said.

I couldn't stop myself from trying to change her mood. I didn't want her to be mad at me. "Isn't that what a hideout is for?" I asked, attempting a laugh. "Hiding?"

Stevie had no response. My efforts looked like they were working, at least a little.

"Also, if I can point out, *you* knew I was here," I told her. It thrilled me to know she'd figured me out. Even when I'd tried to hide, she'd found me.

"I kept thinking you'd show up at the mixer," she said. "Then the band asked where you were, and you didn't magically appear to lead us all in a two-step across the dance floor, so I knew you were legitimately missing. Michelle hadn't seen you. The twins hadn't seen you. My brother, your *soulmate*, hadn't seen you."

It was meant to be a dig, and that's exactly how I received it. Could she not see how little her brother meant to me? How did she not know it was her? It had always been her.

"Your sister said you were probably mad at her, but she didn't have anything else to offer," Stevie continued.

"That sounds like Dara," I said. "And your brother's *not* my soulmate."

Stevie didn't hear me, because she hadn't stopped speaking herself. "I've been walking around the campgrounds looking for you, figuring surely you didn't come out here, because it's way too dark after the sun goes down!"

"I've never been here after the sun goes down," I countered. "I didn't know it was gonna get this dark. I didn't mean to fall asleep. I was just relaxing."

Stevie threw her hands in the air, her flashlight pointed at the sky. Nothing I could say seemed to please her. "Don't you *dare* apologize," she told me, anticipating my next move right as my lips had formed those exact syllables.

"You're so upset with me," I said instead.

"I'm not upset. I was *worried*. If something happened to you . . ." She let the sentence trail off, a thousand different endings playing through in my mind.

"No need to worry. I'm here in one piece."

She harrumphed, stepping closer, then stepping back. "You saved my life, and I didn't say thank you."

"I'm the one who tipped the boat," I reminded her. "There was nothing to thank me for."

"*I* tipped the boat," she shot back.

"I stood up first."

"And I stood up second. It was me standing that tipped us over."

"Right, but you were only standing because I was standing."

"This isn't about standing."

"Isn't it?"

"I wasn't speaking to you," she said, quieter.

"You were ignoring me because I keep making your life harder. Like when I tipped the boat over," I said.

She did not entertain the boat debate. Instead she whispered, "You're not making my life harder."

I stared at her. God, her face was perfect. Even when I could hardly see it. I knew the sweet slope of her nose. The hollows of her cheeks. Her smile lines, crinkling in the corners of her mouth when she grinned. I'd been so flustered when she found me, I hadn't processed the honor of witnessing her. Now the heat of her sunshine spread through me, moving like a fast-acting drug, waking up every nerve in my body.

"Okay, yes, you *have* complicated my life. But not in the way you think," she admitted.

"You've complicated my life too," I blurted out.

"How have I complicated your life?" The frustration in her voice lowered, stretched out. Lingered on the verge of something different.

The two of us were fixed on each other, an exchange of dares between our gazes. Who was I to her? Who was she to me?

"You have to tell me how I've complicated yours first," I hedged.

She backed up even more, making herself small. "I can't."

"Because of Mason?"

She looked away.

"Stevie," I said, the force in my voice pulling her attention back to me. "I can tell you with complete, one hundred percent certainty that I will *never* date your brother. Call down the fake birds and take that information straight to the government. Tell the camp ghosts to post it on the front page of their gazette. I do not care if my own brain conjured an entire world where I ended up with him. It is *never* going to happen."

If Dara could throw out the rule book, so could I. I wasn't ignoring my vision anymore. I was outright rejecting it. Staring it in the face and saying *No, that's not who I plan to be*. It didn't matter if that life was assigned to me by the magic my sister and I had created all those years ago. We'd both grown past those versions of ourselves. If she didn't have to want that anymore, neither did I.

Stevie stepped forward. "You really don't like him?" she dared to ask, after I'd all but cut my thumb and made a sacrificial pledge to Mother Nature that I'd never go near him romantically.

"Stevie," I whispered, her name a secret for the stars to unravel.

After throwing out the rule book, the first decision of my

new life was accepting that I didn't have to move like the universe was keeping score of my generosity at every single moment. I could do the reckless thing intentionally. I could do it with *purpose*.

"I have no idea how I made it three whole days convincing you that I wanted to know Mason more," I continued. "Ever since you crashed into me at our doorstep and I saw the little freckles on your face, you've been the only person I've thought about that way."

If she didn't understand before, she got it then. Her eyes softened, and in them I saw the kind of hope I'd always chased. My bold, confident Stevie had been protecting herself from letting me in. I'd made her think she needed to do that. There was nothing in the world I wanted more than to change that.

"I like you," I continued. "And I know your ex-girlfriend is here, and you guys have some big history that I could never possibly understand, so I totally get it if you do nothing with this information. I've never told a woman I liked her before, and I have to be honest and say that if this is the wrong way to do it, I'm not going to apologize, but as my alliance partner I hope you'd tell me. That way if another woman ever comes along who shines as bright as you, I'll know what to do."

Stevie stepped closer to me. There it was again. The feeling of falling. Standing on the ceiling of the world and tipping over. And I wanted to fall. Because I wanted her to catch me.

"You're doing pretty great," she said, giving me the very grin I loved the most. The light-beam smile.

"Is that alliance information, or 'you're charmed by what I'm saying' information?"

Now she laughed. The bottle-rocket kind that sent birds out of trees. The other campers could probably hear her over the music in the main hall. They'd know her laugh as the purest concentration of joy that existed. "You know, for such a smart person, you've really let all of this go right over your head."

"What do you mean?"

"*Garland*," she whispered in her favorite way. The *years of history between us* kind of way. "I think that the floorboard outside our cabin got loose because the earth shifted when I saw you."

She said things in a way that sent my pulse into my toes. I was feverish. Lit up and terrified and so completely hooked on her every word.

"There's a thing a lot of people say about women when they date other women," she continued. "I'm sure you've heard it. We fall in love too fast. We rent the U-Haul and move in together after a week. And that's always annoyed me, even though to be perfectly honest, it's happened to more than one of my friends. I still thought it was a boring generalization and that people lacked imagination. Until I met you." She laughed, remembering. "I saw you and thought, *Oh yes. Wherever she asked me to go, I'd follow.* And then you told me my fucking brother was your soulmate."

"To be fair, I didn't *exactly* say that," I joked, so flustered and overwhelmed and unbelievably charmed, I truly believed

I had a fever. I thought back to the moment I'd told her. How she'd instantly folded her arms. Backed away from me. The way she'd agreed to help with a wobbly, curious uncertainty.

"Yes, you did," she argued, another tiny laugh slipping out of her. "And all week I've been losing my grip on reality because of it. Especially after we slow danced last night. I haven't been able to look at you since. Because I just couldn't take it anymore. I've competed against Mason for many, many things in my life, but we've never competed over a girl. Not that I thought I had a real chance with you."

I almost laughed in return. In that moment, it felt comical that she'd ever doubt it, even though I hadn't known it for myself. But it had always been her. From that first second. And there was no question about it.

"So I've been going to his cabin multiple times a day, pretty much every time I'm not with you, and telling him every fascinating thing about you I can think of, just to be sure he could see every single detail about you he needed to see," she continued. "Because if he fucked it up, I was going to disown him."

"He would've been the biggest shithead in the world," I joked.

"Exactly. And when he wasn't appreciating everything, I'd just tell him again. 'No, Mason. You don't understand. She has several earrings in her left ear, and they all look great together.' Earlier today he even said to me, 'Damn. You really like this girl.' And I said, 'Yeah. *Obviously.*'"

I hated how little I could see of her through the darkness, because I wanted to drink in every detail of her face.

"You don't secretly still love your ex?" I asked.

"No." She moved in closer to me again. We were less than three feet apart. No standard-sized baseball bat could have fit between us. "You don't secretly have even the smallest ounce of feelings for my brother?"

"Not a single solitary drop."

"Thank fucking god." Her breath blew against my cheek, sending a chill down my spine. Her hands found mine as she pressed herself against me. "Is this all right?"

"Yes," I whispered. The warmth that had flooded me poured another layer of heat over all the spaces that were touching her. Our hands burned together, so much better than hands should feel. "I like everything you do." She laughed against my skin. Just as her mouth neared mine, I dared to speak again. "But I hate that I can't fully see you right now."

She fell into me, not a deflated balloon but one that had expanded farther, charging up against my body. "Then let's go find some light."

Holding hands, we walked until we stood underneath a lamplight. In the distance, the campgrounds' event hall burned bright, twinkle lights and loud music pulsing.

I brushed a curl off her cheek as I pressed her against the cold metal pole. "There you are." I could see the autumn in her eyes, flecks of brown against the green. My heart squeezed again, that same feeling I'd had all week.

I'd been an incredible fool, and I could be a fool no longer.

So I kissed her.

Tumbled onto her lips, really.

She corrected me without faltering. I'd never been kissed

the way she kissed me back. With purpose and tenderness, and an ease I could sigh against. I could taste the lime on my lips. One of her shots for courage. She'd taken it for *me*.

The idea that I wound her up, that I was the one she needed to be brave for, made me press harder. My tongue slipped into her mouth, and she met me with the same confidence she always did. I put my hands in her hair, tangling my fingers in her curls.

Stevie Magnusson was not like any other person I'd ever known.

20

W hat's your job?" I pulled back and asked, suddenly desperate to gather other pieces of information I hadn't managed to collect.

I wanted to hold her in the completion she deserved. Stevie wasn't a stranger I'd kiss at a bar, hoping to get the feeling out of my system. She was someone I kissed because I couldn't bear the distance. Because talking didn't suffice. Learning every piece of her became a burning necessity.

"I kiss you, and you want to know how I make my money?" she teased.

"Proof of income is usually on every rental application, right? For after we get the U-Haul. Just want to make sure we've covered all our bases here."

It was a dangerous kind of joking. Intentional recklessness was truly one path I'd never traveled, and it felt like I imagined it would have if I'd gone across the ropes course. Breathlessly scary. Knee-shaking and intense.

"Would you like us to reintroduce ourselves?" she asked me. "Then we can get back to making out?"

I kissed her once, quick. "That would be nice, yeah."

She twisted around the pole until she was no longer touching me, then she stretched out her hand and said, "Hello. My name is Stevie. I was a park ranger for six years. But I quit a few months ago. Bought a van and started traveling around the country in it."

I took her palm in mine and shook. "Hi, Stevie. I'm Garland."

She didn't let me release her. Instead she pulled me forward, and we walked together toward our cabin holding hands.

"So that's what you meant by living nowhere," I continued, remembering what she'd said at the first nightly mixer.

"My permanent address is at Mason's, but that's just a paperwork technicality. I had to have somewhere to register my van. When I found out Allison was cheating on me, I got rid of everything in my life. I've always been all-or-nothing like that. I wanted the earth scorched."

I knew exactly what it was like to lose your identity when someone else removed themselves from the equation. To need to leave it all behind and start over.

"I came back here because I've forgotten what it means to do something just for my own enjoyment," she continued. "Nature became my literal job. And I *loved* it at first. Then I loved what it gave me financially. When Allison ruined everything, I realized I'd forgotten how to enjoy something just because I like it, not because it gives me something. I'd forgotten how to just *be*."

"I understand," I told her. "I really do."

"What's *your* job?" she asked.

"Oh. Nothing notable," I said.

She was a nature girl who did things in nature. Her work made sense. I had a part-time job in a part-time life. The job itself did not embarrass me, but the contrast between Stevie and me did. It wasn't like I had a great passion for transporting people or anything. It was just a thing I did to get by, as all things were in my life. I had nothing I really loved. No dream I chased for the passion of it.

"That can't be true," Stevie said to me. "Everything you do is notable."

"I really think you'd change your mind on that if you had me pick you up and take you to the airport."

I didn't like putting myself down, which is why I preferred making jokes about the hard things. Laughing was so much better than pity. But I didn't know how to make good jokes anymore. Somewhere after our kiss, I'd lost my defenses.

"I'm a rideshare driver," I said, attempting to move away from pity and into honesty.

Stevie squeezed my hand. "You take people places they need to be. That's an important job! Before Uber and Lyft and stuff, a lot of people used to drive themselves drunk all the time."

"Don't you worry. They still do."

"Yeah, but not as much."

She was trying to make me feel better. With any other person, it wouldn't have worked. But she had *that* face, and *that* smile, and *that* surefire confidence. Who was I to deny her?

"Well, thank you," I said, squeezing her hand the same way she'd squeezed mine.

"If it's not what you want to do, though, what else do you have in mind? What makes Garland Moore's heart race?"

"Other than you?"

She grinned. "Other than me."

We reached our front door. Stevie pulled her key out of the back pocket of her jeans and opened our cabin. All the lights were off, so we fumbled through the darkness, still holding hands, moving down the narrow hall and into our room.

"Did you know the distance between our beds is the same as the average length of a Golden Retriever?" I asked, slipping into the bathroom to wash the dirt off my hands.

"Of course. That's exactly how they described it in the camp brochure." Stevie flicked on the overhead light in our bedroom. "Sit with me in here," she called out. "I won't bite. Too hard."

My face went hot. "What if we pushed our beds together?" I asked as I entered the room. Intentional recklessness at its finest.

"If you insist." She picked up our shared nightstand, dragging it toward the door to prevent any obstacles. I walked around to the far end and pushed her bedframe toward mine.

"I love a strong woman," she told me as I closed the gap between our beds.

"The frame is on wheels."

She looked down to confirm I wasn't lying, seeing the wheels beneath each bedpost. "It takes skill to control that kind of rolling," she said. "Gliding like an ice skater across these knotty wood floors." She picked up the nightstand again and carried it to the open side. We both had a few small belongings atop it, and for the second time, she managed not to drop a single thing.

"Now, *that* takes skill," I told her.

With everything appropriately rearranged, she laid herself across our newly joined bed, rolling onto her side to look at me. "Just so you know, I haven't forgotten what I asked you before we came inside. About what makes your heart race."

You, I thought again, seeing her sprawled out with her head resting on her hand and her other hand patting a spot for me. I couldn't answer the question the same way twice, because she clearly expected something more cerebral than what my sensations were conjuring.

I laid myself down beside her, mirroring the way she held herself. "I don't actually know," I told her. "The life I used to want for myself was just a life that fit what I thought the world expected of me. I got a degree in communications, because that made sense. I married my college sweetheart. Because that made sense. I realize now that none of it actually made sense *to me*. It just made sense on paper. And it's taken me way too long to see that those are different things. It's like I've been in hibernation, and suddenly I'm awake. I'm alive. And I don't know what to do with myself."

She scooted in, resting her mouth atop my ear. "Let me tell you a secret," she whispered. The soft tickle of her breath on my skin made me shiver. "You still have time to figure it out. Even though you're—" She pulled back and dropped her voice to the normal register. "Shit. How old are you again?"

"I'm thirty-two," I said.

She leaned back in and returned to her ASMR whisper. "Even at thirty-two. You are not required by law to understand a single fucking thing about yourself, despite what everyone might want to tell you."

It was my turn to whisper in her ear. I pressed myself against the side of her face and said, "You're younger than me, how do you already have this all figured out?"

She laughed her magical laugh. "Were you listening earlier? I don't have a single thing figured out."

I moved back to trace the line of her jaw with my pointer finger. "Oh, I was listening," I said. "I just have a hard time believing you don't know every single thing. You're the most confident person I've ever met."

She had to put her hand over her mouth to stop herself from laughing again. "Nothing could be further from the truth. Do you not remember me when we didn't win the ropes course? I'm an insecure wreck."

"See? You want to win things. You have that figured out about yourself."

"I enjoy knowing that the things I do in life count for something," she said. "And when you win, it's proof you did the best you could."

"Not winning isn't the same as losing, though. You can do the best you possibly can and still get last," I reminded her. "It's a state of mind. A perspective."

"I told you, Garland, I'm all-or-nothing. If it doesn't work, I drop it forever."

"So why is Allison here trying to win you back?" I asked. "She lived with you. Shouldn't she know you enough to know that's the last thing you'd want?"

Suddenly, Stevie put her thumb on my cheek and tucked her fingers under my chin. Like she just had to hold me, because she couldn't believe I was real. I could feel that urgency, that desperation to understand how I had turned up in her life and we were sharing this moment. I knew because I felt the same way about her.

"Allison loves a challenge," she told me. "Which is part of what drew me to her in the first place. She thinks I haven't been serious when I've told her we're over, because in the past, I wasn't. That was before I knew the extent of what she'd done to me. She didn't just cheat on me with one person. It was multiple people. The entire time we were together."

"How'd you find out?"

Stevie rolled away from me, breaking our touch. "You're gonna think I'm shitty."

"Try me," I said, rubbing her back.

She peeked over her shoulder. Peering deep into my eyes, trying to see if I was worthy of her trust. *C'mon, Stevie*, I thought. *Let's see how far we can fall.*

"I looked through her phone," she admitted.

"That's not that bad!" I told her, meaning it. "What made you do it?"

"I don't even know. She left it unlocked on the couch one day when she went to shower. And I just had this *feeling*. I wanted to prove myself wrong. Instead I ended up proving myself right."

"See? Sometimes it's bad to win!"

She granted me a quick scrunch of her face. "I was out the door by the time she finished her shower. I sent Andrew to get all my stuff for me. Bought the van the next day. I like living on the road because it doesn't feel like I belong to anything. No one can catch me there. But being here at camp again, I can see that I'm just running from my fear. And Allison thinks she's caught me. Which she should know pisses me off. I can't be caught."

"Of course not," I told her with fake seriousness. "You are one slippery fish." I took the opportunity to pull her closer to me again. "This is a woman who can't be tied down. No one can hold her," I said as I did just that. I held her.

The power of it wasn't lost on me. Our bodies seemed designed to be pressed together. That's how well they fit. We were meant to hold each other, telling secrets to each other at summer camp.

"Thank you again for dancing with me last night," she whispered to me. She'd rolled so her back lay against the front of me, and I had my face in her hair, breathing in the coconut of her shampoo. "I know that killed Allison. That's not why I liked it, but it didn't hurt. She told me by the water today that if I didn't take her back by the end of the night, she was gonna leave tomorrow. Seeing as I'm here in bed with you, she should be gone by the time we wake up."

"You know what? I'd say I won't miss her, but if it weren't for Allison's presence, I'd probably be three sheets to the wind again tonight, trying to get Mason to tell me about pour-over techniques."

Stevie faked a shudder against me. "He'd have proposed marriage."

"The nice thing is, I would have said no," I told her. "I have no plans to get married again."

"And you thought you didn't know anything about your life!" Stevie rolled so we were nose to nose. "I don't want to get married either."

"Of course not. Because no one could hold you."

"Exactly."

She moved herself even closer to me. This was the beginning of something big, that much I knew. It used to be hard for me to cherish beginnings because I found myself anxious to learn what would come next. I always got too far ahead of myself. The future had more in store for Stevie and me. Desire hung heavy in the air, a third party to our every action. But the present was perfect too. Sweet and full of hope.

As eager as I was to explore her—learn every curve of her body up close, hear the sounds she made when pleasure overcame her—I wanted just as much to cherish every milestone as we met it. I was *holding* Stevie Magnusson. We were going to sleep in each other's arms. I needed to appreciate that for what it was—a gift. The rest would be here soon enough.

Until then, I wanted to let the magic of the present amaze me.

Day Four of Summer Camp

21

It seemed impossible that we had only two full days left in the mountains before we were due to return to our normal lives. It had felt like years since we'd arrived at camp, and I couldn't imagine it coming to an end. Instead of being reinvented, I'd been rearranged. All the pieces of myself I'd never acknowledged before this week now fit me so well they seemed like the entirety of my personhood.

It went so much deeper than my attraction to Stevie. My queerness shifted the lens through which I viewed my whole life. I could finally see how I had never actually been comfortable in the old molds I used to live inside. They'd been shattered long before I arrived at camp, but with my new perspective, the wreckage no longer hurt to look at.

Holding Stevie in my arms as she slept, feeling the easy rise and fall of her chest, I felt so much compassion for those old, jagged pieces of me. I had been so fearful of inflicting pain on others, I ended up hurting myself. I had fallen over myself to fix things that couldn't be repaired.

When Stevie finally stirred, the first thing she did was roll back to see me. "You're still here," she said, groggy. She rubbed her eyes as if she had to make extra sure.

"Of course I am," I told her. "Where else would I be?"

"Sleeping on a rock in my hideout." She laughed softly at herself. "It's a really nice view in the mornings."

"I've seen better," I said as I kissed her on the cheek. When I tried to pull back, she drew me in closer instead. Our foreheads were touching. We breathed into the quiet, listening to the campgrounds wake up around us.

In a way, my old habit of romanticizing life was one of the only kindnesses I'd granted myself, because it was the only time I allowed myself to believe I deserved a love full of care. I didn't need to shut that out anymore. I needed to lean in harder, because it was a gift to be able to not just see the good in the world but embrace it.

And Stevie Magnusson was all the good in the world. She was warmth. She was sparkle. She radiated the exact kind of compassion I'd only recently learned to have for myself. Pressing my skin against hers had the same grounding effect as being barefoot on grass. I'd hardly slept all night, and I didn't feel tired. I felt calm. For the first time in years, my alarm went off after I'd already woken up, and it wasn't because I'd spent the night heartsick and confused. I'd been content.

"What do you say to a morning swim?" I asked her. The

way her face lit up told me I'd surprised her in a good way. It was addicting, watching Stevie marvel at me. She made taking risks worth it.

We dressed in our swimsuits with regular clothes atop them and headed toward the water. The air had a bite to it, but the gentle pinkish tint of the early-morning sun softened the chill's effect. It all looked so lovely that the breeze invigorated me. Emboldened me.

There was a dock not far from our cabin, and Stevie and I walked down it hand in hand. When we reached the edge, both of us paused, squinting into the light as we took in the beauty of the view. That could have been enough. But I found myself wondering what it would be like to kiss Stevie at dawn. Instead of imagining the scenario, I decided it would be infinitely better to live it instead.

So I did.

I pressed my lips to Stevie's, and she welcomed me eagerly, wrapping her arms around me to pull us closer. The cold air swished between us, finding the gaps where we didn't touch. All the places we did were warm and secure.

I had never felt such a comfort with my desire. It was easy in the way all good things often were, like when you found yourself wondering why you didn't *always* take a nice walk on a beautiful day or cook your favorite meal for dinner. Why didn't I *always* wake up with the sun to kiss Stevie Magnusson on the dock of the lake? In that moment, it felt not only possible to do this every morning of my life, but necessary.

"I could get used to this," I told her, pulling back to see her face.

"I'm afraid I already am," she said back. There was a hint of melancholy in her voice, and the best I could do to soothe it was kiss her again.

Get used to me, I thought. *Be as desperate for my touch as I am for yours.*

Distantly, I wondered if anyone could see us. I hoped they could. There was a thrill in imagining all of camp knowing that Stevie Magnusson spent her morning making out with *me*. It was equally exciting to consider that this moment existed only for us. We were not just the only two people at camp but the only two people who would ever live that morning in that way. The dock, the lake—all of the campgrounds, really—belonged to us, if only for a little while.

Stevie moved her lips from my mouth to the bridge of my nose. She kissed it quick, then threw her sweater off, kicked her flip-flops down the dock, and dove into the lake headfirst, gliding under the water until she emerged a few feet out.

"I couldn't think about it too long," she told me. "I had to just do it."

I wanted to be as bold as her, but seeing her teeth chatter behind her beaming smile gave me pause. She swam up to where I stood, and I lowered myself down to sit, marveling at her. When I dipped my feet in the water, I let out a little yip of shock.

"It's so cold," I said. The world's most obvious statement.

"It's warmer by me," Stevie teased.

"Are you telling me that because you're nearing hypothermia and my body heat will help regulate you?"

Stevie laughed. "Yes. Save me, Garland. I need you."

She was joking, but it worked all the same. I took off my top layers of clothing one by one, folding each piece and making a neat pile beside Stevie's hastily discarded sweater and shoes. When I stood at the edge of the dock in just my swimsuit, I hesitated, trying to decide if I was going to count to three or just jump.

"Never mind," Stevie said, breaking my train of thought. She was treading water a ways out. And also staring at me. Grinning. "Stay right there."

I instantly posed. "Why? Are you admiring me?"

"Of course I am," she told me. "Have been since the moment you arrived."

At that, I cannonballed into the lake. The plunge of cold didn't feel like shock. It felt like relief because it meant I was on my way to her. No matter what my vision had shown me, I had always been on my way to her. And that was exactly where I wanted to be.

22

The referees started the daily color game by reminding us of the standings. With seventy points in total, Red Team held strong in first place. Blue Team was in second place with fifty points. Green and Yellow were tied for last at forty.

We weren't underdogs. We were legitimate contenders.

The referees brought us back to the same starting spot as yesterday—the field beside the obstacle course, vast and previously wide-open. It had been altered. There were wooden crate stacks of various heights positioned throughout the field. The referees stood next to several buckets of what looked to be water balloons. There was a folding table beside them, with a pile of clear ponchos laid atop it.

"You can probably guess what we'll be doing today," one of the referees said.

Frank pounded his fists into his chest. "Water balloons!"

Everyone laughed.

"Close!" the other referee told him, quieting the amusement. "These balloons are filled with paint. Hence the ponchos. Every participating team member will receive one to wear over your body and hair. The paint's washable, but we know you may want to protect yourself just in case."

It was a small detail, thinking of whether people would want to be dirtied up by the challenge. Another mark of the level of care the twins had put into all this.

"Once everyone is appropriately dressed, we will move the buckets to the center of the field for a good old game of paint-balloon tag," the referee continued. "When we blow the whistle, all teams are welcome to run and grab as many balloons as possible. This is an elimination game, though. If you get hit by a paint balloon, you're out. There is no second life. The first team to lose all their members will come in last, and so on until only one person remains. The last one standing will clinch the victory for their team."

"This is more about strategy than it is speed," the first referee added. "Though you're welcome to go about this in just about any way you want. You can hide behind the crates, stock up on supplies, ambush other teams. Anything goes, so long as there's no physical violence involved. But if you drop your own balloon and it splatters on your foot, you're out. If someone hits you with a balloon and it does not break, you're safe. You have to remain completely paint-free to stay in the game."

Once the rules were finished, Blue Team huddled together for a strategy session. "Anyone want to sit this one out?" Captain Aja asked.

All eight of us were silent. A rare first. Even Marge believed she could be an asset. "I've seen all those Hunger Games
movies dozens of times," she told us. "I know I don't need to
be fast to be clever."

Aja nodded. "This might get messy. Literally, but also personally. Julianne? Garland? Stevie? Tommy? All four of you
are personally connected to people on other color teams. When
it comes down to it, will you be able to throw a paint balloon
at your loved one?"

"Obviously," Stevie said before the rest of us could gather
together a case for our participation. "I will hit any of my
brothers gladly. In fact, I want all of you to leave them alone
so I can be the one to personally eliminate them."

"Noted," Aja said. "We've got Marge and Stevie on the
field. As your captain, I would like to participate as well, if
everyone agrees."

"Of course," we all told her in near-perfect unison. Aja had
shown repeatedly that she had not just enthusiasm but skill.

"Then we need three more," she told us. "Julianne, Garland, and Tommy, we still haven't heard whether or not you
think you can participate given the circumstances."

"I'm on my husband's team in life, but not when it comes
to the color games," Julianne offered.

Aja nodded.

It was down to Tommy and me to plead our cases. I looked
over, fully expecting him to take the floor before I could find
a way to articulate my Blue Team loyalty. Instead he stayed
curiously silent, not at all like the Tommy of days prior. Seeing
my opportunity, I cleared my throat. "Um, if it somehow

comes down to my sister and me, I won't let her hit me with a paint balloon."

"Will you throw one at her?"

It wasn't Aja who asked me. It was Stevie. She had a hand on my forearm and all her sunshine spotlighting me. In truth, I *didn't* want to throw a paint balloon at Dara. Not that it was going to hurt her. I just knew she'd hate losing, and I didn't want to be the one who provided that experience for her.

"Not winning isn't the same as losing," Stevie said. "Just in case you're worried about Dara's feelings or something."

She'd seen through me as she always did, returning my words to me and reminding me that I not only said them, I believed them. I wasn't responsible for Dara's feelings. I was only responsible for my own.

"I can do it," I assured my team. "I can throw a balloon at my sister." My tone mimicked the same thick-as-thieves sincerity as Julianne's, and it didn't even amuse me. I meant what I said.

Tommy bobbed his head in approval. "I'm good with sitting this one out. If it came down to Tim and me, I wouldn't eliminate him. I'm compromised."

Sky nominated themself as the second person to sit out on account of not really wanting to make a mess with paint. Which, fair enough. So representing Blue Team were Stevie, Aja, Marge, Julianne, Laurie, and me—six women from all different walks of life, united in our goal of domination.

During our pregame strategy, Stevie and I got put in charge of obtaining as many balloons as possible. Aja and Laurie were going to secure a spot for us behind the crates.

Julianne planned to spy on other teams. And Marge got the job of being our secret weapon. She would feign helplessness in a way that would make other teams pity her, like we'd forced our oldest player onto the field and she was suffering through the experience at our cruel hands. She should have been an easy target, but we knew everyone at camp would be too nice to eliminate her right away.

"It's brilliant," Marge said, loving every moment of it. "They'll never see me coming."

When the game started, Stevie sprinted full speed toward the balloons, beating everyone else by a long shot. Only Mason came close. When he successfully reached the buckets, Stevie already had two balloons in her hands. Mason tried to grab some of his own. Stevie, with the precision of a sharpshooter, pinged his shoulder.

Mason became the first person eliminated from the game.

"Are you kidding me!" he screamed, looking at the neon-pink splatter on his poncho-covered shoulder blade. He even touched his fingers to the paint, like it was a fatal wound he couldn't quite believe was real.

Stevie blew him a kiss. "Love you!"

The ruthlessness with which Stevie took out her brother made most other people pause on their way to the balloon buckets, creating a perfect window of time for me to approach. I ran forward and gathered half a dozen balloons, cupping them in my Blue Team shirt and waddling back to our safe haven behind the tallest crate stack.

As the game progressed, Stevie's early actions made our team a major target. Aja had a great arm, and she managed to stave off several different teams that attempted to attack our hideout.

The more people we picked off, the bigger our target became.

"They want me dead," Stevie said to me as she returned with a fresh set of balloons. She was heaving and sweat-slicked, having sprinted back and forth as fast as possible.

"I think you have to stay at the crates from now on," I told her. "It's not safe for you to get balloons anymore."

She wheezed out a laugh, too out of breath to give much life to the sound. "I'd rather die than give up. Besides, I'll be fine. No one can touch me." She handed her latest collection of balloons to Laurie and Aja, who used them to launch a simultaneous attack on Frank.

Laurie nabbed the edge of Frank's shoe.

"It's barely on me!" Frank yelled, instantly devastated. "It's like a speck! I could get that just from walking right now, there's so much paint on the field!"

"Please leave the game, Frank," the referee called out.

Frank sulked off the field, tossing his poncho to the ground in anger along the way. Of the Magnusson family, only Andrew and Stevie remained.

I hadn't seen Dara once. I didn't even know where she was. Red Team's safe zone was not far from ours, and she wasn't among the people protecting the balloons, but she did not run out to capture them either.

Stevie sprinted out again, performing amazing acrobatics while dodging missiles, dive rolling and leapfrogging to keep herself out of the line of fire. When she made it to the supply, she turned back to wink at me.

"Told you I'd be fine," she said.

Right then, Dara darted out from behind a tree with a balloon tucked into her shoulder like a shot-putter. She hurled it as hard as she could, and it smacked into Stevie's chest, an appropriate explosion of bright yellow. Shocked, Stevie sunk to her knees beside the buckets.

The game came to a complete pause. Everyone stood stock-still, watching Stevie process her unexpected elimination. Even though the other teams had been desperate to get rid of her, the mood was oddly somber. It was a bummer to see the best player taken out before the game ended.

Once Stevie's initial grief passed, she stood up and walked off the field with her chin held high, maintaining her dignity. Dara took the moment to start clapping. The spectators followed suit, erupting into applause for Stevie's gutsy performance.

That's when I threw *my* missile.

It got Dara by the hair, a splatter that edged the bottom of her long, exposed ponytail. It was less paint than what had landed on Frank's shoes, but Dara knew better than to protest. The rules were the rules.

"If only I'd had you cut my hair already," she called out to me as she walked off the field.

In that moment, I had grand plans to win it all. I'd already done the hardest part. I'd taken out Dara. I could charge the field and eliminate every player until only I remained. All guts and glory. Balloon tag was ruthless, and I'd proven myself to be a dangerous contender. Everyone needed to fear me.

But Andrew—my supposed friend!—got me out with a balloon to the back.

"Really?" I said, giving him my best *et tu, Brute?*

Andrew smiled. "A game's a game!"

I dragged myself into the growing spectator section, the third person eliminated in as many minutes.

The remaining numbers dwindled quickly after that. Red ended up as the first team with every player eliminated, securing their last-place position. Green Team got out next. Eventually there were only two players left on the field—Julianne's husband from Yellow Team. And Marge. Our secret weapon.

"He knows she's not fast," Julianne whispered to all our eliminated Blue Team members. "I never should have told him that."

"Good lesson here," Aja said to us. "Keep internal details to ourselves. They might matter more than we think."

Julianne's husband charged Marge.

Right before he launched his missile, Marge pulled a paint balloon out from under her shirt. She smashed it to her stomach in an act of protest, eliminating herself before the other balloon reached her.

"Wow. She really does love *The Hunger Games*," Stevie whispered.

23

You're not dismissed," Tim announced after the referees read us the updated rankings. He moved away from his Green Team members until he faced our makeshift spectator section.

Tommy gently nudged my shoulder so he could skirt past me and join his twin. They stood beside each other with matching mischief on their faces, desperate for one of us to ask what was going on.

"What's going on?" I called out, letting it be me.

"We can't tell you that!" Tim teased. "But all of you need to meet us at the mess hall in about an hour. We have a surprise for you."

"We'd love to tell you more, but that would ruin the surprise for *all* our campers," Tommy explained. "So we ask that you head back to your cabins and put on your best daytime attire. No athletic clothes necessary, unless you want to wear them, of course. Or sport your paint splatters to remind everyone what you sacrificed on the field today."

After the laughter faded, chatter grew. The crowd walked toward the cabins in a tizzy. Everyone was gossiping, asking some version of *What's going on?*

"It's definitely visitors' day," Frank said, loud enough for most campers in his vicinity to hear.

"So much for a surprise," someone else snipped back.

"Visitors' day like our parents are going to appear here with snacks and hugs?" I asked Stevie. The title of the event did seem pretty self-explanatory, but I was positive I would keel over and die if my mom or dad appeared in the middle of the woods in Georgia, of all places.

Stevie snickered at me. "My parents absolutely will, yes. It can be anyone, though. Visitors' day is open to all friends and loved ones. It's not really a secret if you've been to camp before. Sorry if you like surprises. Hope Frank didn't spoil it." Stevie looked at her brother chidingly.

"I do like surprises," I said, wrapped up in her for a moment. "But I appreciate the heads-up on this one. It helps me manage my disappointment. There's no way I have anyone here to visit me."

"The old owners used to make it their business to make sure every camper had a visitor," Stevie said. "We used to joke that they hired private investigators to find everyone a guest."

"It was probably the birds."

"Shit," she said, grinning. "You're right."

"If either of my parents are here, it's because someone has

gotten married or died nearby," I told her. "They haven't left Arizona in three years. Since my wedding."

"Maybe a friend will come to see you." Stevie said it without a trace of doubt. As if I had dozens of eligible friends eager to arrive in the Georgia wilderness for a day just to see me living my best summer-camp life.

"Maybe," I said, drifting off. She could believe the best of me a bit longer. I didn't want to spoil the joy of the occasion by convincing her that no one was coming for me.

Her hand found mine as we broke off from the larger group. Other campers who passed us clocked the gesture and reacted with a mixed energy. Some people gave thumbs-up. Others did a double take. It was fun to take people by surprise.

"By the way, Allison's gone," Stevie told me. "I confirmed it with the twins a little bit ago."

I blew a kiss to the sky. "Goodbye to the past."

Stevie blew a kiss to me. "And hello to the present."

Picking an outfit for my visitors' day with no visitors proved harder than I expected. I'd gone through most of my clothes already. There were only a few options left—my bottom-of-the-bag clothes, packed as suitcase padding, never intended to be worn. One of which was the white sundress I'd put on for the airport on the way to my honeymoon. It was just a dress. I'd thrown it on many times throughout the years. It never had particular significance to me, until suddenly it did. It represented the beginning of the long, winding path that had led me to the very moment I was experiencing.

Underneath it, at the very bottom of the bag, sat my heart

bracelet and Dara's. I wasn't sure why I'd packed them, only that I thought I needed them with me. Now they both belonged to me forever, beads and twine and memories. Discarded hopes made of dull sequins and cracked buttons. I swallowed back my pang of hurt. Dara was allowed to make her own decisions about her life.

My white dress accentuated every interesting line the sun had marked on my skin. Edges around my swimsuit that I'd missed with sunscreen were echoed in a V down my chest. They were temporary reminders of the permanent changes to my life that had occurred here. The dress looked brand-new on me because I wasn't the woman at the airport, proud to let the world know I'd gotten married. I was a woman who had nothing to lose and everything to gain. On the precipice of starting her life in earnest. A whole new version of myself.

Stevie changed in the room with me, not bothering to turn her back when she put on a new top. The flash of her skin was something I was allowed to see, and I felt in that moment all the times I'd filtered myself around other women—a laundry list of instances I'd made a point to look around and examine the floorboards with intense interest. For everyone else, it really was to respect their privacy. It had started that way with Stevie too. Now I knew there was more to it. Attraction. Desire. It was a flush to my system to know that when she undressed, I was someone who was allowed to see. She threw on a loose yellow cropped tee—her best color, my favorite on her—and what I'd come to learn was her favorite pair of cuffed jeans.

"You look like sunshine," I told her.

She glanced me up and down, taking in the white dress. "Then you're clouds."

"Blocking you? I'd never."

That's Allison, I thought.

"No. Softening me."

"Fair. I'll accept it."

"Good." She drew me in for a kiss. My bottle rocket. Firecracker. Sunshine. She held it all, and when she kissed me, it gave me strength I forgot I had. I could do exciting things. I could be liked. I could be *loved*, if I wanted.

Outside the mess hall, the doors were closed with a sign in front that said **DO NOT ENTER (YET)**. Enough alumni had guessed about visitors' day that the news had spread through camp with surprising efficiency and speed. We could barely use our real phones here, so word traveled through a good old-fashioned game of spoken-word telephone instead. We knew one another as campers here. Not as anything more. This would be our first glimpse into who and what everyone had left behind.

Dara lounged against the wall of the mess hall, right next to the doors, wearing what I knew to be her favorite outfit: a black tank tucked into ankle-length brown slacks, her long hair hitting her waist. She'd even worn this exact look to my rehearsal dinner, and one of our aunts had gotten really upset, thinking she didn't look nice enough. But I'd seen my sister and grinned. She looked exactly like herself. Put together without embellishment.

The nice thing about fighting with her—if that's what we

could even call it—was that we knew no matter what, we could talk again. Fights never meant silence. They were mosquito bites between us, and a lot of times, the less we interacted with the source, the faster the bad feelings went away.

"Think Mom and Dad are behind those walls?" I asked her.

"With confetti and a handmade banner that says 'We Love Our Daughters'!" she joked.

"Matching shirts," I added. "'Proud parents of Dara and Garland Moore.'"

We laughed. Not loud. Not drawing attention. Just for us. Then Dara took a heaving breath and squared her shoulders. "You wanna fist-fight me in the parking lot or what?"

I grinned. "Are you trying to ask me if I'm mad at you?"

"No, I'm trying to join the Camp Carl Cove fight club, and if they don't see me tussle with someone soon, they're gonna think I'm lying when I say I mean business," she said. "Especially since you're the one who took me out of balloon tag."

"I'd hate for you to lose an opportunity like this," I said. "All right. Stand still. I'm aiming for your nose."

"Can you go with gut? I don't wanna get blood on Mom and Dad's banner." Her smile shifted to her keen *I know you in your bones* gaze. "No grand plan to convince me that love is real if only I'll let Mason Magnusson toss me over his shoulder like a firefighter and whisk me off to the woods?"

"I think he's more likely to cradle you like a child. He seems sensitive like that." Our eyes both found him in the crowd, where he was, no joke, waltzing with Andrew.

"When's the haircut?" I asked her again. "We don't have a lot of time left here."

"Soon," she told me.

"Attention, campers!" Tim stood atop a picnic table with a microphone in his hand. "Tommy will be opening the mess hall doors soon. Please enter in a single-file line. A surprise awaits you inside!"

Tommy waved his fingers mysteriously, then yelled out, "You heard my brother! Single file! I won't be stampeded."

Dara and I were closest to the door, so we ended up at the front of the line. Our conversation had ended before it really began, but we both knew we'd pick it up again.

"Are we gonna like what's inside?" I asked Tommy.

"Guess you're about to find out!" he said as he opened the door.

24

The mess hall was filled with people I didn't recognize, positioned strategically throughout the large room. Each person sat with about five feet of space between them and the next. Being the first to enter the scene probably made it a lot stranger than it should have been.

It was visitors' day, all right.

Some campers had small children waiting. Some had adult children. Some had lovers with flowers. Some had parents with signs, just liked Dara and I had joked.

A familiar, agonizing lump formed in my throat—a tiny pebble of embarrassed regret that lodged itself in my esophagus. I already knew our parents wouldn't come. Even in my most fantastical imagined scenario, I'd learned to stop having one where they showed up for me anywhere. It still stung all the same.

"How do we play this?" I asked Dara. "Everyone else has a guest but us."

"We walk straight out the back exit and into the lake," she said. "We're mermaids now. Goodbye to our mortal forms."

"We had a good run."

"Legendary. They'll erect a statue in our honor here."

"I hope they use a good photo of us for reference," I said.

"Maybe the one we took last Thanksgiving?"

"I don't like my smile in that one."

A voice cut through the crowd. "Dara. Garland."

It was our older sister, Bess. Her gentle, shy tone—never one to yell—fighting to be heard all the same. She sat all the way on the other side of the mess hall with her fingers laced together, not even picking a hand up to wave. We found her all the same.

The shock of it—the genuine, gut-punching surprise—set us both running. Suddenly Dara and I were kids again, and Bess had shown up at the house to take us mini golfing, and we had our oldest sister around to lend a sturdier roof to the flimsy, makeshift safety net we'd created around ourselves.

Bess was the best of us in every way someone could be the best. The nicest. The most patient. The funniest too, when she let herself be. She was just so much older—sixteen years from me, fourteen from Dara—that she was more like a parent than a sibling. She had a different mom from us, not that it mattered in any real way. She'd also had a completely different life from us. That never stopped her from making as much effort as she could to know Dara and me, though I recognized as an adult how hard it must have been for her to willingly return to our childhood home every so often and extract us from that pit of unhappiness. I'd never resented her for not coming over more. Every moment had been a gift.

I fell all over her, already sobbing in happiness. "I thought you said this wasn't your idea of a vacation." It was so good to see her face. I'd loved camp, but I didn't realize how much of the real world I missed until presented with a taste of it. Bess had always felt not like home but like promise. The potential for something better.

"Those twins are incredibly persuasive," Bess explained. "A little scary, actually. I'm pretty sure I didn't have a choice about attending. Not that I was going to say no."

"Are you spending the night here?" Dara asked her.

"No, no. Just the afternoon. Dave and the kids are here too, but the girls got carsick when we started driving up the mountain, so it's just me at the top."

Dara and I both hugged her again. Bess was the only person in the world who could make Dara become this emotional this fast.

"It's so cool that you're here," I said.

Bess took a long look around. "This place is . . . interesting."

She didn't understand, which made sense. She really did have a different life from Dara and me. A harder one, I knew, having heard some of the stories. They were hers to reckon with, so maybe she didn't need to be healed in the same way Dara and I did. Or maybe she didn't trust herself enough to see that she could want this kind of thing. To revisit her childhood and have a second chance at getting it right.

"It's honestly great," I told her.

"Are you in bunk beds and the whole bit?"

"No! Some people are, but Dara and I have our own rooms.

I mean, I'm sharing my room with someone else, actually. One person. She's my—"

As I paused, attempting to come up with a word that captured what Stevie was to me without having to sit and spell out the entirety of my journey, both of my sisters looked beyond my head.

A shiver ran up my spine. I'd never been sent to the principal's office, or had a deadly spider crawl up my shoulder, but I imagined the feeling wasn't much different than what I experienced in that moment. Because the way they looked told me the killer was behind me, and I had a split second to survive.

I turned around slowly, savoring every moment before my reality surely changed.

Ethan.

He'd shaved again. And he looked taller somehow. Or it had been so long that my brain had forgotten how he filled rooms, built both physically and emotionally like a large, sturdy tree, incapable of shedding so much as a single leaf. I'd rewritten him to take up less space. The last place I physically saw him was outside the courthouse. In that moment, he and I were nothing more than bugs to the universe, so easily smushed.

In the mess hall, he held a bouquet of flowers to his chest, a pretty collection of dusty blue hydrangeas. They were the same flowers we'd had at our wedding. It gave me a carsick feeling. Everything moved faster than I wanted it to, and if it all would just stop, I could catch my breath and make sense of things.

He handed the flowers to me. I think he even said my name, but I was still trying to make this picture make any sense. I couldn't hear him. I couldn't feel anything. My mind had been slingshotted into outer orbit.

"Are you her visitor?" I heard Dara ask on my brain's crash landing back to Earth.

Ethan gave me the exact sheepish grin he'd invented in front of my eyes in college. He used to make that face at professors when his grade was a little lower than he needed. It was a forgiveness smile. A *please see me for the good of my heart* expression. He'd never used it on me before—and I realized in that instant that it was because I'd always granted him forgiveness without conflict.

"I am." He leaned in toward me. "I was hoping to talk to you alone, if that's okay?"

I looked to my sisters for permission, as if they were the ones who could grant it. I needed someone else to give direction. Move my limbs. Speak in my place. Be me for me.

Dara nodded, and so I went, following Ethan to the back of the mess hall. *My* mess hall. He was here, in the white banded collar shirt I'd gotten him from Urban Outfitters for his twenty-eighth birthday. He'd pulled out every stop for this. Plucked every heartstring for whatever melody he intended to play me. I could somehow see it all outside myself, as if Ethan's decisions got sent to me early for review and I was watching them on a playback loop before he even made them.

I bit my tongue so hard it actually hurt. My manners wanted me to say thank you for coming, but my heart wanted me to be above that.

I settled on, "What brings you here?"—trying to sound casual, which was the last thing in the world I'd ever managed to be. I finally embraced the fact that I wasn't casual about lunch. Or summer camp. Dating. The products I used to wash my face. What I bought someone for their birthday. Anything at all.

I'd chosen that particular button-down for Ethan because that year he'd become obsessed with the reality show *Homestead Rescue* on the Discovery Channel, and it looked very similar to the shirt the main guy on there always wore. It was not a casual gift. It required deep knowledge of many small, personal things to make sense.

When I was around Ethan, I always tried to be casual anyway. That's what he made me think I needed to be. All my big emotions sapped him of his energy.

Attempting to be that person again felt like putting on clothes that had been tailored to fit someone else—the old version of me. I couldn't be her anymore. Not after all I'd been through here to set myself free.

Ethan and I moved to a new bench. Michelle was sitting farther down from us, beaming at two very cool-looking people I knew were her best friends in New York. I recognized them from her Instagram, where she'd written more than one heartfelt caption about their bond, and how they were all artists who'd grown up together in the city. I'd wanted that for myself even then. A friend I liked enough to write long, sincere captions about. Ethan was the reason I didn't have any of my own. Everything had been *ours*—including friends—and when we split, I surrendered all of them to him.

Michelle looked down the table at me with the unbridled

happiness of someone truly overjoyed by a surprise, and I smiled like I too was happy. Like this had all gone exactly as I hoped it would. I wasn't casual, but I *was* in survival mode. The exact kind Dara and I knew from our childhood. I would see this moment with Ethan to its completion. I owed that to myself.

"You look beautiful," Ethan told me. There was a barely perceptible shake in his voice. My brain was like an earthquake monitor, designed to pick up on his nerves.

I accepted the compliment with nothing more than an exhalation of air.

"I first found out about this place from your sister," he started.

That was a shock. "Which one?"

"Dara. She asked me to come for the week. I kept almost signing up, then backing out."

How many times had I—somewhat jokingly, but mostly seriously—told Dara that I wanted Ethan to show up? How many times had she looked at me flatly, not entertaining that road of thought?

"I didn't end up going through with it, obviously," Ethan continued. It was the closest he got to fumbling. He adjusted the collar of his shirt, tugging for room he didn't need because he wore two buttons undone. Not as many as the guy on the *Homestead Rescue* show, but close. "I guess there was a question on the application about visitors, though. And you put me?"

My mind raced back, accelerating faster than my wild heartbeat. Dara and I had filled out the camp applications so late at night. It was a longer process than both of us expected, requiring paragraph answers to unexpectedly deep prompts like *What do you hope to gain from this experience?* By the end, I was working as quickly as possible. The last question had been *If you could have anyone in your life come visit you at Camp Carl Cove, who would it be?*

I'd put down Ethan's name because I wanted to finish the application, and writing him down seemed equivalent to saying I hoped Tom Hanks would find time to see me. I didn't imagine it was the kind of question that would result in Ethan's actual presence at camp.

I was the one who had given the twins access to Ethan. Made them think he'd be the one I'd want to see. Up until a few days ago, I'd thought he was.

As he sat before me, I knew with complete certainty that was no longer true. He wasn't at all the person I hoped to interact with at camp. He represented my past. The very thing I'd come here to shed.

"I've realized that my life doesn't make sense without you," he told me. He wasn't used to me being such a stone wall. It disarmed him in a way my crying never had. "It's been a whole year and I still haven't stopped buying that weird granola you like. I eat every bag because I tell myself that I have to finish it. When the twins emailed me that you wanted me to come, I realized it was a sign. That I was waiting for you to come back."

To call it a sign felt both cheap and significant. Cheap in that he knew it was a way to get my attention when his other tactics weren't working. He was always the first to tell me he didn't believe in signs. But it was significant in that it was true. It *was* a sign.

Signs didn't just exist to tell me where to go. Sometimes signs reminded me of what I needed to avoid.

"This is the first time I've been propositioned via flaxseed granola," I told him. Ethan had to see it. How wrong all of this was, comical even in its absurdity.

Instead he smoothed his already gelled hair, patting down invisible flyaways. It took a lot to get him nervous. In another version of this moment, it would make me feel unstoppable to know I was the one to do it. That my presence had finally cracked the uncrackable. I was a lightning bolt through the world's sturdiest tree.

"I came here because I want our life back," he said. And with that, he wrapped up his speech. Over a year without seeing each other, and that was all he'd cooked up to win me over.

I could feel how the old me would respond. Something muted, desperate to cover up the intensity of my actual emotions. Something like, "Lucky for you, I have our life right here in my pocket." I'd pretend to pull the past out of my jean shorts. And that would be that. We would be together again.

Instead I said, "I don't."

Ethan's face scrunched up in confusion. "You don't what?"

"Want our old life back," I told him, unflinching.

Stevie called out my name. I turned to see her with two blonds who could never be mistaken for anyone other than her parents. They had not just the same hair but the same spirit. The Magnussons all did.

"Garland! Come meet my mom and dad!" she yelled.

25

Stevie gave Ethan an openhearted smile. She had no idea who he was, and she clearly never expected him to come visit me at camp. Which, join the club. To think she could look at Ethan and me together and not see a sprawling history between us felt so liberating that I didn't even feel awkward getting up to meet her parents in front of him.

We were not Ethan and Garland here. We weren't college sweethearts, permanently linked. I was my own person. And Ethan was just someone who'd visited me. Someone who had never really seen all of me. Or hadn't understood it, at least. And never would.

The fact that Stevie wanted me to meet her parents could have completely overwhelmed me, if the surprise of Ethan's presence hadn't managed to stun my senses in such a profound way that there was no curveball that could stop me. I felt invincible in my shock. I strutted toward the Magnussons without so much as a sideways glance at Ethan, who followed me, saying nothing. I had already given him my answer. If he wanted to stick around beyond that, it was his decision.

"I hear you're quite the gift giver," I said to Mrs. Magnusson as she kissed my cheeks hello.

She blushed, tossing a hand over her heart. "I can't believe you know that!" I caught in her voice the same youthful wonderment I'd been picking up in Mason.

Mr. Magnusson offered up a strong handshake. "Nice to meet you."

"Garland is my roommate," Stevie explained. We had no other name for what we were. It seemed from her look at me that it was a top priority to create one. "She's my favorite person here."

"The feeling is mutual," I said, grinning at her.

All the while, Ethan lingered behind me, waiting to be introduced.

From the moment Ethan served me papers over Valentine's dinner, I'd thought of myself as divorced. I had the bumper sticker and the perverse sense of humor to prove it. But I'd never thought to call Ethan my ex-husband. Divorce had to do with *me*. It was a personal journey, and a quick way to let people know I'd been through a lot more shit in my life than they'd expect when first meeting me. To me, Ethan was not my *ex-husband*. He was just Ethan, this absent presence I'd spent over a year waiting to return to.

Not quite ready to reckon with how to redefine him, I said, "This is Ethan," to all the Magnussons. "I haven't seen him in a really long time."

"Oh, that's so lovely," Mrs. Magnusson gushed. "What a wonderful surprise."

I understood exactly what Stevie meant about her mother. She was so nice there was a kind of reckless abandon to her love, completely unearned. What if it was a bad surprise? How could she know? All I'd said was his name.

Ethan shook everyone's hand. "Nice to meet you all."

He always had a habit of tossing me into new situations headfirst without giving me any context. I had to navigate his college friends, his work friends, and his family without being made aware of any land mines I should avoid, instead gracelessly falling onto them on my own. For the first time ever, I got to be the one doing that to him. As far as he knew, he was meeting my roommate's parents. He had no idea I'd spent the morning kissing her.

In fact, Stevie and Ethan on either side of me was like the final boss of brain-melting situations—my former husband and my very special roommate. My solution was to treat it all as something mundane. Like every single day of my life, I went around having to introduce my—*shudder*—ex-husband to my love interest's parents at summer camp. Snooze, yawn, we'd all been there.

"Oh! My oldest sister is here," I told Stevie excitedly. "I want you to meet her."

Stevie followed me over to meet Bess, who was a study in shyness in comparison to Stevie's mom. She did not get up to hug Stevie or shake her hand. Instead she waved and asked Stevie if she appreciated the surprise of seeing her parents. A classically thoughtful Bess question, making sure the surprise was good.

The twins, triumphant over the success of visitors' day, announced that dinner would be served at the picnic tables, and we'd be having an outdoor party instead of the usual nightly mixer. They didn't have guests of their own, I noticed, so I immediately called them over, folding them into our growing group of campers and visitors. All the while, Ethan remained a silent shadow, trailing me as I met the family and loved ones of all my camp friends. He endured hours of me introducing him only by name, never explaining who he was.

"Everything good?" Dara asked at one point, her eyes narrowing quickly, then returning to normal. Ethan was busy telling Tim and Tommy about his landscaping company.

"Everything's *interesting*," I said back.

"Very interesting." She nursed a drink. "I have to admit that I'm the one who told him to come to camp. You kept bringing him up, so I messaged him and—"

"I already know," I said, cutting her off. "That's not why he's here, though. I listed him as a potential visitor on the camp application."

"Oh god. I didn't even realize that was a serious question. I put Bess because I didn't know who else to write."

"Further proof you're smarter than me, and you always have been!"

Dara didn't laugh. "That's not true." She glanced back at Ethan once more, making sure he wasn't listening. "You have managed to make this monumentally weird situation into something that actually feels kind of normal. That takes a level of intelligence I do not have."

"That's because I haven't told anyone who Ethan is. If anyone but you and Bess knew, the vibe would be significantly different."

"Exactly," Dara said. "You're always looking out for everyone like that. Trying to make sure no one's day is ruined except your own. Sometimes it backfires, but sometimes, like now, it works."

"My day's not ruined," I told her. "It's super uncomfortable, don't get me wrong, but I think I needed Ethan to do this. It was the only way I'd ever know for certain how I felt about him."

"And how do you feel about him?"

"I feel grateful to have this closure," I said. "And excited for him to be on his way soon."

We laughed. Dara always took me at my word, and that was why I loved her so much. I didn't have to fall over myself explaining how it was possible that I could see Ethan and feel nothing after wishing for this exact moment for over a year. It had been just that, a wish. I'd made many in my life. And not all of them were meant to come true. Not all of them were the best solution to the problems I had.

Dinner was sloppy joes and mashed potatoes. Guests and campers smiled over their food, sharing stories of childhood and memories from the past. Ethan sat beside me, watching as he always did. An observer of life not unlike my sister. A lot of the time, I'd felt it was up to me to be the one who shimmered enough for both of us. And I didn't want that anymore.

I wanted a teammate.

Stevie had coordinated a seating chart for all our friends and our guests, making sure we all could have an opportunity to chat with the people we already knew and also with their loved ones. It was thoughtful and generous. Exactly like Stevie herself. She was good at things that I wasn't. She could see a crowd and think about all the ways we could be reconfigured. I liked that about her. I liked it so much. I felt like I could give her the things I couldn't do, and she could do the same with me. We worked in harmony, not in contrast.

It wasn't a study of extremes like Ethan and I had been. Stevie liked to talk to people maybe even more than I did, actually. But she was direct in ways I was effusive. We balanced each other out.

When the sky darkened, the string lights created a starscape below the real one. The firepit blazed as people roasted s'mores around it. Ethan and I moved to the outskirts of the party, passing by campers who waved and said hello to me.

"You're really settled in here," Ethan noticed.

"I guess I am," I told him.

"You really don't want another chance?" he asked, getting right to the point. He'd been waiting hours to pose the question again.

For an entire year of my life, I'd been living with Dara in North Carolina, fixated on the possibility that Ethan would come back to me. Now he'd done it. He'd told me he missed me. That the flaxseed granola didn't taste the same without me there to purchase it for, and I finally knew my old hope had been a curtain, hiding the truth from me. Now that I'd learned that truth, I could never go back.

"I always thought real love required complete acceptance," I told him. "So the things I didn't like or didn't agree with, I just kept quiet about, because I thought it would turn into an ugly fight, and that was the last thing I wanted."

His calm face betrayed no hint of emotion. If my words affected him, he looked determined not to show me.

"You know better than most people that all my parents ever did was nitpick each other," I continued. "I'm sure they still do it. They're forever at each other's throats, the only two people in their house, bitter about the fact that they've chosen to be stuck together for life, acting like they don't have a say in the matter. So I fought with you over none of it. I shared no observation that seemed less than kind. Which means you were right about what you said when you left me. You told me I romanticized everything. That was true, just not really in the way you explained it."

For once, Ethan let a bit of surprise show. It was nothing more than an exaggerated blink. Something that could be attributed to dry contacts. But I knew better.

"I wanted to see the best in you because I didn't want to be bad at marriage," I said. "I didn't want to admit that things ever felt wrong between us because I never wanted to fail in the same way my parents had. You were just as bad as me about it. Except you weren't a romantic. You were lazy. You never wanted to do more than someone asked of you."

He squinted his eyes again. Maybe the lights were too low.

Or maybe he'd never really seen this in me. I hardly recognized it in myself. I could feel regret beneath my words, but the regret didn't win over the need to speak my truth without censoring it to be more pleasing.

"I might be wrong to even say things like this," I continued. "It's not the nicest way to put it. I haven't had time to figure out how to communicate this in some way that gets my point across without sounding too harsh. And that's the whole problem. I'm so afraid to be right or wrong with all my choices that I don't end up making any. I don't even have a real career. I've never let myself pick, just in case I chose something that wasn't optimal. So I've cobbled together a life of side jobs, always waiting for the big event to arrive." I threw my arms up. "There is no big event! And I'm finally learning how to put myself out into the world without being so worried about how I'll be received. No more stressing over who is gonna feel upset about what."

All these examples I'd never really let myself examine for what they were now seemed to be on the lowest shelf, easiest for me to reach.

"Remember how we'd watch a show together, and I'd pause to talk to you about why that character had made a certain decision or something?" I asked. "You know what you'd do almost every time? You'd look at me and say, '*Why do you care so much?*'"

The phrase echoed in my mind. Every time he made me feel small for having too many feelings about something that didn't involve me.

"That's the thing, Ethan. I'm *always* gonna care too much,"

I said. "And you're never going to understand that. Your best trait is your patience, though. You'd listen to me all night. You'd let me run out of words, take a break, and launch in again. But when I was done, you'd still look at me and wonder why I cared so much."

He didn't even want to get a word in edgewise. He let me finish my thoughts because he didn't expect me to say no. I'd never once rejected him. Not when he picked our house. Not when he chose our every vacation destination. Never.

"Thank you for coming," I said to him, really meaning it. "I know this isn't how you imagined this going, but it was actually really helpful to me. I know now that I've always felt like too much around you. And I don't want to feel that way anymore. I want to feel like I'm just enough."

His cheeks reddened. He was embarrassed, but he was also understanding in the same way he'd always been. "You're welcome," he offered. "I'm sorry I made you feel that way."

"I'm sorry too. That I couldn't be all of myself for you."

He never had many words to give me, which would have been fine if he gave anything else. But he didn't make up for his silence with any kind of passion or touch or thoughtful gesture.

I'd spent years trying to assimilate to that way of being. Now that I knew how full I could be, how much space I could take up in not just life, but love, I couldn't even *imagine* going back. It wouldn't be a future I could see with him. It would be a revision of our past, done solely because I regretted making the mistake of marrying him in the first place.

"I hope you're happy," he told me. It could have sounded

cutting. The nice thing about spending so much time in his life was that I could tell he really meant it. He did hope that for me.

"I am," I said. "And I hope that for you too."

He gave me a kiss on the cheek, and he took the bus back down the mountain with the first round of departing visitors, walking out of my life the same way he'd walked in, with an ease almost too effortless to be real. I would always love him, in the same manner I loved all my past memories—with gratitude for what he'd given me, and the perspective to know I needed more going forward.

An hour later, Bess decided to leave on the second bus.

"I'm glad you did this," she told Dara and me as we hugged her goodbye. "I like what this place has done to you both. I keep picturing you as kids again." She nearly cried. "It's really sweet."

"Join us next year?" I asked, hugging her tightly.

"Probably not," she said, patting my back. Her honesty made all of us laugh. "You two are making the changes I never could," she admitted, whispering. "I hope you never stop."

Dara and I sent her off with waves and tears.

Once all the guests were gone, I headed to my cabin to wind down. I appreciated the chance to go to bed earlier than usual. Dream about what the hell had just happened and hope that it made sense to me in dream logic land, because it sure didn't on my waking planet.

My husband had divorced me over Valentine's dinner. We'd filed the papers and paid the fees and got it all done without incident or issue. That night at camp, *I'd* divorced *him*. I'd let the hope of a future together drift into the trees and float off, gone like a paper lantern wish, designed to self-destruct.

I lay on my bed and closed my eyes, not even washing my face or changing. It was that kind of day.

Then Stevie tapped on my shoulder and said, "What do you think you're doing, trying to sleep? Get up! It's lake night."

26

Attending a summer camp required knowing a lot of rituals. Having never been to one, I was surprised by every custom. "Lake night always follows visitors' day," Stevie explained with all the obviousness of someone who had done this so many times she'd never *dream* of lying down between events.

"Sorry. I didn't see it on the itinerary," I said.

"This is the Camp Carl Cove secret menu. If you have a visitors' day, you have to have a lake night."

"Weird. That's exactly what I ask for at Starbucks."

She laughed at me, then tugged on my white dress. "You need to change. Put on a swimsuit with some warm clothes over it."

My green suit hung in the bathroom over the shower, still air-drying from our early-morning swim. I left it there, wanting to keep that memory preserved. I opted instead to wear my blue bikini with an oversized sweatshirt over it. I returned to find Stevie in a similar outfit, waiting with our bedroom light already turned off.

"Wait, I forgot to ask. Who was that guy who visited you?" she whispered into the dark.

"My ex-husband," I said calmly.

Stevie flicked on the light again. "Ethan is your *ex-husband*? The chill guy with the red hair who sat with us at dinner?"

"That's the one. Who did you think he was?"

"Your relative or something," she said. "A third cousin twice removed who the twins found by sending in a swab of your spit to a private investigator who located him, then forced him to attend so that every individual person had a visitor on visitors' day."

"I'm *thrilled* to announce Ethan and I do not share DNA," I said. "There are four of you Magnusson kids, and you only had your two parents come."

"That's not true. Frank's firefighter *best friend* was also here. And Andrew's weird neighbor, weirdly."

"Best friend?"

Stevie shrugged. "I don't ask questions. Since I'm the resident gay sibling, they know they can come to me with any news."

"Well, my visitor was in fact Ethan, my ex-husband. But don't worry, he and I have nothing between us anymore," I said.

This made Stevie walk right up to me until our noses were touching. "Do I look worried?" she asked playfully. Her breath tickled my cheek.

"Hard to tell when you have your face smashed against mine."

"I want you to be able to examine every detail. Really *see* how unworried I am."

On someone else, it may have felt like a "lady doth protest too much" thing. Not Stevie. She had a calm about her that I trusted. And I liked how much she trusted me in return. She believed me. "You seem to be one hundred percent unworried," I told her.

She kissed me once, quick. "Exactly. Besides, it's nice to see the guy who lost to me." She laughed a quiet—but slightly evil—laugh.

I couldn't help but laugh with her. "There's no contest," I said.

"Garland, there's *always* a contest." She hit the light and grabbed my hand to bring us into the hallway. When we passed Michelle's door, she put a finger to her mouth to shush me.

"Michelle can't come?" I whispered anyway.

Stevie refused to answer until after she closed our cabin door with utmost caution, careful not to make a single sound. "Lake night is a very exclusive event." She led me down the familiar paths, past all the buildings and back into the places the lamplights couldn't touch. She shone her phone's flashlight on our feet to make sure we didn't trip over anything. "It starts farthest from the cabins. That way we don't get in trouble."

I stifled my laugh. "I'm asking this with completely openhearted curiosity—how could we possibly get in trouble as adults?"

"Camp rules don't abide by real-life ones," she said. "Trouble is an idea."

When we got to the designated starting spot, which was the edge of the lake right before her hideout, there was enough light that we weren't swallowed whole, but we were mostly cloaked by night. I expected to find the twins waiting for us. The twins attended everything at camp. Instead I found the three Magnusson brothers and no one else.

"No Tim and Tommy?" I questioned.

"You can't invite the owners to lake night," Mason told me with the same obviousness his sister had used earlier.

"You're not supposed to invite *anyone*," Frank elaborated.

"Really wishing for a lake night infographic," I said. "Something compact and shareable so I'd stop committing so many faux pas." It was chilly, and I was already shivering in my sweater. Any event called lake night surely required getting into the water, so I did my best to mentally prepare for that. "If this involves nudity, I just want to say that I think it's weird you do it as siblings. Putting it out there, but letting you guys know I'm committed all the same."

"There's no nudity," Andrew told me. "Not literally."

I didn't have the energy to explore what that could possibly mean.

Mason had a big backpack with him. From inside it, he pulled out four boxes. Stevie shone the light on them, revealing pool floats that had not been blown up—a pineapple, a flamingo, a strawberry, and a crane, to be exact.

"Lake night is a family tradition," Mason said as he

distributed the boxes to his siblings. "We blow these up, and we put them out on the water."

"I'm proud to announce I guessed that," I said.

Stevie took her box from Mason. "That's all we can really tell you right now. You and I can fit on the crane together."

"Not to be a downer, but we did have a near-death experience in the rowboat yesterday," I reminded her.

"And we had a perfect morning in the lake today," she said back, grinning. "Don't worry. We're just floating."

It took a long time to blow the rafts up. The siblings insisted on doing it with their mouths, which was as weird as it was sweetly noble. They worked on their individual floats with focus and complete attention. Stevie wouldn't even let me help her. No one would. The Magnussons took lake night as seriously as they took everything else, and I found it poignant that it was a family tradition instead of a competition. At least, I didn't *think* it was a competition.

I expected we would each lead our raft into the water and float in different directions into the terrifying dark. Once the floats were ready, Mason pulled a rope from his backpack, and he tied each raft's handle to the next until all four were linked together.

"That's so we don't lose each other," he told me.

"You guys explain all the stuff I can already figure out on my own, but you leave out all the details I actually want to know," I said.

He patted my head. "You'll get it, Gar. Have some faith."

"It's time," Andrew announced. He kicked off his flip-flops and left them at the shore.

Gamely, I followed suit, and so did the rest of the family. We had to wade into the water before we climbed onto our respective floats. The cold around my ankles reminded me again of the previous day's disaster. Trudging through the lake in layered clothing with Stevie was one occurrence I didn't expect to ever re-create.

Before the rafts floated in earnest, we climbed atop them. Mason tossed his backpack onto the pineapple, then hoisted himself up. Frank took up the strawberry. Andrew went to the flamingo. Stevie and I had the crane. She put her legs on either side of the bird's head, and I had mine on either side of her. I clutched her torso tight as could be, as if we were riding the world's weirdest motorcycle. It was nice to hold her all the same. I'd take any excuse for it.

"See? The water is calm," she told me. The lake did in fact rock us like a lullaby, soft and serene.

For a long while, we floated in silence. Fireflies blinked out quick flickers of light that put me further at ease. I continued holding Stevie tightly, no longer in fear. Just contentment. Even the cold didn't seem too bad. That's how good it felt to be that close to her. The lake water had dried on our exposed skin but stayed wet in all the places our bodies touched, sealing us together.

"Are we ready?" Andrew asked.

We seemed to be in the middle of the lake, judging by the size of the buildings in the distance. Andrew was only two floats over from us. I couldn't see him. I barely saw Mason right beside us. Only the outline of his moving body.

"Yes," Mason, Stevie, and Frank all offered in unison.

Mason passed something to Stevie. She opened her palm and showed me two pennies. "Don't worry. It'll all make sense in a second," she said, anticipating my question.

After Mason distributed pennies to his brothers, Andrew spoke again. "Welcome to our first lake night as adults. We come here to remember our past, and to honor our bond as a family."

I laid my head on Stevie's shoulder as I listened. Andrew made no mention of me being an outsider. Instead he folded me into their family tradition without judgment or qualification.

"We will start with sharing our favorite memory from the week," he continued. "Then we will sink that memory to the bottom of the lake, remembering that no matter where we go in life, a piece of us will always live here."

Whether he gave this speech every year or he did it for me, I wasn't sure. It sounded practiced all the same. Careful and sacred. I felt the history wrapped up in the tradition. How many pennies were there at the bottom of the water? What memories did they represent?

"I'll go first," Frank said. He took a deep breath. "My favorite memory so far this year was when I found out what color team I was going to be on, and all of you clapped for me when I got picked for Green. Nobody claps for me anymore. And that's not me being dramatic Frank or whatever you're gonna say. It's just the truth. There's not much to clap about in my everyday life."

"You're literally a firefighter," Stevie interjected, inducing gentle laughs from all of us.

"People don't wait outside burning houses clapping. They want their pets and their belongings," Frank told her.

Stevie shook her head. "They should clap more."

"Let him finish, Steve," Andrew said.

Frank cleared his throat. His voice had thickened with tears, rumbly and full of emotion. "After Andrew got picked for Green, he hugged me and told me he was so happy we were on a team together. I was so happy too. I just felt really lucky to be your brother. That I had someone who would put up with me no matter what." He stopped to let out a snotty sigh. "That's it. That's enough from me."

"That's beautiful, Frank." The water rocked as Andrew leaned over and patted Frank on the back. "Send it out."

Frank hurled his penny into the water. It landed with a soft plink, a tiny ripple in the surface that calmed within seconds.

"I'll go next," Andrew offered. "My favorite memory is right now. Never in a million years did I think we'd get a chance to have a lake night again. None of you know this, but I started this tradition because Mom told me during visitors' day that I wasn't being grateful enough."

"*Mom* said that?" Stevie asked.

"I know," Andrew responded. "That's how you know it was bad. It was the first year all of us got to come to camp together. You guys were pretty young, so you probably don't remember, but I hated that you were all here with me. When Mom asked me what I'd done with you guys during the week, I had nothing to tell her. She said I better change that, because I needed to appreciate how lucky I was to have three siblings who were obsessed with me. You were like my little ducklings, trying to follow me everywhere. I'd been wanting to go out onto the lake at night ever since the first year I came to this camp. That year I'd finally planned ahead and packed a big pool float to do it. So I decided to bring you all with me, and that could be the one thing we'd do together. It ended up being the best tradition we ever started."

"How old were you?" I whispered to Stevie.

"Eight."

"Four children on a raft in the middle of the night," I said, louder.

Andrew chuckled. "Listen. No one's ever accused me of being smart. But everyone loved it so much, we had to keep it up. The fact that we're all in our thirties now, and we're out on Lake Carl at midnight again? That's the greatest gift I've ever received. So thank you for this. And thank you, Mom, for reminding me to be a better brother." He tossed his penny into the water.

I understood exactly why they'd want to come back out on the lake like this. It was reckless and a little terrifying being out on the water in the dark, but it was also full of contentment.

"My favorite memory was the other day at dinner," Mason offered, not bothering to announce he was going next. "When Stevie was upset about *you know who*. I know that sounds like a weird pick, but I liked how it felt like if we had to, all of us would've started a war for her. It made me proud to be part of this family. We look out for one another. We always have."

Like all things Mason did, his memory had an exquisite simplicity to it. Succinct and true. He tossed his penny so far out I couldn't see where it landed, or even hear the soft plop against the water.

"My favorite memory is similar to Mason's," Stevie started. "When I found all of you by the water after you'd gone on the Jet Skis. I'd had a real roller coaster of a start to my day, and I was prepared to be in a terrible mood for the rest of it. But I saw you guys hanging out with Garland like you'd known her all your life, all because I told you she was someone important. I watched for a while before I walked over. I couldn't be upset anymore, seeing all of you like that. I actually thought to myself, *No one is luckier than me.* And that's still true. I'm the luckiest person alive with the four of you in my life."

Four. She'd counted me.

It sparked in my heart. A firecracker eruption that left me in awe of my good fortune.

She underhand tossed her penny into the lake. It arced up past the sly smile of the crescent moon, then plinked down in front of our crane, sinking right beneath us.

"Garland, do you want to offer a memory?" Andrew asked.

I sat up straight, lifting my head from the crook of Stevie's neck. "Is that okay? I don't want anyone to be mad."

"You should do one," Frank told me.

He was the sibling I'd really been asking, so his approval pushed me forward. "Before I give a memory, I do quickly want to clarify whether it needs to be one that involves all of you?"

Stevie cackled.

"Sorry, I just, I know this is a whole rules-unspoken ritual, but I don't want to do it wrong," I said.

"It doesn't have to involve any of us," Andrew said. "We just usually do it that way."

"One time Mason's favorite memory was getting a blow job from Chloe Hannity," Stevie announced, which prompted Mason to kick our raft. "Sorry! I just needed Garland to understand we're not always this earnest out here. That seemed like the fastest way to illustrate the point."

I let the beat between them die before I spoke. It helped to have a little more time. How could I possibly limit this week to one memory?

"Dancing at the mixer with Stevie," I said, throwing it out before I could overthink how much I should tell her siblings. "I learned a lot about myself that night. And I think when I look back on this weekend, I'm always gonna return to Stevie and me under the disco ball."

She leaned back into me as I spoke, tilting her head up so her curls brushed my collarbone. I held my penny over the water and dropped it straight down. My first contribution to lake night. Proof of my existence.

Silence blanketed us again. We floated, lazy on the lake, lost to time. Eventually our rafts made their way to shore again, spitting us out in front of the main buildings.

"Whoa. We never land over here," Mason commented as he unlinked our rafts.

Andrew left to retrieve our shoes from the starting point.

Frank went into Mason's backpack and pulled out a knife. "We pop the rafts," he told me.

"That's sad," I said, looking at our sweet crane friend.

Mason took the knife from Frank and plunged it into his pineapple. "Nothing's permanent, Gar."

Stevie shielded my eyes as Mason killed our blow-up crane. "We finish the night in the event hall," she told me.

"Am I allowed to ask what you do there?"

She grinned her sly little grin and took my hand. "You'll see."

27

Somehow, Andrew had unlocked the back door of the event hall. After he handed us our flip-flops, we followed him inside, dripping water puddles behind us. The huge space felt hollow with no band or other guests inside to fill it. The disco ball sat idle at the peak of the ceiling, dull without other lights to shine on it.

Andrew stopped behind the bar and grabbed two bottles of Coca-Cola, then led us up the loft stairs, where he'd already turned on a few lights. Just enough to keep it from being spooky. One by one, we sat in a circle on the rug behind the beer pong table, watching Andrew unscrew the lid on one of the Coke bottles.

"We used to take these and mix them with whatever alcohol I could smuggle in from home. But it feels right to do it with no booze this time," Andrew said, taking a swig. "I don't want to steal that from the twins."

Frank took the next sip, then passed it to me. "I agree."

"I haven't had this in years," I admitted. The sweet, carbonated sugar rush gave my nose the same weird tingle that chlorine did. I suspected this element of lake night used to be more illicit and exciting. With all of us in our thirties, there was a lot more yawning involved.

Stevie took the bottle next. "What can I say? We live on the edge in my family."

When she handed the bottle to Mason, he looked at it with a sad kind of disappointment. "I think I have to go to bed?" he said, presenting it as a question instead of a statement. "If I have caffeine right now, it's gonna keep me up. And I'm too tired to stay awake."

Andrew let out a sigh of relief. "I'm so glad you said it, man. I'm *exhausted*."

"Aww, really?" Frank had the other bottle of Coke hovering below his lips. "All right."

"We can still drink some more," Andrew offered.

Frank waved him off. "No, no. It's okay. The best part already happened. This part isn't really the same anymore. We can drink whenever we want. And I don't really need a bottle of Coke after midnight."

The boys got up. I went to follow, and Stevie stood beside me, wrapping her hand around my elbow to keep me from moving. "I'll lock up," she told her brothers. "I wanna show Garland something first."

"You guys have keys to this place?" I asked.

No one answered. The boys went one by one down the stairs, leaving Stevie and me alone. The click of the back door latching shut echoed through the cavernous space.

"Thank god," Stevie said.

"What did you want to show me?" I asked, confused.

Stevie laughed. "Nothing. I just wanted you alone."

My cheeks flushed. I moved to wipe my last tear from my cheek as quickly as possible. It wasn't the time for it.

"Are you *crying*?" Stevie asked. "A little river of tears, running right down your perfect cheek." She kissed the wet spot. "What's making you cry?"

Historically, the world's hardest question. It pressed on something primal in me. A crying activation button if I ever met one. "It's just so nice to be a part of someone else's good memories," I said, my crying turning to full sobbing. No one had ever been impressed by my sentimentality, that was for sure.

"Garland," Stevie said, so softly. "Come here." She pulled me into her arms and held me, dragging us down into the leather chair underneath the artwork. I sat in her lap then, curled up and content. "This is the best lake night reaction we've ever gotten."

"How many other people have even gotten to know about it?" I asked through sniffles.

"Just one, actually. I brought this girl Holly Beekman to lake night when I was in eighth grade. Andrew was a senior in high school, so it was his last year of camp. I had it so bad for Holly. But she liked Andrew."

"Uh-oh."

Stevie smiled. "I know. It was mostly fine, though. I knew Andrew would never date someone that much younger than him. And I was still a baby gay who believed I could manipulate the situation to be closer to her."

"*Hmm.*"

"Oh, I'm an expert-level queer now. And you picked *Mason*. Different brother. Different rules."

"The biggest shithead in the world," I said.

She grinned. "Exactly. When I told all my brothers I was bringing someone to lake night, they were mad because it's our family thing. But I said that Holly would totally get it, and they didn't know what to say to that, so they let me do it."

"*Did* Holly get it?"

"Not in the least. She put her hand on my arm and said, 'Do you think Andrew likes me?' right in the middle of his introductory speech about memories."

"Why the hell was she thinking of that then?" I asked.

"Exactly." Stevie smiled. "When we came to the event hall to drink, she kept finding weird ways to be next to him. Andrew missed every single cue she sent him. And she sent him *a lot*. He just kept being like, 'Do you want me to give you some space?'"

I knew the brothers so well I could perfectly picture the moment unfolding. "Frank got pissed, didn't he?" I asked.

"Frank was so offended I brought her, I thought he might never forgive me," Stevie said. "He kept saying, 'She's ruining lake night!' to her face. Holly was resolute, though. She was willing to do anything to get to Andrew."

"You Magnussons really cast a spell."

Stevie grinned. "Faulty magic, if you ask me. Never seems to land on the right Magnusson at the right time."

"I think it's worked out pretty okay in the end."

She brushed her thumb across my cheek. "Even when we did a few lake nights without Andrew, no one was allowed to bring anyone new. But I knew you'd be different. I felt a lot better about my chances this time." She pulled my chin down toward her and kissed me.

When Stevie put her mouth on mine, I didn't see stars. I didn't even have thoughts running through my head. I was all feeling and movement. Pulsing heart. Urgent tongue. Heavy breathing.

Stevie twisted her hand through my hair, and I turned so I was no longer sideways in her lap. I straddled her legs instead, giving in to the pressure between us. She arched up against the weight of me, closing every gap she could find. Her hands found their way under my T-shirt. The damp remnants of lake water had made my skin sticky, letting each print of her fingertip scrape against me, nerve endings waking up to the feel of her.

"Are *you* tired?" she asked me.

"Not at all. If someone asked me to, I'm pretty certain I could lift up a car right now," I told her.

"Good," she whispered in my ear. "Because I want my mouth on every part of you."

No one had ever spoken like that to me. I didn't know I wanted it. Didn't know I needed it. Every joke I'd made to her without meaning to hadn't been a joke at all. I'd held myself back in more ways than one. Stevie knew where I was vulnerable. She saw me, as she always had.

"I want that too," I told her.

"Whatever shall we do?" she teased.

Before she could make the first move, I dropped my hand down her body until I found the hem of her bikini bottoms. I slid past the tuft of hair until I could feel the slick heat of her. She gasped in a good way. "That's one option," she said, shuddering.

"I'm sorry. I don't know what I'm doing," I teased, even though it was true. But I knew what *I* would like. And I knew how gentle Stevie could be when no one was watching. If anything, I knew more than I ever had. "Can I keep going?"

"Yes." She bucked her hips into my hand as I started drawing circles against her. My blood boiled to the surface of my skin watching her breath quicken. "I think you know *exactly* what you're doing," she said, exhaling. She moved to touch me too.

"Not yet." Watching her rock against me, looking at me the way she did, needing more of me, I wanted her to lose herself first.

She started moving faster. So did I. When she let out moans at the accelerated speed, it made me dizzy with want. I couldn't believe I was the one making that happen. She tried again to reach for me, but I wouldn't let her touch me yet.

I had never been so lit up by someone else's pleasure. Seeing her fall apart, it vibrated through me the same way my own orgasm would have. If she so much as breathed too hard on me, I would be right there with her. So I breathed alongside her, pressing my nose to her face, climbing into the moment with her. More than physical closeness, there was an emotional string between us that tightened, knotting the two of us into place together.

When she came back to herself, her eyes had a steady focus that exceeded all the other times I'd watched her look at me before. Her desire had no filter over it anymore. She did not fight it, or hide it, or deflect with humor. She stood from the chair with her arms wrapped around my back, lifting me up with her.

"*Oh, Garland*," she said. Once upright, she hooked her hands under my knees, then she knelt down and laid me on the rug. "You beat me at my own game. And you know I don't like to lose."

"Remember, Stevie, not winning isn't the same as losing," I teased.

Flat on my back, my arms went up so she could lift my sweatshirt over my head. She worked her hands up my sides, letting goose bumps pinprick every inch of skin she covered on her way to taking the fabric off my body.

"Since you *don't know anything*, mind if I teach you?" she asked.

I lay there in my bikini, shivering. The pinprick chill made my nipples peak against the fabric of my swimsuit. "Teach me," I breathed.

Stevie moved the fabric of my swimsuit and cupped her mouth over my nipple. Every nerve ending sparked against the wet heat of her lips and tongue. "First things first, we take our time around here."

I put my hands in her hair, holding her close to me.

Her tongue moved to lick the space in the center of my chest, drawing a line up the hollow of my throat and then lifting to my mouth. Then she dragged her lips along my cheek until she reached my ear. "No one has ever made me finish that fast," she said, nipping at the tip of my lobe.

"Good." I liked being someone significant to her.

"I told you I wanted to touch every inch of you," she reminded me. "You won't be finishing fast."

I shuddered at her words. My legs contracted around her body, pinning her in place. Testing my limits, she slid her hand down the space between us, and the shock of her fingers beneath my swimsuit made me gasp.

"Guess I'll have to stay up here a while," she said, feeling my wetness. She kissed at my neck and along my collarbone, not even granting me her lips atop my own.

"Stevie," I panted out, agonized by the distance.

"Not now." She pinched my nipple between her fingers. "I'm busy."

"Stevie," I panted again.

Exactly as promised, she moved her mouth across the surface of my skin. I surrendered myself to her as she mapped me out with her hands and lips, learning every inch. She found parts of me I didn't even know were tender. My ribs. The outsides of my hips. The crook of my elbow.

She circled around my bikini bottoms, making a point to keep away, because every time she got close to the pulse between my legs, my body clenched around her, trying to pull her in. When her fingers *finally* threaded through the fabric of my bikini bottoms and she tugged them down, I started to tremble.

"Please," I managed to say.

She looked up at me from her spot between my legs, grinning. "Finally, you use your manners." She pulled the fabric down until every inch of me was bare. "Beautiful," she said. "My Garland."

I'd never been so locked into the moment. No shame. No worries. Just sensations.

When her mouth found its place between my legs, she licked and sucked with a tenderness that clenched every muscle inside me. She was sunshine to the blaze of pleasure coursing through my blood. She lit me up from the inside out.

I cried her name into the hollow silence.

Stevie.

28

Naked, Stevie scooted in closer to me until she had her nose pressed to my cheek again. We were lying side by side on the rug, wrapped up in each other.

"Are you trying to show me how unworried you are again?" I asked. "Trust me, after what just happened, I definitely believe you."

She blushed through her smile. "Actually, I'm trying to climb inside your brain," she told me.

I laughed. "Oh, casual. How's that going for you?"

"Not great."

Putting my palms on her shoulders, I backed her up until we were a slightly more normal distance from each other. "What do you want to know? I'll tell you."

She stilled in my arms the same way she had in the water. I was capable of helping her, I realized. All the time I'd been thinking I didn't contribute anything meaningful, but something about my presence quieted her in a way I could never do for anyone else.

Oh.

It was bad.

So bad.

The way I saw myself in her. How I realized that I changed her. How we moved together through the world, always on each other's sides. I could see in my reflection in her eyes that I even looked at her with a soft fascination I gave no one else.

This wasn't just a crush. Or a summer-camp thing. This was so much more.

"I'm just wondering who I'll be to you when we leave," she said.

The fact that she had questions about anything to do with me was a marvel in and of itself. She didn't know me as the person I'd been before this week at camp, too transparent for my own good.

"I'm afraid whatever I say will sound too intense," I told her honestly.

"I'm an intense person," she said. "I can take it."

I could spend a lifetime trying to tell her how much the last four days had changed me. How meeting *her* had changed me. Brought me to life. Pulled me up to the surface. Shown me the realest parts of myself. To get it out right, I had to sit up straighter. Put my bikini top back on, so I didn't have to think about all the ways I was physically exposed in addition to the emotional exposing I was about to do.

Stevie mistook my actions as apprehension. "If you want to

keep this thing casual after camp, I get it. We haven't even known each other a week."

"No, that's not it at all," I said urgently, my top pressed against my chest without being clasped in the back. I let it fall off, as if to say, *Look at me. Remember all the places you've just touched.*

"You just saw your ex-husband," she continued. "Allison was here. Maybe casual is good for us."

"I could never be casual about you." I scrambled to fasten my bikini top. "I don't believe in casual."

"I couldn't be casual about you either," she said back.

I shimmied into my swim bottoms. Found the sweatshirt I'd worn over it all and pulled it over my head. There was that energy in the air. My least favorite kind. The crackle of uncertainty that our words didn't seem to erase. We both agreed that neither of us was being casual. But what *would* we be when we left?

My gut curdled. This was what it always came down to. The kind of moment where I'd opt to leave my feelings unsaid for fear of making things worse. It would be so easy to do. We'd walk off toward our cabin and let the next day arrive, hoping that in sleep, the unease between us would dissipate.

Just then, a bird started singing, pitched as high as a whistling kettle, with the sweet musicality of a flute. Both Stevie and I cocked our heads, stunned by the sound cutting through the echoing silence of the empty event hall.

"Hermit thrush," Stevie whispered. "They like to sing at night."

What's a sign, really, but something that's always been there, you just forgot to notice it before? I'd never noticed the birds. Never thought to make note of their calls or learn how to differentiate them or think about when they made them.

Until Stevie.

She claimed she welcomed my intensity, and I believed her. But I didn't have anything to offer her beyond myself. No home. No job. I didn't know who we'd be to each other when we left camp. It was exactly why as kids, it seemed like everyone's summer-camp romances didn't last beyond the week. Logistics got in the way of passion. Stevie and I weren't cabinmates in the world outside Camp Carl Cove. We were two women with totally different lives, and we needed to figure out how they might fit together.

"The bird sounds so pretty," I said. We listened to its call in appreciative silence.

"Should we go back to our room?" Stevie asked, standing up. "Big day for us tomorrow. Last color game." She was going to let the moment pass. She was offering me an escape route.

"You're everything to me," I blurted out. If I didn't have a real answer, at least I had that truth to give.

She turned back to grin at me. There was a tinge of sadness behind her smile. A knowing that went both ways. She'd asked the question because she didn't have an answer either.

How would we make this work beyond the week?

The answer would come. I believed that, because that's who I was in my core—a person who believed in magic. Who found secrets tucked into the fabric of the universe. Who wished on shooting stars and took leaps of faith based on nothing but gut feelings. And my gut told me I'd find a way to take Stevie home with me.

Until that answer came, all I could do was appreciate the present. I stood up, pressed my lips atop hers, and savored the moment. Then we slipped into our shoes, and we walked each other home.

Day Five of Summer Camp

29

The sun didn't wake me. Stevie did, rolling away to get out of our two-mattresses-as-one-bed setup. I opened my eyes and saw her pretty spine, bare, curled away as she pulled a sports bra over her head.

"Going for your morning hike?" I asked her.

She looked over her shoulder. "You know me well."

After she dressed and left, I felt the dread of the coming day. Tomorrow afternoon, camp would be over, and we'd go down the mountain and return to the lives we'd left behind. I couldn't bear the thought of leaving without Stevie, but I still had no idea how to take her with me.

Michelle sat in the common area, as she so often did. She could see from my open door that my bed and Stevie's had been made into one. "Is it safe now for me to guess who you like?"

"What do you mean?" I asked, playing coy.

She laughed and went back to working on her laptop. The nudges I gave other people were usually nudges I wanted to receive too. Michelle had told me she needed someone else to stop her from working. That could be me. I could push us both toward something new.

"Do you want to go do archery together?" I asked her.

The way she laughed told me exactly how ridiculous my suggestion sounded. It was barely six thirty in the morning.

"We're two people who have a habit of committing to our habits," I explained. "I think we'd be great partners in failing at something random together. And archery is one of the only things I haven't tried here this week."

She took mock offense to my words as she put her laptop on the coffee table. "What makes you think I'm not good at archery?" she asked.

"Have you ever done it before?"

"Of course not. But I'm very gifted at focused tasks. I might be a prodigy." She stood up, revealing the full glory of her lavender utility jumpsuit and platform sneakers.

"We better go find out, then, before anyone else gets there," I said. "We have to take control of the narrative in case you're an archery sensation. We don't know how Marge from my color team will handle it. She's a big Hunger Games fan. She might be really upset if you're the real Katniss around here."

As I initially predicted—like the vision-having prophet I was—Michelle and I were very bad at archery. With much sighing and many words uttered under his breath, our instructor tried his damnedest to teach us the proper technique. If nothing else, he had to appreciate our early-morning commitment to the craft.

"I hate this," Michelle said when her arrow flew well past the target again. It barely even hit the haystack behind it.

The rising sun was already bright. I blocked it out with my hand to be able to see her. "What was it you told me the other day?" I asked. "We miss out on so much life when we hold ourselves back."

"You are like an elephant with that brain of yours. Sometimes I just put words together and say them. They're not definitive truths," she told me. "Nothing is."

I put my next arrow into the bow and lined up my shot. "Except your newfound hatred for archery."

"Right," she said. "That's fixed. But everything else? Fluid and free."

"Just like me." My words slipped out before I could process them. I startled myself so much I accidentally released my arrow.

Naturally, I hit the bull's-eye.

Our beleaguered instructor burst into hearty applause. He even threw a finger to sky, like God had to be the one who'd orchestrated my success, because I sure hadn't done it of my own accord.

Michelle slipped into her signature deadpan to contrast the exaggerated reaction of our instructor. "Gender or sexuality? Or both?"

"Sexuality," I said. "But I don't feel like I get to really say that yet. I don't actually know anything at all about myself. Every morning, it's like I'm meeting me for the first time."

Michelle pulled her phone from her pocket. "Do you want a picture with the bull's-eye?"

"I haven't taken a picture here all week," I told her.

She walked around, searching for the best lighting. "Is that a yes or a no?"

"If I take this, the only picture that will exist of my time here is me standing beside the bull's-eye I *accidentally* hit when I *accidentally* came out to you."

"First of all, you already came out to me," she said. "You and Stevie moved your beds together. That's not something gal pals typically do unless they're diddling each other. Second, I *love* accidents. Imagine explaining this picture to your friends."

"I don't have any friends anymore," I admitted to her.

"What the hell am I, then? Some random loser you coaxed into early-morning archery as punishment? Jesus, Garland, have some decorum."

I stood beside my arrow plunged into the bull's-eye as Michelle snapped a picture. "You're definitely my friend. I meant outside of here."

"What did I just tell you?" she asked.

"That your words are meaningless, pretty much."

I managed to snag a rare eye roll from her. "I said nothing is definitive. You're not a friendless hack. Or any of the unkind things you think about yourself. All of that passes. It always does. The best gift you can give yourself is permission to keep figuring shit out, no matter how messy it is. You can be a different you tomorrow. You can also own the person you are today. You don't have to hide away because you might one day change."

I started shaking my head, pretending to empty my ears. I kept going until I forced a smile from Michelle.

"What are you doing?" she finally asked.

"Oh, sorry," I said. "I was just shaking out any memory of your words so that I didn't go around quoting you like an elephant loser who valued the wisdom of her friend or something. I'd never be that graceless."

Michelle smiled. And it was so simple, really, the beauty of it.

I'd made real friends, just like I'd always wanted.

30

The color teams gathered for the last day of competition. What had started as something I dreaded somehow turned into the most important element of my daily camp ritual. Putting on my blue shirt. Sitting with my team. Wondering what the competition was going to be. Reaching deep within me to find the courage to try for the sake of trying.

At eighty points, Blue Team was in a three-way tie with Yellow and Red in the overall rankings. Green trailed behind everyone at sixty. We had not been counted out, despite my first-day efforts to put us as far from victory as possible.

I didn't see Stevie until we were seated together to hear about the final day's activity. I put my hand out where she could grab it. She didn't take hold. There was a charge in the space between our fingers, like we were magnets not yet connected.

"Campers," Tim started. "I can't believe this is the last day."

Tears welled in Tommy's eyes. "This has been such an incredible experience for us. Thank you for committing to this with everything you've got."

Tim picked up where Tommy left off so his brother could cry in peace. "Growing up, we always felt like camp was our real home. The summer weeks we spent here meant more to us than anything else in our lives. Tommy and I found that as adults, we really missed that summer feeling. We didn't know if we'd ever be able to replicate it."

"But we did," Tommy whispered, trying to interject but unable to say much.

"We really did. Thank you for committing to our silly color games the way you have. It's turned out even better than we ever could have imagined."

Tommy pressed his hand over his heart. "We love you all so very much."

At that, all four color teams got up to smother the twins in the biggest bear hug in existence. They deserved to know what they'd created was so special. Out of their pain, they'd built a safe space for everyone to enjoy.

"Okay! Please get off us now!" Tim shouted from the center of the hug. "It's so nice that you love us this much, but we can't be injured before the last game!"

We dispersed, making room for Tim and Tommy to runway walk to their teams, soundtracked by our cheers. When Tommy joined us over at Blue, I rested my head on his shoulder.

The referees took the place of the twins, standing with the

same seriousness they had all week. "Today's challenge will be the obstacle course," they announced in unison.

The reveal was met with cheers and gasps and instant back patting, almost everyone saying a version of *I knew it*.

Except me.

I hadn't guessed it. I had not guessed a single thing all week. In fact, if we'd been given a guessing game, I was sure to be the one to lose it all for my team. It should have been obvious. The obstacle course was the biggest element of the camp, shaped like a giant U. Pieces of it had been in the background of every other challenge we'd completed throughout the week.

"Marge is out," Captain Aja said. "Who else is with her?" She moved her finger between Julianne and me. "The heights part is only at the end, but it *does* need to be done."

I tried to look at Julianne. Do a Rock Paper Scissors or something. She avoided my gaze, instead staring forward with her hands on her tool belt fanny pack as she said, "I'll try."

It was a generosity of spirit I had not yet encountered from her. "Oh my god," I said. "That would be amazing. Thank you, Julianne."

She nodded once and walked to stand beside Aja in some sort of symbolic acceptance. It took all of ten seconds for me to process that if Julianne, who for all of camp had been thoroughly lukewarm toward me, was willing to push past her fears for our team, why wasn't I?

Why wasn't I?

"No," I yelled, so loud I startled Marge. "I have to do this."

I put my hand on Julianne's arm and moved her over, taking the symbolic place beside our captain.

"Are you sure?" Julianne was so openly skeptical of me, I had to appreciate it. She did not have a single drop of faith that I could do this. Weirdly, it helped.

"No," I told her. "Being sure is overrated, though. I know you don't want to do this, and neither do I, really, but I have something to prove. Not just to myself but to our team. So let me go. Please."

I looked at every person one by one. Exuberant Captain Aja to my left, who loved leading us. Softly serious Tommy, who was doing his level best to hide that he was still crying. Brassy Marge, with her hands in the air, saying "Welp" and sitting on the ground for the second time in a week, apparently unconcerned with getting dirt on her ass. Julianne, who'd started the week disliking me pretty openly and had offered to fall on her sword on my behalf. Sky and Laurie and their sweetly consistent camaraderie.

And Stevie. My sunshine.

"I'm going to be the sixth member," I told them all.

Everyone reacted with the same skeptical energy Julianne had, albeit much softer versions.

"This isn't the same as the ropes course," Tommy told me. "This one matters for everything."

"I know," I assured him.

Marge rubbed her knee. "It's gonna be a hell of a challenge. I'm getting sore just thinking about what you're all gonna go do."

"I'm ready to meet it," I told her.

The obstacle course started with a dozen tires placed in a zigzag pattern, leading to a series of small walls, no higher than ten feet, designed to be climbed over. On the other side of that were tunnels to crawl through. From there, the ground opened up into a small body of water, where two long logs spun atop it like spit roasts. They fed out to a monkey bars setup that culminated in a quick zip line, not very high off the ground. The weighted sled push that followed stretched out roughly fifteen feet, finishing at the base of the main event—a fifty-foot-high rock climbing wall. Plastic rocks were scattered upward in varying primary colors, leading to a giant red buzzer on the top ledge. It could only be pushed when every team member had climbed the wall and completed the course.

Each team would go through the course one at a time. The team who finished with the fastest time would win. Simple as that. Since Green Team was in last, they'd compete first. Because the other teams were in a three-way tie for first place, the referees pulled names from a hat to determine the competition order.

Blue Team got picked to go second.

"You don't have to do this," Stevie told me when it was announced.

She knew me as someone who didn't take many risks, and she was willing to let me live that way, even though losing would mean she'd walk away from this competition devastated. I'd never completely understand why it mattered to her that much, but I didn't need to grasp all of it to know that I could be the one to help. What was love if not holding someone else's hand through their chosen journeys? Our ups and downs didn't have to match to matter. I never wanted to be Ethan asking *Why do you care so much?* It was enough to know she did.

It would always be enough.

"Yes I do," I told her.

31

At thirty-two, in a summer camp tucked into the Blue Ridge Mountains, standing at the beginning of a long, challenging obstacle course, I finally understood that the questions I used to ask myself all the time were the kinds that had no answers. Like, why did my home always feel dark, even in the daytime? When would I learn how to make myself into a person who didn't cause trouble by feeling too much? Life didn't come with a guidebook, or a checklist, or a set of accomplishments that had to be fulfilled to succeed. I got to determine what success looked like for myself.

When the bell rang for the course to begin, I asked some new questions. How much more could I grow? What pain did I carry that I no longer needed? When would I stop judging myself?

I ran, charging toward the unfamiliarity. Greeting it with open arms.

Stevie kept up with me as she always had. The two of us leapfrogged from tire to tire in near-perfect unison. I felt freer than I'd ever been. More daring than I could have ever dreamed. It was a bit like my time on the Jet Skis, but better because I had Stevie next to me. Stevie to challenge me.

She made the hard things better. She made the scary things fun. Could she not see all the ways she'd touched me? Every inch of my skin had already been covered in her, long before she'd ever put her mouth over it.

When we got to the series of wall climbs, I let Stevie take the lead. I wanted to follow her strategy, re-creating her every lift and jump.

"You doin' good?" she asked me.

"I'm great. You?"

"Great."

We didn't have time to say more. We had to run.

She leaped down from the last wall and charged off toward the tunnels, moving at a pace I wanted to match. She needed to know that no matter how fast she sprinted, I'd do my damn best to catch her. We were headed toward the same destination. At the tunnels, we dropped into a crawl. Each of us slithered down parallel paths, emerging on the other end with barely a second between our times.

Behind us, Aja had stopped at the end of the wall climbs to motivate Sky and Laurie to keep it moving. She'd really developed into a captain in the truest sense—a no-soldier-left-behind leader who knew that not all of us needed her to stick by us and cheer, but Sky and Laurie did. In order for our team to work best, she had to be there for them to ensure the success of *all* of us.

We reached the spinning logs. With quick, tiny steps, Stevie sailed across them, holding her arms out for balance like a gymnast on a beam. I did the same, right behind her. Forever in sync. Tommy started the log walk right as Stevie and I finished. I looked back to see him spry and focused, light on his feet as he took careful steps forward.

I thought again of Ethan's favorite question. *Why do you care so much?*

He wasn't ever asking it for an answer. He was asking it to be judgmental. Subtly, because everything he did was subtle. But judgmental all the same. In that moment it occurred to me that it was the wrong question, anyway. It wasn't about the why. It was about the how. *How* do you care? That's what mattered.

I cared through my words. My generosity. I cared through the way I supported people's plans and dreams. I cared through the challenges I pushed through.

Everyone at this camp had opened their arms to me since the moment I'd fainted at Mason's feet. No one had ever once judged me for being who I was. Except maybe Julianne, but to her credit, she was right to judge me for being distracting. The other people here had no way of really knowing how much they'd all changed me over the course of the week. Completing this obstacle course was one way I could show them at least a small piece of it.

We made it through the monkey bars and the weighted

sleds. Stevie and I ended up as the first two to reach the rock climbing wall. There were safety supervisors there to get us into harnesses before we began climbing.

My stomach lurched. All my exhilarated pride and excitement began to drain out of me—an unseen puncture in my boat of courage. My adrenaline no longer had a pleasant, buzzy tremble. It turned into a shake in my legs, and an air-gulping desperation to catch a breath that wasn't available. I'd managed to trick myself into thinking my fear of heights was some abstract, conceptual thing. In some ways, it was. But it was also literal. Very, very literal. A terror that, when confronted, did not retreat.

"*Oww*," Stevie said softly. "Fuck." She shook her wrist. Her harness was nearly secure, and she was due to take off in seconds.

Tommy slammed into the wall from the full-throttle force of his run. "What's wrong?"

"I hurt my hand pushing the weighted sleds," Stevie told him.

I'd been right beside her, and she'd not so much as skipped a beat as she moved. We'd been standing getting harnessed for close to a minute. How had the pain just appeared?

Stevie didn't look Tommy in the eye and hold his gaze in her Stevie way, all resolution and pride. Instead she focused all her attention on her unswollen wrist—though a beautiful one, as far as wrists were concerned—and pretended to nurse it. It looked so unnatural that in any other scenario, I'd have laughed. Because I did not have to know Stevie long to understand she was the type of person to run a marathon on a broken ankle. Not that she *should*, but she would. She did more than necessary when it came to competing, and here she was trying to get out of the biggest competition of the week.

She was lying.

And she was doing it for me.

She saw me panicking, and she was trying to save me, as she had so many times before. She knew my shaking was coming from fear, and she wouldn't be able to carry me up the rock wall like she'd wanted to do across the ropes course. So she was going to throw the competition instead.

The resolution that only seemed to find me when I was around her—that spine-straightening assuredness I'd never known before—came charging forth. "I'll carry you up," I said to her.

"You're not carrying an entire human up a fifty-foot wall." She looked at one of the safety supervisors. "Will you let me out of the harness? I won't be able to compete."

"Don't take her out yet," I told the supervisor.

"Please do," Stevie said.

The man lingered with his hand over Stevie's harness, utterly confused.

"I'd do anything for you," I said to Stevie.

"I don't need you to do anything for me. I can do it for myself. Just not right now." She moved the supervisor's hand and started unclipping the harness herself.

I put my hand atop her wrist—her *injured* wrist—and pressed down. "You don't need to do it for yourself anymore. This isn't all or nothing. I'm here."

Tommy, to our left, had already started up the rock wall.

Aja, Sky, and Laurie arrived together, getting harnessed on the right side of us.

I saw it then. What Stevie tried so hard to hide. *Her* fear. She did everything to avoid showing it because it had depths that terrified her, so she made herself scary to intimidate everyone out of acknowledging it. She was afraid I'd leave her behind. That when we went down the mountain, I would give her up because I didn't know how we'd fit our real lives together.

Instead of backing away from me, she was going to sacrifice everything she cared about to help me through. That was how she cared for me.

"Attention, Blue Team," I yelled. Tommy looked down for a split second before deciding that whatever I had to say, he could listen while he climbed. Aja, Sky, and Laurie stared down the wall at me while helpers clipped them into their harnesses.

I still had my hand atop Stevie's. I let her go. She didn't need to be held down by me to know what I meant was real. "This is going to sound absolutely wild, but it's one hundred percent true. I am in love with Stevie Magnusson," I announced.

Tommy, a good ten feet above us by that point, let out a quick whoop.

"She knows this," I continued. "I can tell she does. But she doesn't *trust* it. Which is understandable considering the mess I've been all week. So I'm going to attempt to prove to her how serious I am. I am going to climb this terrifying fucking wall. And our team might not win. I don't know how fast I'll be, what with the whole fear of heights thing. But I am still going to try! Because I care about all of you, but I care about Stevie more than anyone else. And this is how I plan to show her."

With that, I began climbing.

The first several feet came easy. So easy, in fact, that I actually went faster on account of how mad it made me that I could do it. What else had I missed? What else had I held myself back from?

Then I looked over to see if Aja and company had started their climb. I didn't look down. I knew better than to look down. But to my right, about twenty-five feet up, I could see almost the entirety of the camp through the trees. The halls, the lake, the cabin—all of it was visible from where I was.

My body did its favorite little trick—lock up and freeze. I clung hard to the plastic rocks that dotted the wall. My knuckles turned white from the sheer force of my squeezing. Inside my head, I yelled, *Go, Garland. Move!* but a sleep paralysis demon's worth of fear said, *No, bitch, you're stuck here.*

Blue Team was going to lose again. And it would be my fault. For the *second* time.

Stevie had tried to help me and I hadn't let her, and now it was going to be my fault even if Stevie never put a foot on the rock wall. I'd stuck my neck out. Begged to be the one who competed instead of Julianne. Made all these speeches about how brave I could be. And there I was stuck on the rock wall with the last remnants of my past baggage in my metaphorical pockets—my fear that I could be so small in this life and still feel so big. When I saw how large the world really was, I felt like I didn't matter.

"My favorite hangout spot. Thanks for reserving it for us. It's really hard to get in here." Stevie had climbed up to meet me. She wrapped her leg behind mine, pinning me tighter to the wall, creating a sense of security.

"I thought your wrist was hurt," I whispered. I wanted to talk louder, but the noise of my own voice startled me. I needed complete stillness.

"And I thought *you* were afraid of heights." She gripped me tighter. "We can go back down together. I'll make sure you're safe."

I dared to turn my head and look into her eyes. I saw the green of her irises, and the countless freckles highwaying across the slope of her nose. I kissed her then, long and hard. The kind of kiss that should have knocked us off the wall, because it felt exactly like falling. Like the moment Stevie had tumbled atop me at our doorstep. She'd thrown herself into my life, and I'd never be free of the mark she'd left. I'd carry her with me everywhere.

Even if I had no control in any real way, I could do this one thing. I could climb.

For her.

So I did. Pull by pull, feeling my muscles surrender to the effort, I climbed. I tore through my own barriers until there was nowhere to go but toward the fear itself. I climbed inside it. The darkness. The void. The unknown. The loss of control. All of it belonged to me. When I brought myself to the top lip of the wall, Tommy stretched his hand out to help me over. Aja, Laurie, and Sky came up next.

"You did it!" Tommy said in disbelief.

Stevie spidered her way up behind me. "Celebrate afterward, fuckers. We need to hit the buzzer and lock in our time."

The second Stevie's feet stood steady on the top of the wall, I slammed my hand onto the buzzer.

The sound rang through the sky. Our own birdcall.

We had no idea if it would be enough to win. Somehow, that didn't seem to matter to any of us. We hugged and screamed and cried like we'd done it anyway. We'd made it to the top of the mountain. We'd seen it through to the end. We celebrated the journey to get there. Not the destination.

"By the way, I love you," Stevie said to me. "In case it isn't obvious."

"Oh, it is," I told her. "Now let's get the hell off this wall."

32

Back on the ground, my limbs still working through the aftershocks of what I'd accomplished, we watched Red and Yellow teams compete. I kept the stopwatch on my phone running, monitoring our competitors. I didn't know what *our* time had been, but I had a pretty good idea of everyone else's. It was funny, me peeking at the phone in my pocket, breathless over milliseconds. Yellow was the last to go. When they punched in their time, I stopped my clock. I didn't know enough to say for sure, but I suspected we had a real shot.

The referees did not announce the winners outside. Instead all the color teams had to gather in the event hall for the results. It was a full-scale awards ceremony, complete with trophies and medals and sashes, as well as a big fake check. The entire camp had come to hear the results, and all the tables that were normally pushed to the periphery of the floor were now centered around the stage. There were two confetti cannons poised to explode, and a host of streamers tied up overhead. I saw all the machinations put in place to turn this into a celebration. And I wanted it for Blue Team. Badly.

Stevie held my hand as we took our seats at a table up front. It was a bright day, muggier than it had been all week. The stickiness glued me to her. I thought of her hands on me—her mouth on me—in that very room the night before. I didn't dare imagine what kind of moments between us were yet to come. I wanted to experience them instead. Learn everything I could have with her in real time. Because there would be more. There *had* to be more.

The band hosted the award ceremony. They fist pumped and air guitared their way onto the stage to set the scene for all of us. "Welcome to the first annual adults of Camp Carl Cove award ceremony!" the lead singer said into the mic. "We've got lots of fun stuff to get through today. From announcing the color games winner to passing out some very special camp-wide awards, this is sure to be one hell of a rocking good time! Hee-haw!"

"Hee-haw!" everyone yelled back.

The awards started with the color games. The drummer pattered an anticipatory beat on his legs, building the tension in the air, as the lead singer opened an envelope handed to him by the guitarist. "In fourth place, with a score of ninety, we have Yellow Team!"

Stevie squeezed my hand tighter. The two of us were in it together. No matter what. We hadn't gotten last. That counted for something.

Yellow Team walked up the stairs at the side of the stage

and collected their trophies. They took their spot behind the fourth-place sign that had been set at the edge of the stage.

The lead singer opened the next envelope. He scrunched his brows, then leaned to the guitarist, who showed the card to the bassist, who showed it to the fiddle player. They all whispered over the contents.

"We have a tie," the lead singer explained. "Not for first place," he clarified as the chatter rose. "I just had to make sure what place it would be for. The consensus is that there will be no third place. So we're gonna announce each second place team one at a time. That way everyone can have their moment to shine."

The tension was so thick it had coiled around my throat. *A tie for second wouldn't be so bad*, I thought. *So long as Red doesn't win.*

"In second place, with a score of one hundred, we have Green Team!"

I could have floated through the ceiling and burst the confetti myself. Green Team assembled onstage, Frank and Andrew with arms wrapped around each other. Andrew drank in the moment, staring out at the crowd with tears in his eyes. Frank grimaced as he made direct eye contact with both Mason and Stevie. The drummer quickly swapped out the third-place sign for another second-place one, and Green Team assembled behind it.

It was down to Red and Blue. Stevie and me versus Mason and Dara.

"No matter what place we actually get, we still won," Stevie assured me.

"We only win if we're first," I told her.

She smiled, then gave me one quick kiss. "Very good. I was testing you. We better fucking win."

"*Also* in second place, we have—" The lead singer let it linger, prompting a comically long drumroll to increase the tension. "Red Team!"

There was a pin drop silence before the collective understanding landed.

We did it.

We *won*.

We did our level best to keep our composure as Red Team collected their trophies. They deserved their moment.

The second the lead singer said, "And our first place team—" all hell broke loose. Blue Team shot up, screaming and hugging one another, knocking over chairs on our way to the stage.

"With a score of one hundred and ten, Blue Team!"

I held hands with Julianne and Stevie as we rushed the stage. Captain Aja accepted our gigantic first-place trophy while Tommy held the comically large fake check that announced we had half off our camp tuition for the next summer.

I took it upon myself to hoist Tommy up. As only she could, Stevie saw where I was going with the moment, and she joined me, as well as Sky and Laurie, until we held Tommy above our heads. He deserved all the flowers for what he'd help create.

This place had become a part of me. Even if I never physically returned, every time the wind whistled through the trees or I smelled sunscreen and bug spray, I'd be back in this moment. Back at Camp Carl Cove, under a blanket of trees, safe from the outside world, celebrating a victory few outsiders would ever see as significant.

It didn't matter. I was a winner. A teammate. An adult who'd accomplished so much more than anyone would ever know how to give me credit for, because my accomplishments did not fit into any list I'd ever seen before. And that was more than okay with me. My other campers would always understand. Some awards would never be known by other people. They still mattered. And I was still allowed to be proud.

I got to kiss the woman I loved at summer camp under a waterfall of confetti and streamers.

It really wasn't going to get much better than that.

When we made our way back to our seats, the other campers greeted us with a chorus of congratulations, everyone mingling, needing to shed a little more adrenaline before the ceremony could continue.

"Look at you," Dara said to me. "A winner. Congratulations."

I hugged her tight. "Thank you. Congrats to you too. Second place is no joke."

"But it's no first."

I beamed at her. "It's no first."

Mason was sulking to a Frank degree. Any other person, any other version of me, and I'd have let it pass. But I knew the Magnussons well enough to understand that a little ribbing came with the family. "C'mon," I said to him, patting his back. "Go tell Stevie you're proud of her. It's not going to kill you to show a little good sportsmanship. I promise."

For the first time all camp, it was as if he *really* saw me. I wasn't someone who everyone else had been telling him to like. An easy suggestion he followed, because why not? A summer camp fling sounds good. In place of whatever passing fascination he'd manufactured for me, there was now a genuine respect. I was the person who looked out for his sister.

"Well done," he said.

He found Stevie and hugged her, whispering something as he did so. When they broke apart, she had tears along her lower lash line. She looked at me and mouthed, *Did you just see that?*

I sure did, I mouthed back.

The lead singer tapped the mic, creating an ear-piercing reverb that silenced the room. "Campers, back to your seats! We have more awards to hand out!"

Green and Red and Blue and Yellow were scattered throughout, now intermingled, sitting at tables with other camp friends and loved ones. Stevie and I were at a table with the twins and Michelle.

I learned quickly, as I had all week, that camp awards were a tradition not to be taken lightly. There were the standard awards. Most Helpful. Most Cheerful. And some sillier ones, like Most Bizarre Use of a Pool Noodle. That award went to someone I didn't know. An entire subsection of camp became uproarious in laughter as the woman accepted her medal and sash.

There were whole swaths of campers I never got to meet, celebrating a moment I'd totally missed. It struck me again why kids wanted to come back to camp summer after summer.

You could try to do everything and still miss so much. You never ran out of people to know or things to experience.

"Our next award is for our Most Influential Camper," the lead singer announced. "This goes to the person who has made the biggest impact on our week here at Camp Carl Cove. Be it through acts of kindness or other memorable gestures, this is someone whose impact on camp will not soon be forgotten."

It sounded like a lovely award.

"This year's recipient embodies this completely. She's new to Camp Carl Cove, and she has already made herself a part of the history here. She's coined catchphrases. She's formed new friend groups. We have watched her challenge herself all week, inspiring others to do the same."

Stevie squeezed my hand.

"This year's Most Influential Camper is Garland Moore!"

I rushed up to the stage to receive my trophy, bowled over with gratitude and also a healthy amount of shock.

"Thank you," I told my fellow campers, feeling a bit like a celebrity at an awards show, clumsy and stunned and a little bit light-headed. "This is a truly unexpected honor. I am so grateful you guys think I'm influential. I feel like I learned everything from all of you, so I do not take this lightly. I've changed so much this week. You have no idea. But I never expected it was the kind of thing anyone else could notice. So believe me when I say this award means the world to me. Thank you so much for making this week such a goddamn delight! Hee-haw!"

The referee put a crown on my head, and a sash, and I went back to the fold of joyful campers, proud of myself for making an impact. I'd set out to make friends, and I'd done that and more.

"I feel like you should have won that one," I said to Stevie.

"Oh, no. That's all you. Please. I didn't start full-fledged dance parties two nights in a row or inspire any camp-wide trends." She pointed to a large statue sitting at the corner of the awards table. "I want that one, anyway."

"What is it?"

"Most Valuable Player," she said.

Naturally, she won it. Because Stevie won every award she put her mind to, which is exactly how she won *me* over. My strong-willed, clear-minded sunshine girl.

Forever in first place in my heart.

33

The awards ceremony turned into an impromptu mixer in the event hall, until the twins and the camp staff forced all of us to get ready for the final dinner. It was hard to spend precious moments apart, even though I loved the ritual of getting ready with Stevie and Michelle.

"We really have the best cabin," I said when we convened in our common area, about to head to the mess hall.

It broke Michelle, who up to that moment had not cried in front of us. Her eyes filled with tears as she gathered Stevie and me for a group hug. "I didn't think I was going to like this," she told us. "I hate the outdoors. I don't need new friends. I'm on a deadline that creeps closer every day. But the twins promised me I'd enjoy this. And they were right."

"You're the best adult camp counselor in the world," I said, pulling back to salute her.

She grabbed my hand. "Don't let Tim hear you saying that.

He's the counselor for Cabin Fourteen, and he's with five other people in bunk beds. We're living in luxury here."

Stevie pretended to zip her lips and threw the imaginary key across the room. "Secret's safe with us."

I opened our front door so we could leave. Much to my surprise, Dara was standing on the other side, just about to knock. "Oh," she said, sheepish. "Hey." She had the hair-cutting scissors in her hands.

"Is it time?" I asked.

"It's time," she confirmed.

Stevie and Michelle went on without me as I let Dara into the cabin. She looked around the room with her usual quiet interest, taking note of everything. She had wanted to do this ritual all week, and it occurred to me then that I had a ritual I wanted to do with her too. She wasn't the only one finding ways for us to stay connected.

"Hold on a second," I said as I hurried into my bedroom.

By the time I came back out, Dara had taken a towel from the bathroom and set it under a chair. "I figured we could cut my hair out here," she said. "There's more room than anywhere else. And I don't need to see myself in the mirror or anything." She was attempting to complete this without fuss, as was her way.

As was my way, I was in the mood for a bit of fuss. "Before we do this, I just want to say it was really wrong of me to try and meddle in your life," I told her, thumbing the pocket of my jean shorts. "I never should've tried to get you to be someone you're not. Our heart promise made sense when we were kids because we didn't know any better."

"We knew worse," she said. "But yeah, definitely not better."

"In the end, all we really wanted was to have a happier life than our parents, right?"

"Right."

"I'd say you've done that," I told her. "*Without* someone else. Which is even harder. You have a nice apartment. A great job. You do activities you like in your spare time. You're rarely in a bad mood, and when you are, it's usually because someone else was rude for no reason."

Dara grinned. "I'm begging people to be rude for a reason. Is that so hard to ask?"

I reached into the pocket of my shorts and grabbed what I'd tucked in there. "I'm trying to say that I've thought about this, and I've come to the conclusion that you earned this all on your own."

I held out her heart-promise bracelet.

"When we came up with these, we were too young to really know what adult life was going to be like," I continued. "It's silly of us to cling to every detail of an idea we came up with when we were kids. We can honor the heart of it, though. We got that part right." I took her wrist into my hands and tied the bracelet around it. "It's still our magic. Just not the way we thought it would work."

Dara had tears in her eyes that she tried very hard not to show, blinking furiously to stop them from falling. "If I've learned anything about magic, that's definitely how it works," she said. "Thank you. It means more to me than I can say."

"Don't worry," I told her. "I know."

She laughed. "What about your bracelet?"

"I can't earn it twice," I said.

"Why not?"

I opened my mouth to explain. No good reason came to mind.

"You just said it's our magic. We decide how it works, don't we?" Dara asked. "Why can't you get a second chance? Why can't you get a million? You've earned the bracelet, Garland. Just by being you."

"I brought it with me," I admitted. "It's in my room."

"What are you waiting for, then? Go get it! I want everyone to know I share an accessory with the *Most Influential Camper.*"

I ran to my room and grabbed the bracelet from the bottom of my luggage. Dara took it from me, preparing to tie it onto my wrist. "Up until a few hours ago, I didn't actually want to cut my hair," she said.

Confused, I looked to the scissors resting on the chair beside us. "How can that be possible? You've mentioned it for weeks."

"I never cut my hair more than a few inches," she said. "You know that better than anyone. So I told you I wanted to chop it off because you were so nervous about coming here, and that was the only thing I could think of at the time. Blame it on *The Parent Trap*, I guess. I wanted you to feel less alone in being worried, so I made you think I had something about this place that scared me too. I'd planned to keep putting the haircut off as long as possible, then act like I changed my mind about the whole plan."

She tied the bracelet onto my wrist then, taking care to make the knot secure.

"But all week I've watched you do shit that *actually* scares you," she continued. "Ever since you moved in with me, you've been telling me you're done with love. That it's not meant for you, and you won't ever find it again unless it's with Ethan. Then Ethan showed up here, and not only did you turn him away, you went ahead and found real love too. I *know* how hard that was for you to do. I'm your sister, after all."

She put great emphasis on the word sister, because to us, it meant something so much deeper than family or friend. It was all of that and more—a single word with an impossible amount of history behind it. We'd lived the hardest parts of our lives side by side, and we'd always be loyal to each other for it. We knew the depths of each other in a way no one else ever could.

"When you told me about this camp, I thought it would be a perfect thing for you to do." She tugged on my bracelet, making sure it wouldn't fall off my wrist, then sat in the chair and handed me the hair-cutting scissors. "Your divorce had made you stop believing in yourself. Believing in your magic, really. I thought maybe coming here could remind you of happiness. And hey, I figured I'd get a fun week out of it too. I meant what I said when I told you I wanted to use this place to let go of my bitterness. I just didn't know how much I meant it. The truth is, I really did need summer camp just as much as you. Maybe even more."

She gathered her long hair into a low ponytail and pulled the band down until it sat right above her shoulders. The brown waves cascaded down the back of the chair in a single neat river.

"It took being here to see just how much I've been bluffing, Garland. I hide behind you," she admitted. "All the stuff you feel out loud, I feel in quiet. That's why I don't like change. Change makes me feel like I don't have a grasp on the situation. But I'm never going to have that, I realize. No matter how many angel numbers I find, or signs from the universe I chase, there's no way to know for sure what the future will bring me. It took watching you chase risk after risk to realize I could do that too, and it would bring me good things. Never in a million years did I think I'd ever see you climb a rock wall. But you did. You showed me I could *actually* be brave, not just pretend-brave."

Strangely, it didn't make me want to weep. For the first time, our roles were reversed—she was openly vulnerable, and I had enough composure to get her through it.

"Thank you for letting me help you," I told her as I combed my fingers through the end of her ponytail, feeling the soft strands of hair that had been with her for years. I felt what they meant to her. They meant safety. They meant comfort. They were a part of her protection.

"Yeah, yeah. It's no big deal," she said jokingly, wiping the fast-falling tears from her eyes.

"Of course not. You chop your hair off all the time."

"Exactly. This is a routine experience for me."

I held my arm out to touch our bracelets together. "The world is ours," I reminded her, whispering. "It always will be."

"Yes it will," she said. "Sisters."

"Sisters," I echoed. I put my bracelet hand on her shoulder. "You ready?" I asked.

She took a deep breath. Steadied herself. "I'm ready."

I put the scissors above the hair tie and cut off her ponytail, letting her brown waves fall to the floor.

34

Inside the mess hall, the logs in the fireplace crackled, burning bright into the warmly lit room. It was later than we'd had dinner all week, and it felt secret somehow. More private, because the darkened sky shielded us from seeing anything on the other side of the windows.

Dara's haircut was the source of much chatter. I'd given her a bob that hit above her shoulders, not unlike my own. I wasn't a professional hairstylist, but thanks to my years of cutting my own hair, I'd done a damn decent job on her. She looked great. As we walked by, other campers commented on how much we resembled each other. They hadn't noticed it before. Now they could really see it. It was nice to be linked to Dara in that way, no matter how temporary it was. Hair always changed, but our bond never would.

When Dara saw Aja, she headed toward her. I went for the buffet line at the back, finding Stevie in the snaking line that had formed around the periphery of the hall. It smelled so good inside, warmed bread and the sweet burn of a controlled fire. I wanted to bottle up the feeling of contentment it gave me.

"Camp tradition?" I guessed, giving Stevie a quick kiss. We were waiting to get our serving of spaghetti and garlic bread.

"You're starting to sound like a regular," she said back.

"I mean, I've been to lake night. I'm practically a camp fixture at this point."

"Don't go saying that too loudly. The others will get jealous."

"They should be," I said. "I'm dating you."

My words made her blush. "We're *dating* now?"

"You think I go around professing love to women on rock climbing walls for them to not end up as my girlfriend?"

Stevie examined me from toe tip to forehead, taking her time. "Yes. I do. You look like exactly the type."

"You're right. Will you excuse me? I forgot I was supposed to scale the main hall an hour ago. My other girlfriend's waiting for me there." I pretended to walk off, but Stevie caught my arm.

"Yes," she said.

"Yes what?"

"I'll be your girlfriend."

The heart construction crew stopped their work with one last triumphant thwack. The Stevie tribute had been secured within me. I had a girlfriend. I loved her. After five days. Because I was a romantic. And I always would be. Ethan could never take that from me.

I extended my hand. "Shake on it?"

Stevie smiled. She pulled our rock from her pocket. Then she put her hand in mine and we shook.

"Hell of an alliance we made," I said.

She looked into my eyes, seeing me as only she could. "I had a feeling I needed you in my life."

"It's you and me against everyone else," I said, repeating what she'd told me that very first day. How right she'd been. She'd shown up for me from the very first moment I met her. This beautiful woman had fallen into my life unannounced and taken up a whole corner of my heart I never thought I'd give out, and she had it forever. I didn't need to know what tomorrow would bring to know that she'd be a part of it. And every tomorrow after that.

Once we got our food, we went to our usual dinner spot. Stevie's brothers filled in the seats around us. Mason landed directly across from me, with Andrew to his left and Frank on the right. Michelle, Tim, and Tommy sat farther down on the left. Dara was with her cabinmates at the end of the table.

"Do you mind if I say something before we eat?" Tommy asked. "It's not a prayer. Not traditionally, at least."

Everyone nodded.

"As we prepare to eat our last dinner, I ask that all my friends and found family here find the nourishment they need, not just physically but mentally and emotionally. I ask that their time at camp conclude in a fulfilling way that helps everyone see how loved and protected they are. No matter where life takes them, they are always safe here in the mountains with us. The memory of this place is a shield from harm and a balm to the soul. Cheers."

"Cheers," we whispered.

The conversation quickly turned to reliving moments from the past week. We were already nostalgic for what wasn't yet over.

"Don't forget that Garland tipped a rowboat," Mason boldly offered.

I shot him a surprised glance. He raised his eyebrows to me in an appropriate level of challenge. A deep understanding permeated between us again. That respect I'd felt earlier had strengthened. He was accepting me into the Magnusson family in the best way he could—by ribbing me.

"I heard it was because she was trying to set me up with her sister," he continued, escalating the shock. "Whole time she was in love with *my* sister!"

His risky setup had uproarious payoff. Stevie was so amused she was nearly gasping for air. Her hand caught my forearm as we both laughed so hard I could have wept.

And I saw it.

My vision.

Unfolding before me.

It had all been true.

Every single frame of it.

I lived it exactly as I'd remembered it, but I hadn't understood it before. I'd put my attention in the wrong place. I'd looked straight ahead, when I needed to see that the woman with her hand wrapped around my forearm was the one I loved. Not her brother.

Never her brother.

"Stevie," I whispered, as the rest of our group's attention

got pulled in other directions. The walls closed in until it was just her and me at the dinner table. "Everything I thought I saw was wrong."

"What are you talking about?" She still had the lingering laughter on her lips. She hadn't switched gears with me yet, but she would. She always would.

"My vision," I told her. "It came true."

Her expression slid from joy into something closer to wonder as understanding broke through. "Just now?"

"Yes," I said, breathless from the shock of it. The final puzzle piece had slotted perfectly into place when I thought for sure it wouldn't fit. "It was always you. It should have been obvious from the moment you crashed into me."

She pressed her forehead to mine, right there with me, just as I knew she would be. "You had to live your life exactly as you did to get to this moment. What if you'd chased Mason down that day in the airport? We never would have ended up here. And here is exactly where we need to be."

"I can't even imagine that," I said, first idly, then with a whole layer of meaning that almost shattered me.

For all the ways I'd looked at her, I'd never stop seeing something new.

"I used to spend a lot of time imagining my future," I told her. "I'd make up little scenarios with people as soon as I met them. What would we eat for lunch on a rainy day? If we went to Disneyland together, what ride would we go on first? That kind of thing. I loved to do it. It made me believe that I could one day have so much more than I did. And then I got married for real. I lived out all my scenarios. Ethan and I used to make quesadillas on rainy days. We had Disneyland season passes, and we always started on Indiana Jones. It all looked lovely in the scrapbook of my mind. But the moments between didn't fill me. That's where the real love lives. And I never paid enough attention to that. I was too busy chasing milestones that didn't matter."

I swore I heard the hermit thrush sing again, a surprising underscore to the words of my heart. Words I used to fear speaking. Too intense. Too romantic. Too much.

"When I'm with you, I don't ever want to imagine any moment other than the one we're in," I continued. My voice did not waver, despite my nerves. My certainty was greater than my fear. "It's the weirdest thing. You're the first person who has ever made me appreciate the present for what it is. You remind me to be here, in the now. To imagine anything outside of it always feels wrong, because I never want to miss what's right in front of me. I don't need my imagination or a vision to *know* that you're my future."

She looked at me with such love. Such hope. It was a mirror into my own feelings.

"No matter what happens after we leave here tomorrow, you have moved into my heart and taken up permanent residence," I told her. "That's never going to change. So I don't know what we're going to do about it, but I do know we will figure it out."

I kissed her again. Right there at the dinner table. In front of all our friends and family. Because I wanted her to know how much I meant it.

"We'll find a future together," I said.

35

The firepit glowed an impressive, resilient orange, sparking embers into the night sky, reaching heights that would have scared me if I let them. Off to the side, blankets and s'mores awaited us, as well as stacks of blank paper and markers.

"It's tradition for us to finish out a week of camp with a bonfire," Tim explained.

"You've probably gotten a sense for how much tradition means to us," Tommy added. "When we came up the mountains to spend time at Camp Carl Cove, we found a new kind of family here. And in that family, we got to live by rules that valued our feelings and hearts. Traditions built around finding our courage. And traditions built around letting go."

"The bonfire is a place for community," Tim continued. "It's a place where people gather to tell stories and share food. But it's also a place for things to burn. So in the grand tradition of these sacred grounds, we ask that you join us in writing down everything you'd like to leave behind. Feelings, memories, bad habits. Whatever you want. Tonight, we burn them together. So when we head back down the mountain tomorrow, we're only carrying the things we need."

My heart continued to expand with all the love I'd found here. Camp Carl Cove had truly provided me with more than I had known I needed. But there was so much I wanted to leave behind too, and Tommy was right. This place was safe. I could abandon things here, and the camp would take care of it.

Dara and I got the papers together, meeting in front of the fire with permanent markers and, for once, matching expressions. She had tears in her eyes as she pulled me in for a hug.

"I love you," she told me.

"Are you drunk?" I checked.

She laughed as she held me. "No, you weirdo. I'm just sad. You're leaving me."

"Dara," I said, fully adrift in the tidal wave of my tears. "I'm not leaving. I'm giving you back your space. I've been intruding on your life for a full year. Thank you for putting up with me as long as you have, but we both know it's well past time for me to go."

She let go of me to hold her bracelet up to the light. "I've been thinking more about these. When we made them, we wanted to find a place where we were loved. But we've always had that in each other. Remember the speech I gave at your wedding?" she asked, and I nodded. "I didn't really say much about Ethan. I always liked him. He's hard to dislike. But I see how happy you are with Stevie. She's such a big personality.

She forces me to have an opinion about her. And my opinion is that she's the best thing that's happened to you in a very long time. I've never seen you with someone who made all the best parts of you shine even brighter."

"Fuck," I whispered, laughing at how much she was making me cry. "I love you too."

"Good," she said. "Don't go forgetting it."

That night was different. As some nights just are. An extra crackle in the air. A brighter shine to the stars. And Dara and I took the pieces of paper, and we both wrote down what it was that we no longer needed.

I didn't need to judge my own actions so harshly, or think that I owed everyone in the world the most complete version of my kindness in order to be worthy of good things. I did not need my fear. Maybe of heights. I could keep it a little bit. I didn't need my fear of control. Letting go was the best part. All good things had happened to me when I stopped trying to make them the most perfect version of a moment. I did not need any last shred of belief that there was any sort of rule book for life that I had to follow.

Messy was good. Messy could stay.

And romance could stay. I could have my big heart and my dramatic ideas. I could dress like a kid and still be an adult. I could be young in my heart no matter my age.

When Dara and I finished our papers, we folded them into paper airplanes and we threw them into the flames. Dara's landed dead center. Mine curved unexpectedly, catching the edge of the fire and bursting into burning fragments. I could see my own handwriting as the paper got seared. The word *fear* got swallowed by fire until it no longer existed.

Dara and I pressed our heart-promise bracelets together. "That night we made these," I said, "what made you want to do it?"

"I wanted you to know you had power," she told me. "I don't know. You always used to cry so much."

I was crying then, and she knew it, which made both of us laugh.

"You felt everything," she continued. "And sometimes it was like you were feeling it for me too. So I wanted to help you. I wanted you to know that it didn't have to be pain all the time."

I'd really seen my sister all wrong. She had the softest heart of anyone I knew. I'd always known she'd been protecting me. All that time, I'd been protecting her too. "We had to be the way we were," I said. "And look at us now."

"Adults at summer camp!"

"Exactly."

Our heads connected as we watched other campers toss their discarded feelings into the flames. Dara was my first teammate. My *sister*.

Across the flames, Stevie and her brothers worked on their papers. They threw them together, laughing as Frank's collided with Stevie's in the middle of the fire. I wondered what was on her paper. But I knew I didn't have to read it. Because it was her pain to lose. And I'd be there in the aftermath.

It was hard to go to sleep that night. Holding Stevie, I didn't want to close my eyes. To sleep would be to bring the end. So instead I thought about all the things I'd loved in my life. Everything that had ever brought me joy. I hoped for some great revelation to come with it. Some obvious purpose for me that existed outside of camp.

The truth was, I still had no idea what I wanted my life to be after camp ended. I just knew it needed to involve Stevie.

Day Six of Summer Camp

36

Our last morning was quiet. No Michelle at the couch working. No Stevie on a hike. We all stayed in the cabin, letting the morning rise with us, packing up our stuff and clearing out together.

Checkout was at eleven. Enough time for one last breakfast and a lot of hugs. The twins left the last morning's schedule completely open. No rituals or traditions other than goodbyes. The way we wanted to execute that was up to us.

Reality had begun to sneak in, bleeding onto the edges of the utopia of camp. Down the mountain, Dara had all but built a permanent wing for me in her home. I took comfort in knowing that existed, but I needed to find my own direction. The only way to do that, I knew, was to take the risk and leave.

When it came time for me to wheel my luggage back to my car, against the sadness, I'd developed a weird sort of hope. I looked forward to the challenge of what awaited me. It was a bit like starting at the beginning of an obstacle course I never imagined I'd complete.

For the first time in a week, I saw my car, with my HONK IF YOU'RE DIVORCED sticker displayed on my bumper. It no longer seemed as funny to me as it used to be. I'd been trying so hard to wear my pain as a badge of honor. But it hurt to fail. It hurt to lose. It didn't matter how loudly I laughed about it or how much I tried to tap-dance over the truth.

Maybe one day I'd laugh again about being a divorcée. Maybe it would suit me later in life, like dressing youthfully suited me now. At the moment, I didn't want to be defined that way anymore. I ripped the sticker off my car.

The goodbyes began in earnest. Michelle left first. I hugged her beside the picnic tables, right in the place where we'd met six days prior.

Then Julianne.

Aja and Marge.

Andrew, Frank, and Mason.

One by one, my friends made their way back to the world beyond Camp Carl Cove, driving down the dirt road and into the land of cell phone reception and obligations. I stayed put. I wanted to be the last person left. Close the camp down and walk through the grounds with the cleaning crew. Savor every last bit of what we'd all created here.

After Stevie sent her brothers off, she made sure to walk toward me as slowly as possible. She knew I needed that. Saying goodbye to her in any form seemed impossible. I didn't know how I'd speak those words. Looking at her giant back-pack once again cresting over her head, it reminded me of how she'd crashed into my life. How could I ever send her off?

"Guess the alliance is over," I said when she finally reached me. It sounded so wrong, I wished I could swallow it back and start again.

She pulled the rock from her pocket. "Say that to his face, Garland."

"Sorry, Rock the rock. The alliance is forever." I squinted to see her against the morning sun. "Summer camp really does end, doesn't it?"

"It has every other time I've been here, at least," she told me.

"Sucks," I said emptily.

"It's the worst part."

The twins found us. They had on their camp shirts again, and so did I. The way we matched made me so proud. I was a part of the fabric of this place.

"You two." I hugged the twins so hard I could feel every muscle in my arms straining through the effort. "You have changed my life. I have never had better passengers. Ever."

"We love you," Tommy told me.

"I love you too." It was so beautiful to tell people I loved them and not worry about sounding too intense. If anything, it was hardly enough. They deserved so much more than I could put into words.

"What on earth are you going to do next?" Tim asked me. "Back to driving?"

"No," I said. "No more rideshare driving. I don't know

what I'm going to do. I was hoping the answer would magically appear here. So far, no luck."

"Stevie? What are you doing next?" Tommy asked.

"I guess I'll just keep driving my van around," she told him. "Until I figure out something better."

"Don't you hate driving?" Tommy asked her. "I remember when you got your license. You told me you never wanted to be the one to drive."

"I do hate driving, yes," Stevie said.

I couldn't imagine her hating anything. It shocked me but also pleased me a little, to see a new side of her. There was so much more to know about Stevie Magnusson.

"I like to drive," I told her, taking one last risk.

Tommy locked eyes with me. He understood what I was getting at. I suspected most people thought of the twins as a unit, and a lot of times, I did too. But I knew I was closer to Tommy. We were both young and divorced, for one, but there was just that intangible closeness. That true kind of friendship that spoke without words. We got each other.

"Do you?" Stevie said kindly, interested but not comprehending. She had seen me so clearly all week, but she did not see what I was trying to say. Or to ask, really.

Bolstered by Tommy's silent support, I nodded. "I do. Small vehicles. Or large ones. I can drive them all."

"Some would say she could even drive a van," Tommy told her.

Tim understood then. He winked at me, then said, "I've driven with Garland before. I can attest to her skill. If it weren't for her careful and steady hand behind the wheel, maybe we wouldn't even be here. After all, she took us to a very important appointment with our contractor."

Dara approached, wheeling her luggage up to where we stood. "Are we talking about how good Garland is at driving? She's great. Rain. Shine. Snow. There's no element she can't navigate."

If Stevie didn't get it before, she did then. She fought off a grin. Fought off the hope that had started to grow in her eyes.

"What a shame I don't have anywhere to drive," I said. "There's so much of this country I've never seen. If only I had someone to navigate. Maybe someone who has lived all over? Knows the country better than me? That would help, I think. Because I just use my GPS and let it guide me. It would be nice to not have to do that."

Slowly, the group backed up until Stevie and I stood alone. Or as alone as two people could be with three very eager spectators pretending not to be interested in what they were watching.

I put my hand on Stevie's cheek. Brushed my thumb over her freckles. "What do you say, Stevie? Need a copilot for the road?"

"Are you serious?" she asked.

"Are birds real?"

She laughed.

I pulled her closer to me. "Will you let me live on the road with you? I know we've only known each other six days, and you said the thing about the stereotype and the—" She interrupted me with a kiss I could only assume meant yes, because her lips and her hands and her mouth all seemed determined to merge with my own.

"Gay rights!" Tommy called out.

"Love is love!" Tim said after.

They were kidding. I loved that I understood it. I had always understood it. I had always been this version of me. I'd just never noticed her before. With Stevie's mouth on mine, everything about me made sense.

"I just need to spend a few days gathering up my stuff, and then I'm yours," I told Stevie. "I have nothing but time."

"Let's do it," Stevie said, beaming. She grabbed me so tight we fell over. And just like she had on that very first day, she rolled so her backpack caught the ground instead of me.

"Now, *that's* magic," I said as we landed.

I had no idea where we were going to go next, but I knew that we'd figure it out. Because we were teammates.

And we always would be.

One Year Later

Stevie sat shotgun as I navigated the winding roads up the mountains, praying no one had randomly decided to back out of a summer at Camp Carl Cove. There was no way another vehicle could get past our van. We were selling it at the end of the week.

"Camp always brings a new beginning," Stevie had reminded me every time I cried over the thought.

In the last 365 days of traveling with her, I'd seen parts of the country I'd never before known. Yet nowhere on the map came close to the magic of this particular corner of the Blue Ridge Mountains. We came back here for renewal, as we had the year prior. And I suspected we always would.

When we pulled our rumbly old van into the parking lot, Tim and Tommy waited by the welcome sign. Time had remained kind to them. They looked stronger, more handsome, more equipped for what the week would bring than they'd been before. They were waving without purpose until Tim poked Tommy's shoulder, spotting Stevie and me through the large front window of the van. Then their smiles broke wide, and they chased us down to the end of the lot.

"Our girls!" Tim cheered, clapping as Stevie swung the side door open.

When we climbed out, the twins wrapped us in a group hug, squeezing so tight that it was hard to tell whose limbs belonged to who.

Tommy pulled back to appraise the back of the van. "No more bumper sticker?"

"I got rid of it last year, actually," I told him. "Stevie wanted to do *honk if you think you're gay*, but we drive through a lot of interesting towns, so we decided against it. The bumper stickers live in our hearts."

"Thank you for agreeing to come back," Tim said.

Stevie and I spent so much time together that I didn't need to look at her to know she'd all but certainly folded her lips together between her teeth and quirked her head, looking at Tim like he'd become the most baffling person in the world.

"We were never going to miss this," I said, speaking for us both. "We have half off tuition!"

Stevie wrapped her arm around my shoulder. "That's right. We're the returning color games champions. We have a legacy to uphold here."

A cameraperson appeared, weaving between the rows of cars to find us. Behind them were two more people. One held a microphone. The other wore a silk maxi skirt in lime green, a striped T-shirt with a black suspender-like harness over the top, and black combat boots on the bottom.

"Michelle!" I didn't mean to yell, but excitement got the better of me.

She stepped in front of the film crew to walk toward me. Not run. Michelle wasn't the type. But she had a very quick skip to her step as she came to greet me and Stevie. "You're supposed to ignore the crew," she whispered into my ear as we hugged.

It was only then that I realized I'd been staring directly into the lens. Watching not just the camera but the person behind it. "Sorry," I said, suddenly looking instead very closely at Michelle's shoulder, inspecting the stripes on her shirt.

"Are we going to be famous?" Stevie asked her as the two of them hugged. "I don't know if I'm ready for my fifteen minutes. But I want Sloane Ford to play me in the biopic they make of this documentary."

Michelle's adoption documentary had garnered more success than she'd expected. Because of it, she'd been able to secure financing for her next project—a documentary about Camp Carl Cove's adult sleepaway camp, with a special focus on the queer found family that had sprung up within it. Michelle had been uncharacteristically sheepish when she'd called Stevie and me to ask if we'd be willing to participate. As if we'd ever say no. As if we weren't incredibly starstruck and flattered to be included in her art.

I looked at the film crew one more time. "I fear we won't be very interesting this time around," I told Michelle.

The production wasn't as sweeping as I expected. There was no gigantic camera resting on the cameraperson's shoulder. Instead it was small, practically handheld. If anything, it distracted me more. It seemed like all the equipment should have had more heft to it.

"It's not about being interesting," Michelle said. "Just authentic."

"Okay. Let me know if things are looking desperate, though. We can go do archery and I can pretend to come out again," I offered. "Just in case you need a bigger story. I'll be sure to hit another bull's-eye."

Michelle gifted me with her laughter. "I'll keep you posted."

"Well, *authentically*, I'm dying to see everyone else!" I transitioned. "Who is checking us in this year if it's not you?"

When we made it to the sign-in table, I got my answer. Dara sat where Michelle had been last year. "Last name," she deadpanned as we approached, doing a decent Michelle impression. She'd chopped her hair even shorter. It sat along her jawline now, suiting her perfectly.

"Long time no see," I said.

It was true. I hadn't seen Dara in over six months. But she'd agreed to come back to camp as quickly as I had, though she was less sure of the documentary angle. She ultimately said yes, because I'd come to learn that she actually put a gigantic amount of stock in *my* opinion of things, and I'd been too busy worrying about her opinion to notice.

She told me she'd drive herself here. She didn't want to intrude on Stevie and me. It felt so funny to hear my sister say she could ever intrude on anything in my life. If she wanted to move into the van with Stevie and me, it would have been awkward as hell, but we'd have made room. There would forever be a place for her in my life. We didn't have to live together to make that true.

Lucky for us, we would always have camp.

She lifted her wrist to show me her heart-promise bracelet. I lifted mine to show mine back. We pressed them together.

"Here's to another great week," I said.

"You're in Cabin Twelve this year," she told me. "And Stevie, you're in Cabin Four."

At first I wanted to protest. *I should get to room with my girlfriend!* But I remembered what a gift last year's room assignment had been. It had given me the love of my life. And one of my best friends in the whole world. Whoever waited for me in Cabin Twelve would surely be just as wonderful. And if they weren't, well, sometimes it was nice to be reminded of how much I really valued my loved ones.

In the distance, we heard chanting. It was rhythmic but distant, coming from somewhere beyond the trees. The closer it got, the clearer the words became.

Hee-haw. Hee-haw.

Three blond men emerged in something of a conga line, pumping their fists, with several people snaking behind them. The Magnusson brothers were here, and they had spotted Stevie and me.

Andrew reached us first. "You're finally here," he said as he kissed the tops of our heads.

"You're acting like we're late or something," Stevie teased.

Andrew dropped his voice to a whisper. "No, no. It's just that Mason's made us do the marching line for about fifteen minutes, and every time we circle back around to sign-in and you're not there, he makes us start it over again."

Mason came up then, smiling like he was waiting for a compliment. "I love the marching line," I said to him.

He waved me off with fake humility, disguising his widening grin. "Please. It was nothing."

"We don't have to do that again, right?" Frank asked Mason before hugging Stevie and me. Mason ignored him. Behind Frank stood another man, the same one who'd come to see him last year on visitors' day. "This is my boyfriend, Owen," Frank told me.

"Nice to meet you, Owen," I said. "I've heard a lot about you. Welcome to the best week of your life." It was nice to be the one with wisdom here. The person who could initiate someone else into Camp Carl Cove's secret Magnusson society. "Hope you're ready for lake night," I said with a wink.

Stevie and I grabbed our new room keys and headed toward our cabins. "Can you believe we're back here?" she asked me as we walked.

"Of course," I told her. "Where's our rock? We should honor this full-circle moment."

Stevie patted her pocket, first playfully, then with new-found urgency. "Shit," she whispered, stopping us outside her new cabin. "I lost it."

I tried my best to cover up my devastation. The rock had become one of our favorite inside jokes. Earlier in the month, I'd even gotten her a display case for it for her birthday.

She stopped feeling her pocket and kissed me. I had a whole language for our kisses now. This was the one she gave me when she wanted me to understand she was joking. It was wild how I could feel that. In the pressure of her touch. The playfulness of her hands gripping the edges of the backpack on my shoulders.

"You didn't lose the rock," I said when we broke apart.

She kissed me again. A *you got it right* kiss. Quick and pleased. "The rock is still in the display case. I'd never have it free-floating in my pocket." She pulled her own backpack off her shoulders and rummaged around until she found it. "See? Safe and sound."

Stevie looked into my eyes. "I'm gonna miss rooming with you."

"You know what? Something tells me we're going to enjoy it even more," I said. "We'll have to find new places to *explore* around camp."

The kiss we shared then was my favorite of our collection. It was the kiss we gave each other when we were excited. When we knew we had something good in store for us. There was a teasing within it. And a passion, carefully contained. A "saving some dessert for later" kind of kiss.

Stevie picked up her gigantic backpack and put it on her shoulders again. "I'm looking forward to it," she told me. She stood at the entrance of her new cabin and blew me a kiss. "See you around camp, Garland Moore."

"See you around camp, Stevie Magnusson."

I watched her go through her front door, then continued down the dirt path toward my new home for the week.

I passed Cabin Seven along the way. I had a vision not of my future but of my past. The Stevie and Garland of one year ago, crashing into each other on that very porch. How little they knew then of what awaited them. How little I still knew, though we'd figured out some things on the road.

After camp ended, we were moving to Washington. Stevie had gotten another job in the National Parks, and both of us were thrilled. We loved the angst of the rain there; the breathtaking views; and funny enough, the coffee, though neither of us cared very much about pour-over techniques.

During many, many long conversations on the road with Stevie, I figured out I wanted a job around people like me. I'd gotten a position at a social service organization that focused on building community among LGBTQ+ youth in Washington. It excited me just to think about it. I couldn't even imagine all the people I might meet, and that suited me just fine. I didn't have to imagine things anymore. I preferred to live them.

But all of that waited for me down the mountain. For six days, none of it mattered.

Summer camp needed me first.

Acknowledgments

As a reader, I always look at the acknowledgments before I read the book. I like seeing whose love and attention made that particular story possible, and I appreciate the brief glimpse into the life of the creator. So here is *my* glimpse, though I'm not sure how brief I'll be.

First, to all my fellow queer people who have listened to my story over the last decade while sharing their own with me, I am so very grateful. You've truly made this book possible. Our conversations (and realizations) have proved to me that there is no guidebook for how a life should unfold. With every passing year, it gives me such great joy to see all of us grow into more fully realized versions of ourselves. I hope I captured even a fraction of that wonder in these pages.

Thank you to my editor, Kerry Donovan, and my agent, Taylor Haggerty, for the care and attention you both put toward bringing this particular story into the world. While every one of my books is filled with queer characters—and some have even been main characters—this is my first sapphic romance, and it means a great deal to me how seriously you both took it. I am very glad to be in such thoughtful hands, and I am deeply grateful to everyone at Berkley who worked on this book: Mary Baker, Fareeda Bullert, Janine Barlow, Chelsea Pascoe, Pam Feinstein, and Lindsey Tulloch. Special gold star thank-you to Vi-An Nguyen for yet another beautiful cover design and to Rebecca Mock for the perfect illustration. And shout-out to Jasmine Brown and the rest of the Root Literary team for all your hard work on my behalf.

My early readers Hollis Andrews, Provvidenza Catalano, and Taylor Smith—I can't tell you enough just how much I needed your feedback and support. Thank you for reading a version of this story that had brackets like [EMOTIONAL SCENE HERE] and loving it anyway. And Hollis, thank you for letting me know how much I use the word *slacks*. Someone had to say it, and you were the only soldier brave enough.

I am nothing without my friends. Hol, we're in the arena together in every version of reality. This one is for Katniss and Peeta (as all things should be). Ryan E., you are a steady and calming presence in my life. Thanks for coming up with the title of this book, among many other things. You are forever my Aquarian brother. Alex, may we never stop revisiting our own past and reacting to it with laughter and awe. My Bengals: Brittany, Caeli, Jake, and Vince—my love for you all is deeper than my love for Oak Forest, which is saying a lot.

Emily and Austin, this timeline is the best timeline, because it's the one where I am friends with you two. Arden, coaching gymnastics with you every day is joyful, ridiculous, and unforgettable, which is exactly how competitive sports should be. Enza, we owe it all to steampunk Hedda Gabler, and no one can take that away from us. Mia, I'll enjoy a twenty-two-dollar omelet with you any day. Ryan S., you are truly the best of us. Lindsay, thanks for always being game to meet up at a coffee shop and write together.

This is also a story about sisters, so big hugs to my own: Liz, Rose, and Raina. There are pieces of you all over this book. Major love to the rest of my family too: Mom; Dad; my brother, John; and all of my nieces and nephews.

And finally, thank you to the readers. I hope my version of summer camp treats you well.

KEEP READING FOR AN EXCERPT FROM
BRIDGET MORRISSEY'S NOVEL

A Thousand Miles

AVAILABLE IN PAPERBACK
FROM BERKLEY ROMANCE!

Dee

It's very hard to break up with someone you were never really dating. Which is why a man named Garrett I met three weeks ago on an app is currently crying in my bathroom.

He doesn't know I saw the tears. It would probably embarrass him if I mention it, so I am sitting on my couch reading listener emails while I wait for him to finish up, wondering if I should put on a movie or put him out of his misery and suggest he leave.

My extremely nonchalant request that I "take a little more time for myself" was met with the classic "that makes sense" from him—a veteran move that made me entirely too comfortable with the whole process. I skipped right past the usual assurances: what a fun three weeks we've had, how great it's been to get to know someone new after a recent rough patch. We've been having sex in my apartment and sometimes ordering delivery. I've never even tagged him in an Instagram story. I truly thought he understood what was going on with us.

We have a similar dry humor. It's how we connected in the first place. But tonight, for the first time ever, we went out to dinner together. He was so rude to the server in the name of being snarky that I thought I might walk myself straight to Lake Michigan and take up boat living. In the middle of a rainstorm, no less.

My choice to continue our breakup conversation by saying, "We clearly aren't the kind of people who should ever go out in public," did not land as I'd hoped. He let out a hollow, wounded kind of laugh that made me immediately backpedal, even though what I said was true. In front of an audience of restaurant patrons, our connection had dissolved like cotton candy in water. All that sweetness between us vanished into nothingness. But I dared to call attention to it, and next thing I know he's telling me he has to go to the bathroom, and tears are rimming his eyes.

He doesn't even have my number saved! Just three days ago, I texted him a meme while he was taking a shower, and from my nightstand I saw my full ten-digit phone number flash up on his screen. How could he not feel the straining awkwardness throughout our meal tonight? Is it really possible that my empty *yeah*s and colorless *wow*s came off as anything other than detached? It's all so absurd it makes me cackle. By the time he's back in my living room—tears dry and brow furrowed—I am laughing louder than the thunder that booms outside.

"What did I miss?" he asks.

Everything, Garrett. You missed everything.

"What's my last name?" I prompt.

"Um . . ."

"Do you know my job?"

"You record a podcast or something."

"How many siblings do I have?"

"I don't know."

"Your name is Garrett Matthew Robertson. You work in finance, in an office near the Hancock building. Your little sister Hannah just graduated from college. Communications degree from DePaul. Send my congrats, by the way."

"Okay, so you're a stalker. Good for you."

There it is. The darkness that always comes out at the first sign of real trouble. A bruise that blooms from whisper-soft pressure. It's amazing how quickly it happens. How little effort it requires on my part.

"I'm a stalker?" I ask.

Predictably, he has no follow-up.

"We've been hooking up for weeks and I follow you online," I continue. "Your full name is in your bio. You post a skyline shot almost every day. I watched part of your sister's commencement ceremony when I accidentally clicked into your graduation livestream."

Garrett glances forlornly at my door. He pushes back the top part of his hair—a truly aspirational sandy blond, if I'm honest—then lets it fall again down his forehead. "Look, this clearly isn't working." He says it with such finality, you'd think it was his idea. If it gets him out of my apartment, he can keep thinking that for the rest of his life.

Still, it's hard to resist a comeback. "Good observation." I give him a thumbs-up.

"Dude, why are you so fucking mean? Like what the fuck?" At once, he gets teary again.

Now I recognize it for what it is: a manipulation tactic. No one gets the upper hand over a handsome man who is crying.

"I'm mean?" I ask, incredulous. "For asking if you know my name?"

"I don't have time for this shit."

He picks up his overnight bag and huffs to my door. He's still wearing his shoes, because no matter how often I ask, he never takes them off right when he enters. It's such an irritating little detail that I almost throw a pillow at him, but he exits too quickly for me to react, slamming my front door shut with an aggressive theatricality my nosy neighbors will certainly register. Add it to their long list of grievances against me.

It devastates me to realize my heart is racing—that Garrett Matthew Robertson the finance bro has gotten any kind of reaction out of me at all. In an effort to release every last ounce of residual adrenaline, I slip off my bra and lean back into my couch, letting the green velvet cushions hug the sides of my face. Not the most orthodox of calming methods, but it gets the job done.

I can't believe I put on nice clothes for this. What a waste of a powder-blue halter jumpsuit and teardrop earrings. I could feel myself overdoing it when I was getting ready. It's been months since I bothered to curl my hair into long copper waves. In spite of every piece of evidence to the contrary, there was a part of me that wanted to believe that Garrett and I had the potential to be something more than hookup buddies.

No choice but to incinerate that part of me to dust!

Three minutes later, he's knocking. He may not know my last name, but it's nice to see he remembers that my apartment door automatically locks and he can't just barge back in and yell, or whatever it is he thinks he needs to do to prove this was all a part of his plan, not mine.

"What do you want?" I call out.

He doesn't answer.

It infuriates me to imagine him waiting for me, ready to unleash a list of grievances he made up on his walk toward the train station. I gave him a chance to go quietly, and he's not taking it. Neighbors be damned. I want a fight.

With as much gusto as possible, I swing my front door open and bark out one loud, aggressive "What?"

It is not Garrett Matthew Robertson the finance bro waiting on the other side.

Instead it is the last person in the world I ever thought I'd see again.

Ben Porter stands in front of me.

It takes me a second to orient myself. Surely this is an alternate reality intersecting with my current one, and Garrett accidentally got swapped for Ben, and soon the ceiling will become the floor and I will learn that we all speak colors and smell numbers.

He has one battered duffel bag slung across his taut midsection and three dark beauty marks dotting his left cheek. Those moles are my very own Orion's Belt, because that's the only constellation I ever bothered to learn, on the only face I've ever cared to memorize.

His eyes are still brown and bashful. His hair is long enough to curl at the ends, soft brown waves ringleted by the rain, contrasting with the new sharpness in his cheeks. A stipple of scruff further accentuates the angles. No more worn-out Chucks and rumpled band shirt. No more baby face. He looks steady. And well aware of how good a drenched navy blue tee looks clinging to his skin.

"A promise is a promise," he whispers, soaking wet and breathless, dripping puddles onto the carpeted hallway of my apartment complex.

My hands lose feeling. My mind insists on running a highlight reel of memories for me, making sure I haven't forgotten that this is a person I've slept with, and dreamt of, and written intensely embarrassing Notes app poetry about that I've already asked my cohost, Javi, to read on our podcast in the event of my untimely demise. Just so Ben would really feel my absence.

Now I feel his presence, and my first instinct is to close the door, lock myself in my bathroom, and stare at myself in the mirror until the pores on my nose upset me for a week straight. But as impulsive as I can be, I am occasionally great at silencing my first instinct and waiting for a better one to emerge.

It turns out in the event of my high school best friend arriving unannounced in the middle of a thunderstorm—after an entire decade of complete silence between us—my second instinct is to intimidate. I fold my arms across my chest, mostly because I am furious at myself for daring to answer while not wearing a bra. Lucky for me, the gesture lends to the steely mood I'm hoping to strike.

"What does that mean? What are you doing here?" My foot taps against the floor as if my time could be better spent looking anywhere but at Ben Porter's face.

If he's expected a kinder greeting from me, he doesn't show it. Instead he smiles. A heartbreaking, earth-shifting, choir-of-angels-singing kind of smile.

"Hi, Dee." He pauses. "It's good to see you too."

At once I'm flooded with the same bone-deep nostalgic longing that makes me open YouTube at three in the morning and watch all the videos we posted together back in the day. I've made all of them private so my listeners don't stumble across them and uncover the one thing I refuse to directly discuss on my show. The first time Ben was ever mentioned while recording, I made Javi bleep out his name in post. Now Ben is known on the podcast as Name Redacted, an infamous, mysterious side character in my otherwise very open-book life.

One of our YouTube videos is ten minutes of us walking around our hometown. We spend the first half coming up with an elaborate undercover identity for our science teacher, Mr. Davis, all while navigating the aftermath of the previous night's snowfall. The video takes a turn when Ben steps into a snow pile that's not sturdily packed, and he ends up chest deep. Instantly, the two of us are nearly heaving we're laughing so hard. I can't grab on to him tight enough to pull him out because my arms are getting a tickle sensation. It's so cold his cheeks are flushed berry red. I set the camera down on another snow pile, and for the rest of the video, all you can see is his face and my back. And the way he's looking at me. It's like I created the universe with my own bare hands.

Here's that very same Ben Porter. And the way he's looking at me right now—it's really not that different from the old clip of us. Even though everything is different. Down to the shade of red in my hair and the city we're in and surely every single thing about our lives.

"Can I come in?" he asks, because I have been standing here waiting for the sky to fall through the roof. "I can explain everything once I'm inside."

"I don't know if I want you to," I accidentally admit.

Ben backs up until he's against the wall across from my door, a trail of rainwater marking his path. He slides down until he's sitting, all the while never breaking eye contact. "I understand. This is a lot."

"Yeah," I say weakly. Leave it to Ben to understate a thing.

"I'll wait here. And if you still feel the same way after an hour, I'll leave."

All those well-practiced talking points I've assured myself I'd launch into immediately if I ever saw him again? I can't remember a single one. In this moment, I truly cannot recall why we haven't spoken or why it is that I'm not supposed to be nice to him. It's a marvel I even know my own name.

Second instincts be damned.

I slam my door shut.

Bridget Morrissey lives in Los Angeles, California, but hails from Oak Forest, Illinois. When she is not writing, she can be found coaching gymnastics or headlining concerts in her living room.

CONNECT ONLINE

BridgetJMorrissey.com
BridgetJMorrissey

Ready to find
your next great read?

Let us help.

Visit prh.com/nextread